Model Wave

ROMANCE, BOATS & BAD BUSINESS IN THE NORTHWOODS

THE BACKYARD MODEL MYSTERIES, BOOK TWO

T.K. SHEFFIELD

Identifiers: ISBN: 979-8-9905631-0-0 (ebook) | ISBN: 979-8-9905631-1-7 (paperback)

Title: Model wave : the backyard model mysteries, book two / T.K. Sheffield.

Description: Genesee Depot, WI : Making Hay Press, 2024. | Series: Backyard model mystery, bk. 2.

Subjects: LCSH: Murder--Fiction. | Models (Persons)--Fiction. | Internet personalities--Fiction. | Wisconsin--Fiction. | Cozy mysteries. | Mystery fiction. | BISAC: FICTION / Mystery & Detective / Cozy / General. | FICTION / Mystery & Detective / Amateur Sleuth. | FICTION / Mystery & Detective / Women Sleuths. | GSAFD: Mystery fiction.

LCC applied for.

Other books by T.K. Sheffield

Model Suspect

Model Ghost

Making Hay Press, d.b.a. Making Hay Productions, LLC

Life is mostly froth and bubbles, but two things show you're a Midwesterner: You bring a casserole for another's trouble, and bake carrot muffins in your own.

— FERN BUBBLE

To my dear husband.
Life's waves are smooth and rough, but no matter the conditions, I am blessed to fly over them with you.

CHAPTER 1
Friday Afternoon

Pontoon boats aren't monsters. They're not Leviathans prowling Northwoods lakes disguised behind groovy fiberglass panels and putt-putt motors to harm vacationers.

Or are they?

I, Mel Tower, occupied a table on the outdoor deck at the Glass Bottom restaurant. I watched whitecaps roll across the lake and pontoons buck against their tethers. The boats were opposites—big, small, new, old—and tied tightly to the pier.

They seemed to have violent opinions about such restriction, though.

No wonder. The sun blazed now, but the forecast called for storms.

A sixty-ish fellow with smoke-colored eyes approached with a menu. "Good afternoon, ma'am. What's made of cheese and haunts Lake Minocqua?"

I smiled. "The Loch Minoc Muenster."

He laughed. "You read the cartoon over the bar. My name's Curtis Grey." He handed me the menu. "Try the fried cheese curds ... on me. It's a new recipe I developed."

I ordered a small portion of the curds. Grey, who wore a T-shirt saying "Fry More, Worry Less," delivered an overflowing platter. (When dining in Wisconsin: a small is large, and a large is, well, Leviathan.)

Grey said he'd bought into the place and was improving the food. "I want to make this restaurant a destination stop."

I nodded toward the pier. "You're already popular with the pontoons."

"Nah, they don't eat unless you count gettin' gas from the pump." He pointed to a vessel tied to the pier. "See my boat? It's the big shiny one on the end. *No Bullship*. Just got her."

I sampled the curds while studying the boat. It was a mega, a tritoon with dual motors and plush captain's chairs. *Impressive*. Different from the others, which were mostly charming older models. Station wagons of the seas, as beloved in the Northwoods as stars, s'mores, and campfires.

As for the curds, they were delicious. Crispy, fragrant. Slightly salty. I only ate a few. I had a date later with a handsome sheriff and didn't want to spoil my appetite.

It was spoiled, it turned out.

No Bullship, indeed.

* * *

THE LOCH MINOC Muenster joke was for sale. Twenty bucks bought a framed cartoon of a lake with a snake made of cheese that curled its head above water.

The purchase included a free drink, too.

Not a bad deal. I'm a fashion industry refugee, er, retiree, and current art mall owner. I encourage supporting local artists and businesses.

I'd been up north for a few days, pursuing R&R in Copper Falls, the Land of Pines, Lakes, and Historic Supper Clubs. My regular job was owning a craft mall in Cinnamon, about five hours south.

Just as I was exiting the restaurant to prepare for my date, my friend Susan Victory strode in.

No, stumbled in.

She and her friends sported cover ups over their swimsuits, their faces tanned from the June sun.

Susan wore a white caftan. Delicate fish-shaped earrings dangled from her ears, and a matching pendant circled her neck.

I knew she'd made the baubles. Susan was a silversmith, one of the first artists to open a booth in my mall. I adored her—when she wasn't drinking.

I gestured to a table. "Susan, sit down. I'll order coffee."

"Mel, my bestie!" she cried. "Where've you been? I've barely seen you since I got to the N-Northwoods." She waved toward the deck. "Ali and Ericka wanna sit on the patio and have a drink. Have you met 'em?"

I nodded. "Ericka is the woman who found my rental. And you introduced me to Ali the first night here."

"How come we haven't spent time t-together?"

Susan looped her arm through mine and towed me toward the deck.

"Because I enjoy my cottage on the quiet side of the lake," I said. "You have your friends and condo on the busy side."

"Hey, I have a joke." She hiccuped gently. "You'll love it as a former m-model. What did the photographer say after he'd spent all day taking pictures of lake birds?"

I thought for a moment. "He had no egrets?"

"Egrets ... regret." She laughed. "Get it?"

I looked toward the table where her friends had parked themselves. They already had glasses and were pouring rum runners from a pitcher.

Regret?

I wasn't the fun police. I loved a day on a lake with a cooler of refreshments, but I felt Susan and her friends would regret their actions in the morning.

* * *

CURTIS GREY BROUGHT A STEAMING platter of cheese curds to our table. He passed out the golden orbs like they were candy. If I didn't know better, I'd say he was the captain of the *Good Ship Pepper Jack* instead of the *Bullship*.

"You gotta try these. It's our new recipe. Don't worry about the bill. It's on me."

I smelled spices and cheese. If one has never enjoyed fresh curds robed in batter and served while seated by a Northwoods body of water, one should do it, posthaste.

Susan and her friends ogled the fragrant orbs. She reached for a sample.

Too quick, I feared.

The curds were direct from the fryer. Steam rose from the plate, and oil still crackled.

I began, "Susan, wait—"

She waved me off. "Don't mother me. We came here for a vacation, remember? YOLO, you only live once." She selected a crispy morsel and bit the bread coating.

She jerked—burning grease spattered her chin. "Ouch, help!"

Susan's chair, shaky as a newborn foal, wobbled—*CRACK!* She went down as the chair broke, drinks and curds flying.

"Whoa!" I cried. "Susan, are you okay?" I stood and stretched out a hand.

She groaned and touched her lip. "I need water."

"I'll get some!" Ericka jumped up and dashed to a server.

Ali flew to Grey, who was a few tables away. The woman barely reached the man's elbow but thumped his bicep with force. "Curt, stop serving things so *hot,*" She snarled. "You wanna get sued? I need antibiotic ointment!"

I knelt by my friend, shocked to see her splayed on the deck, her dress torn, the necklace broken. The rickety chair was in pieces.

"Don't move," I said. "Let's make sure nothing is broken."

Susan waved me off *again*. "Get me a fresh drink, Mel."

"But—"

"After this embarrassment, I need a stiff one." She touched her lip where a blister already bubbled. "Ask the bartender to make a 'Scotch Tape.' Maybe that will patch this old girl back together again."

She giggled.

I didn't.

Eating a piping hot curd was a foolish decision, Susan.

Not her first one, though. She and I had problems last winter. She suggested this vacation to mend our friendship.

Seeing her on the floor asking for a drink made me feel awful. It was the opposite of what I expected of our time in the Northwoods.

Little did I know the day would get worse.

* * *

I PICKED Susan up and served her sparkling water.

Ali secured a new chair. "I told Curt to get rid of those old ones," she complained. "Replace 'em all with the Yaack Three Thousands. They're my top of the line stool. Expensive, but worth it."

Ali von Yaack is heir to the furniture von Yaack's of Chicago. Upon meeting her, she'll tell you all about it.

After listening to her sales talk when I first met her, I asked if she gave out *stool* samples.

It was a joke. I think that's why Ali doesn't like me much.

I looked at Susan, who was perched in her chair. She appeared disheveled but otherwise unharmed.

I brushed hair from her face. "I'll call you. Drink *water*."

"Where're you headed?" she asked.

"I have to let Max out."

"Give my favorite rescue dog a hug from his Aunt Susan. What're you doing later—"

"Gotta run."

I made a quick exit. I hadn't told Susan about my date with the sheriff. She'd tell her friends, and I didn't want rumors to start.

Loose lips sink new relationships.

I crossed the parking lot. A village squad cruised by, and the officer waved. I thought about Sheriff Cole Lawrence. He and I had met months ago. He'd visited Cinnamon when I was a suspect in a murder case. (The village librarian had tried to frame me for a murder, but I was never *booked*, fortunately.)

I also had an on-again, off-again relationship with a pilot. We'd decided to divert for now.

It was tough beginning for Cole and me, but he and I kept in touch, texting and chatting during the past six months. When I said I was coming north, he suggested going out for frozen custard as our first official date.

I accepted. It was my first *first* date since, oh, George Washington crossed the Delaware.

A day, time, and custard stand was selected. Cole was picking me up at my rental at eight. I had time to take Max for a walk, boat-watch from my little pier, and then shower and get ready.

I hopped in my car, an ancient Saab convertible, and turned the key. At the same time, lightning cracked on the horizon.

I jumped.

I immediately felt cursed, guilty. Like I caused the jolt somehow.

* * *

I DON'T DO guilt and curses. Well, except for boiling rival NFC-North football team jerseys in a cauldron under a full moon each autumn, but every Wisconsinite does that. The spell is taught in schools along with the art of throwing tailgating parties, for Vince Lombardi's sake.

I stood on the dock of my rental, which hugged the channel between Glass Lake and Lake Minocqua. Max, my furry best friend, was near me. We'd taken a walk. And, since we'd arrived in Vacationland, the collie had discovered a new favorite pastime: reading boat names.

Yes, collies can read, and Max's sense of humor is positively *pawsome.* The air felt chilly and the wind had picked up, but we still saw a parade of party barges cruising the water. *National Pontoon's Vacation* was followed by *Toon-Tastic.* Those boats were my favorites, slow-moving vintage gems with beach chairs for seats.

Max seemed to prefer larger vessels. He woofed and tippy-tapped at *Big Nauti,* a wakeboard boat with splashy paint and graphics.

Its captain waved at us. "Beautiful dog, ma'am," he said.

"Thanks. Nice boat."

He trimmed down the giant motor. It moved into position—*CLUNK*—and the driver throttled up. The *Nauti's* engine rumbled like a Harley-Davidson. The pier vibrated under my feet, and I suspected the monster could fly across the lake.

Sure enough, it glided past cottages and docks, and then on open water, it conquered the choppy waves like a fiberglass warrior, its green LED lights giving off a spooky, spaceship aura.

I thought about Curtis Grey's *No Bullship*. That boat had double the engines of this one, a twin pack. Dual 300 Mercs that could race the wind.

I'd never been on a pontoon like it. I wondered how fast *No Bullship* could go.

I'd find out, unfortunately.

CHAPTER 2
Friday Evening

Sheriff Cole Lawrence sat in the driver's seat of his truck. He smiled at me, his grin sweetly lopsided.

A turtle sundae sat between us on the console.

"Ope, sorry," I said as our spoons clashed. "Just call me 'Quick Draw.' Fastest utensil in Wisconsin."

"How are you with a spatula, Mel? The department has a pancake breakfast soon, and I could use an extra flipper."

"I'm better at buying a ticket and eating, but I'm happy to help."

"I'll deputize you as a volunteer."

Our frozen custard treat diminished quickly. Melting due to the humid air, *not* my fast spoon.

We were parked in front of the Lake Minocqua, the custard stand behind us. An illuminated ice cream cone warned boaters of the shoreline.

I nodded at the glowing orb. "Only in Wisconsin would a giant cone act as a lighthouse."

Cole looked at the water. "Another storm tonight. Could be a bad one."

Lightning flashed. A gust ripped over the lake and hit the windshield. It felt like invisible hands grabbed Cole's one-ton and shook it like a toy.

The frozen custard hit my teeth.

Oh, brain freeze!

I jerked sideways, and my head bumped Cole's spoon.

Caramel—fudge—my hair. The wooden dipper stuck like glue.

Cole looked shocked. "I didn't mean to—"

"Sheriff Lawrence, call dispatch." A voice crackled from the speaker under the dash. As he reached for his phone, and his elbow knocked the custard off the console.

Right on my lap. "Oh, that's c-cold!" I cried.

"Mel, I have to respond." He looked at my legs. "Geez, I'm sorry."

He grabbed his cell and stepped out, the wind fluttering his jacket.

I looked around for napkins but didn't see any. I would *not* search for some. Think about it: What could one find in the glove box of a law officer's vehicle?

I didn't want to know. It was our first date. I'd wear the custard, thanks.

I tugged the spoon in my hair, which made it worse. I used the custard cup to corral the goo in my lap.

Fat raindrops began pelting the windshield. *Tap ... tap. Tap, tap, tap.*

After a minute, Cole climbed back into the truck, looking dismayed.

He probably was embarrassed about the spilled dessert.

Well, Mel Tower's mantra is that when life hands her custard, she makes custard jokes. "It's no big deal, Cole. Did you know a deer's favorite custard flavor is cookie *doe*—"

"We have to leave." Cole said, lines etching his brow. "Curtis Grey was just found dead on his pontoon. The boat's being towed to the launch in Copper Falls, near where you're renting, about fifteen minutes away."

"Oh, no."

"It's Curtis Grey. Didn't you and your friends talk with him earlier at the Glass Bottom?"

I nodded, the spoon wiggling from my head like a minnow. "Yes, he brought us turds, er, cheese *curds*." I felt my face flush. "Custard, curds. They're, ah, close."

"You spoke with him?"

"Not long. He'd talked about a new recipe."

Cole started the truck. The engine roared, and we bumped onto the road. "One of my officers will chat with you."

Lightning flashed. I saw a jagged, white scar rip the sky. It looked like it could tear the Northwoods in half.

I was covered in caramel goo and had to speak to police about Curtis Grey, who'd been found dead ... on my first date with a sheriff.

The night had turned into the opposite of what I'd expected.

What a mess.

* * *

COLE DROVE from Minocqua to Copper Falls with both hands on the wheel.

"Watch for deer," he ordered.

What Cole revealed about Curtis Grey's accident was frightening. "A fisherman found him adrift on his new boat. That mega-pontoon could go sixty miles an hour on the water." He pounded the wheel with a fist. "Grey could have lost control, especially in this weather."

We traveled a road that bordered Glass Lake, the storm tracking us like we'd jumped bail. Waves boiled on one side of us, black as lava. Pines as big as Redwoods towered on the other.

Lightning flashed. It seemed like a typhoon was giving birth to a string of atolls.

My thighs felt chilled. The custard had soaked through my dress and onto my legs. The spoon still dangled in my hair.

Cole piloted the truck like a stunt driver. "Why was Grey out so late?" he asked. "Did he mention anything about night boating?"

"I barely spoke to him," I replied. "He brought over a platter of curds and mentioned a new recipe. Are you sure it's Curtis? Maybe there's been a terrible mistake."

Cole swung his gaze to me. "Did he seem fearful? Agitated?"

I saw red lights flash against pine trees. "An ambulance is coming down that hill—look out!"

I heard a siren. It sounded odd, like the ambo had swallowed a goose.

HAYonk. HAYonk.

It blew a stop sign and veered toward us. Cole threw an arm against my chest. "Hold tight!"

He jerked the wheel—we slid across the center line.

Please, Lord, don't let us hit boulders or go in the water!

Cole slammed the brakes. The spoon in my hair whipped like a fishing lure swinging from a pole. I tried to catch it but missed. I grabbed the "Oh, Shucks" handle instead and braced a hand against the dash.

The rocks came closer—tires hit gravel and roared—but praise to the patron saint of brake pads, the rubber gripped. We lurched sideways, then stopped.

We sat in oncoming traffic, wipers slapping, truck idling. No headlights came toward us, thank God, and I saw the ambulance's lights fading in the distance.

"That was close," Cole said. "I did *not* see that guy coming. Are you hurt?"

I released the "Oh, Shucks" to capture the twirling spoon.

"Did we almost get hit by an ambulance?" I asked. "Or an out-of-control pontoon?"

* * *

What happened to Curtis Grey?

Whoever hurt the man—*if* someone did—his boat seemed determined to take the secret to a watery grave.

The time was eleven, but it felt like Midnight at the Pier of Good and Evil. Lightning jagged across the sky, thunder boomed. I feared the lake would split and swallow us all.

I watched chaos unfold from Cole's truck, holding my phone to record the recovery operation.

My effort probably was fruitless. A spotlight blazed from the Glass Bottom restaurant but barely cut the darkness. Two police cruisers idled with their headlights on, too far away to illuminate much.

Grey's boat, *No Bullship*, appeared demonic. Officers tried to lash it to the dock, but it bucked in the waves and smashed itself into the pilings.

Cole shouted directions from the boat launch, looking like a ranch foreman in a yellow slicker and cowboy hat. He tried to move about the steep, greasy surface but kept slipping.

"Stay up," I murmured.

Boat launches are like hockey rinks but coated with lake slime and vehicle oil instead of ice. If Cole went down, the waves could swallow him.

I looked at the pontoon. Grey's body was still on it, apparently. A fellow with a camera, Hilarious Wilde, stood on the pier, fighting the wind, photographing the scene.

I knew Wilde. I'd met the lanky Ichabod Crane-looking fellow a few days ago at a charity dinner. An officer near him clutched an umbrella, shielding the camera from the storm.

An ambulance idled on the steep ramp, its red lights swirling. It was an old-style paddywagon with bubble lights—no wonder its siren had sounded odd earlier.

When we'd arrived, Cole had words with its reckless young driver. I wanted to, also, but the better part of valor had been to remain in the truck, out of the way.

I shook my head, stunned by the day's disasters: First, there was The Great Bar Stool Collapse with Susan on the restaurant deck. Now, a dead man on a pontoon.

Crazy—who'd have expected it? I'd heard of Lake Time, but this day's abuse of the clock—its hours felt like both instant and a year—was beyond what I'd ever experienced.

Crack!

What was that? A gunshot noise came from the dock. I zoomed in with my phone camera.

Holy unnatural disaster, Batman!

The monster pontoon had snapped a piling. It was like the boat opened its jaws like a shark and chomped the wood!

Boards snapped, splitting upward, looking like jagged teeth. Wilde grabbed his helper to keep her from falling into the waves.

Cole waved frantically, signaling the pair to get off the pier.

A red flash caught my gaze.

The ambulance.

Its lights had been flickering in a steady beat, but did the vehicle move? The driver's seat was empty. Either the Ghost of the Glass Lake was driving, or the top-heavy vehicle was slipping.

There—it moved!

Curses to the boating version of Murphy's Law: Whatever can go wrong at a launch will go wrong. Either the ambo's emergency brake released, or the launch was too slick.

The vehicle began sliding backward toward Cole, who couldn't see the danger. He focused on the photographer and officer stumbling from the pier.

I dropped my phone and shoved open the truck door. I teetered on the wet ground. The wind choked my words. "Cole, behind you!"

He looked back, then ran.

Or, tried to. If the scene hadn't been so horrific, his scramble would have been funny. He churned his arms, his legs spinning like wheels. The tails of his coat fluttered like sails.

I fell on the uneven ground, of course. I used to be a model, not a ballerina. I timbered like a sawed-off pine, my dress wrapping my legs like a snare. I rolled and clawed the earth, but it was black quicksand.

I propped on my elbows. "Cole, get out of the way!"

This scene was nuts! I met the sheriff for custard, then within hours, a man is dead and Cole is scrambling for his life?

I lost sight of him from my awful vantage point on the ground—did he go down?

I heard metal crunching, then *CRASH.*

The wind blew harder. I wiped my eyes. The stupid spoon was still attached to my head.

I'd have used the thing to dig my way toward Cole, but I couldn't see him.

What happened?

CHAPTER 3
Friday Evening, Later

Hilarious Wilde pulled me from the mud, wrapped me in a blanket, and stuffed me into his Saab.

"It's got a few dents, but the car is safe," he promised. "It'll get us back to your place."

I shivered under the blanket. "W-where's Cole?"

"Took a fall, but he's okay. He's waiting for the police boat. Once the storm's over, they'll head out, then tow the pontoon back to the dock."

Hilarious and I had met at a charity dinner in the basement of a church in Minocqua. He'd been with Cole. Hil had carried an impressive-looking camera and said he'd been a photographer in the Big Apple. I'd replied that I was a mannequin in the same city, but ate *only* apples because that was all I'd been able to afford.

We'd hit it off.

In the car on the dark road, I looked over at him. "Are you okay? That was h-horrible."

"I'm fine." He stared out the windshield. "Did you record what happened?"

My teeth chattered. "Y-yes, I had my video going."

"Send it to Cole. Email the file from your laptop if you have one. Cell phone service is challenging up here."

I discovered that when checking into my rental cottage. "Sure."

"Cole said I should speak to you about Curtis Grey."

"Mind if we do it tomorrow?"

"Yes, but—"

A firetruck roared past. Hilarious watched it in the rearview. "I wish that guy would slow down. No sense in wrecking another vehicle."

"What can they do at this point?"

"Wait until the storm quits, then search with the police boat. Stuff won't go far; the lake isn't that big. It's too dangerous to do anything right now. The crime scene was destroyed, but we'll find the boat and the body as soon as we can."

"How do you know it was a crime scene?"

I shouldn't ask. None of my business.

"Cole isn't positive that it is," Hil said. "He's just a thorough guy. He said he's sorry he couldn't drive you home."

Cole and I had shared frozen custard, but the treat ended up in my lap. A dead body showed up in a thunderstorm, and a dock and an ambulance were destroyed.

Not sure if I'd go out for frozen custard anytime soon.

The rain gushed, and the wipers swished. We drove for a few minutes, then the headlights flashed onto a sign, Lollygag Lane.

Hilarious turned onto the road leading to my rental. The sure-footed car growled its way on the stones.

"Is your camera okay?" I asked.

"Don't know, maybe, if the water didn't affect it. Dropping it didn't help. Comedy of errors back there at the launch. We don't process crime scenes very often."

Hmm, another mention of a skullduggery.

I glanced at the backseat. The camera bounced on the cushion, its flash attachment dangling like a broken arm.

"Is there anything I can do?" I asked.

"Call Cole tomorrow. Let him know you have the video file. And keep calling—don't give up."

"What are you saying?"

He sighed. "My friend has a job that sucks, and he works too much.

But I've known Cole Lawrence all his life. I've never seen him react to anyone like when he met you."

CHAPTER 4

Saturday Morning

I awoke to caramel-colored light, and the sun bold and red as a cherry. Even dawn in the Northwoods looked like a sundae.

But my mood darkened, as they say, when I recalled the storm, the lost ambulance, and Curtis Grey, the fellow who had been "pontooned."

That was the term for what had occurred last evening. "It doesn't happen often," Hilarious had said when dropping me off. "Now and then, we find a poor soul on his boat who's gone to the great dock in the sky."

From my window, I watched an eagle soar, hunting for breakfast. Max tapped toward me, his nails clicking on the tile.

I bent down to scratch his chest. "We'll go out in a sec. Let's see if Aunt Susan sent us a text first."

I glanced at my phone.

Nothing.

"Rats," I said.

Max heard me and took the word as an order. He dashed to the patio slider, seeking something small and furry to chase in the backyard.

I opened it. "Go easy on 'em, Max. Don't get squirrely."

I'd had the dog since last November. He'd immediately become the greeter at the Bell, Book & Anvil, my craft mall in Cinnamon. Max had gotten me through a murder investigation and the breakup of my long-term relationship.

He also tolerated my frugality and corny jokes.

I suspected Max rescued me, but neither of us was keeping track.

I rechecked my phone. Susan was still sleeping, probably.

When we'd arrived a few days ago, she'd discarded me like an old beach towel to party with her friends on the busy side of the lake. I didn't mind because I preferred the quiet side with its small cabins and rustic vibe. She'd asked me to stay at her condo, but I'd gotten a rental.

Like Paul Bunyan, Mel Tower is a tall, solo act.

Susan was one of the best artists in my mall, and clients were mad about her work. She'd made awful mistakes, though. Last fall, she'd had an affair, wrecking her relationship with her partner, an attorney, a genuinely nice fellow.

And she'd told a whopper of a lie that put me in danger.

She'd apologized, and I'd forgiven her.

But since arriving, Susan had been a different person. She and Ali von Yaack had been partying like Reality TV stars. They'd caused a scene over a barstool a few nights ago at the Glass Bottom restaurant.

Not over who sat in the thing, but who *made* it, who was responsible for its existence.

Ali began arguing with a man, and I'd witnessed her haughtiness. I'd wanted to tell Ms. Von Yaack that Max *yaks* fur balls under the stools in my home with perfect timing—just before guests arrive because, of course, because dogs *know* somehow.

I'd stuffed that *yak* joke down where it came from. No sense in being rude to someone I'd *yust* met.

I sensed Ali did not like me.

Max woofed. I opened the door and stepped onto the deck, inhaling pine-scented air. The dog dashed about, a black-and-white blur sprinting from deck to lake to tree, and then stopping to stare up at squirrels.

They chattered at him but didn't seem worried.

I looked up at the critters. "Max won't hurt you. He'll just herd you. You guys will have to learn to coexist."

I loved the cottage as soon as I'd arrive in the Northwoods. I toured the knotty pine paradise and immediately inquired about buying it because the place was for sale. Even though I had a mall to run, and a new bookstore venture, I'd written a check for the earnest money, given it to the real estate agent, and now awaited a purchase inspection.

Agent Ericka Dimblé, the other woman at the table yesterday, hadn't gotten back to me yet.

I thought about Susan again. I would not abandon our friendship, even if she distanced herself. I treasured our closeness and sought to repair what was wrong.

I'd planned to stay two weeks in the Northwoods. Maybe I'd stay longer to fix things with her.

There was another reason to hang around. If I were writing a romance novel, I'd cast Sheriff Cole Lawrence as its lead. The keeper of peace, sharer of custard, had swept this former model off her feet like a leaf blower wearing a badge.

We hadn't spent much time together, but something about the handsome sheriff made this forty-five-year-old woman take risks. Release her inner Reality TV star, perhaps.

No, I wouldn't go that far.

But Cole Lawrence had given me an excellent reason to stay.

* * *

SPEAKING OF LEAF BLOWERS, I needed one. M. Nature had *yakked* pine needles all over the deck during the storm.

I swept it clean. Then Max and I took a constitutional down Lollygag Lane.

Few things are as lovely as a Northwoods morning. The air smelled fresh, crisp as well-done bacon—wait, that aroma was due to a hole-in-the-wall breakfast spot.

The Sunny Side Inn was a hundred yards from the cottage. It was one of those places that served scratch bakery and pancakes too large for the plates. The entire restaurant seated about twelve.

I stopped walking to read the sign advertising the special: "Sheriff & Eggs—get some while he's hot!"

Okay, maybe not.

I looked at Max. He appeared to roll his eyes in disappointment.

"Sorry, Max," I said. Dogs save their humans from themselves, sometimes.

We continued on. The sun powered the sky to bright blue, and I watched clouds form unusual shapes. It was as though the white puffs worked the Wisconsin sky for the summer, posing as silly-looking animals for tourists to photograph.

I saw a puffy white lizard with saber-tooth teeth and spikes down its back. It looked like a hodag, the legendary monster of the Northwoods. Hodags were a cross between a reptile and a bull, or an alligator and a Tasmanian devil, or a—

My phone vibrated. I checked it. The image showed a pair of spurs —my cousin Louella Jingle, speaking of devils.

Lou's vocals are a mix of stadium announcer and marching-band trumpet. She doesn't need a phone to communicate. All she has to do is stick her head out her kitchen window and add diaphragm.

I answered, which I hated to do because a morning stroll was sacred time. But Lou, Jason, her husband, and our mutual friend, Steven, would be arriving soon. There was a delivery-driver competition in the Northwoods and Steven was on a team.

"Hiya, Mel. What's new?"

"Not much. Enjoying a walk."

"Does Max have a new dad yet? How'd the date with the lawman go?"

"Fine."

"Anything happen?"

I glanced at the sky and saw another hodag. "No. Custard, then home. Nothing unusual."

"What's his name again?"

"Sheriff."

"Dillon? Andy Taylor?"

I sighed. Giving details to Lou was the equivalent of renting a billboard. "It doesn't matter, Lou. Two people shared frozen custard. That was it."

"You didn't eat it all, did ya?"

"Of course not."

She laughed. "What'd ya wear?"

"Sequins. And turquoise bell bottoms."

"You're jokin'."

"Yes."

She clucked, "It's bad luck to tease your only relative. But I'm gonna get ya into somethin' other than black. I'm bringin' suitcases of glitzy Western Wear. Carrot muffins, too. We'll be up there shortly."

I changed the subject. "Lou, have you ever heard of being 'pontooned'?"

She laughed. "It happens up there, too? *Dang.*"

"What do you mean?"

"Jason water-skied on Lake Cinnamon in high school. He spent time with that crowd. Every now and then, a city fella would be found belly-up in his pontoon. Boat would be blowin' around the water like a tumbleweed."

"No way."

"Yeah, guy from Chicago usually. And the poor sap didn't get out there under his own power. He got help. Sometimes a business partner. Sometimes an ex. Why?"

"No reason."

"Hold on, gotta get the muffins out."

I heard the whoosh of her convection oven. Lou was a baker-volunteer extraordinaire and made treats for any nonprofit or charity that asked.

She continued, "Me, Jason, and Steve-O will be up tomorrow. Bringing the cashboxes for the Deliveree Games. I'm running the box office—get it? Delivery drivers use lotsa boxes, *hehe.*"

The Deliveree competition was for messengers, drivers, and couriers. The knights of the road who delivered in rain, snow, and sleet. Our friend Steven had been an expert deliverer for years and was a competitor.

"We rented a cottage down the lane from ya," Lou said. "You buyin' your place?"

"Yes, just waiting to hear back from the real estate agent."

"Get her on it! We'll stay with ya spring, summer, fall, *and* winter. Nothin' like family time."

"*Great.*"

"Stay outta trouble, or at least wait 'til I get there to start some." She hung up.

Max and I turned toward home. Lou was a font of wisdom. Her font, or fountain, was made of cement, barbed wire, and decorated with spurs, but that didn't make her wisdom less valid.

I *should* stay away from trouble. But with the mysterious death of Curtis Grey, the disturbing behavior of my friend Susan, and my attraction to the lawman, I sensed trouble had found me.

CHAPTER 5
Saturday, Custard o'Clock

A law officer delivering frozen custard?

Only in Wisconsin.

I was on the deck, texting Susan, when I heard a truck door slam, then boots clacking on stones.

Cole stood at the fence to the backyard. His knuckles struck the gate post. "Knock, knock."

"Who's there?" I asked.

"Police, but I ask the questions, ma'am."

I smiled. "Permission to enter, sir."

Cole opened the gate, then stepped onto the grass. He wore cargo pants and a tan shirt. Gadgets and police gear encased in leather were attached to his uniform by snaps, buckles, and zippers, making him squeak as he moved.

He was Oz's Tin Man reinvented in leather and khaki. What I noticed more than pips and squeaks was the wicker basket he carried. I spied plaid napkins and tempting ingredients.

"A call came in from this cottage requesting a build-your-own sundae," he said. "Buck County law enforcement aims to deliver, ma'am."

"I'll get spoons."

* * *

WE SAT at the table on the deck. Temps had warmed quickly. The lake and narrow channel had become a mirror reflecting the pines, sky, and clouds.

I savored a bite of custard. "I feel like a lawbreaker. Having a sundae this early must be against village ordinances."

Cole smiled. "The statute about frozen dairy is clear: Thou shalt enjoy at any hour."

We'd each fixed a treat. Max even had a small one, vanilla with crushed dog biscuit on top.

When scooping custard, thou shalt include one's dog.

The Commandments of Copper Falls sounded promising. I wondered how many there were.

"We also have a regulation about second dates," Cole said, as though reading my mind. "Thou shalt be offered a compensatory evening when the first didn't go as planned."

"Sure, when you have time," I said.

"Let's get together this afternoon." Cole's eyes sparkled.

Max woofed at a kayaker floating along the shoreline.

I wanted to woof, too, because I'd spotted a hunk. If Cole were a sundae, he'd be a triple-scoop with a chaser of human lightning.

I looked at the lake to avoid staring at him. I did *not* want Cole to know how I felt. This was only our third meeting since I'd arrived. A few days ago, when he, Hilarious and I met by chance at the church dinner, Cole kissed me on the cheek and acted delighted to see me.

"Join us," Hil had said. "You need the 'Up-Nörthgåsbord' experience. Pasta and red gravy on a board in the middle of the table. You'll never get that from takeout."

And so, it came to pass that the three of us had shared a table. We shared pasta, sauce, and meatballs, knifing out sections, then dragging the food to our respective sides.

Cole had been straight man to Hil's Opening Act. When your friend's name was Hilarious Wilde, the spotlight naturally shined there first.

Hil had explained his unusual moniker with one line: "My parents had a unique sense of humor." Then he turned Act Two over to Cole, the lawman.

That night, I felt like I'd been cast under his spell. Perhaps it had been the spiritual location of the church, or, it was Cole. We shared stories and laughed.

A lot.

I observed him now on the deck: His skin—tanned and smooth. A result of fifty years of exfoliation by clean air, ice, and pine needles. His slightly one-sided smile—a sweet flaw that revealed a sense of humor behind steely eyes. And those eyes—blue-green ghosts.

I feared Cole could read the thought-bubbles in anyone's mind. I would *not* want to be interrogated by the guy.

"By the way, thanks for sending the video about the incident at the dock," Cole said. "Let Hilarious know what you observed yesterday."

* * *

I'D ALMOST FORGOTTEN about the disaster that occurred twelve hours prior. "Shouldn't you be at the boat launch? Don't you—"

He held up a hand. "The storm passed like they always do. On a scale of one to ten, that one was medium. The wind calmed, and the police boat towed everything back to the launch. Mr. Grey was still on his pontoon." He looked at me. "The police chief is leading the investigation."

I sensed tension.

Don't mention the wrecked ambulance ... not your business.

"I hope the chief isn't blaming you for the ambulance," I said.

A grimace flashed over his handsome features. It was easy to miss. So fast it could have been a cloud casting a half-second shadow. The frown meant Cole probably was being blamed for mismanaging the situation.

Cole nodded. "Believe it or not, a few vehicles have been lost at that dock. We have the recovery process down pretty well."

"What happened to Curtis Grey?"

"I can't reveal that, but folks are working on a theory."

I thought about my encounter with the man. "I barely spoke with him at the restaurant. I don't know if I can offer anything helpful."

He set his custard on the patio table. "Speak with Hil. He's deputized to do police work. I shouldn't be the person taking a statement from you."

"Will do."

"I have a few things to finish up. Then my day is free. I'll pick you up in about an hour. Wear jeans."

"Your day is free?"

"Mostly."

That surprised me. It was the opposite of what I'd expected, in fact. But law enforcement got Saturdays off like regular people, too, I guessed.

Cole stood, then wandered to the deck railing, looking at the water.

Had he slept? He appeared fresh as the proverbial daisy. He intrigued me, and I wanted to know everything about him.

I observed his body language. He stood tall, his shoulders square, arms stretched along the rail—a confident pose. I'd describe him as a Midwest Sequoia: A healthy specimen with dark hair and a trunk-like body that soared beyond six feet. Appeared to thrive on dairy products and church spaghetti.

"I'll be ready," I said.

He turned around. "Great. Max can come, too."

CHAPTER 6

Saturday Morning, Later

I showered, then put on jeans and a plaid shirt. I usually wear black, as Cousin Lou complained. It was a habit from my modeling career.

I was on vacation, though. The vibe of the Northwoods called for wearing bright patterns. It's not just fashion here. It's in the DNA. Northwoods babies are born plaid, and bald eagles are known as plaid eagles.

Okay, I'm exaggerating.

Northwoods newborns aren't plaid. Well, they are but don't stay that way. They take their first breath, then turn orange, the color of cheese, Wisconsin's official dairy product.

I smiled at my reflection in the bedroom mirror. The blue, yellow, and orange shirt was a nice change of pace. On the dresser, my phone pinged.

Susan.

I read her text, then reread it. Her sentences were written in odd patterns. Susan was texting in plaid—was she still tipsy from yesterday?

Susan wrote:

> Ali and I are going shopping. No, we're going on Ali's boat, My Alibi, then eating water for lunch. No, eating on the water.

I tapped back:

Did you hear about Curtis?

After a few seconds, Susan responded:

Terrible! A police guy questioned us. Ali's upset. Curtis is her ex—he wrecked that $$$ new pontoon!

She added a heart emoji, then wrote:

Give kiss to Max.

I called her. "Max says he 'hearts' you, too."

"Thanks," Susan said. "I'm, ah, in a rush."

"Where are you headed?"

"Shopping. I told you."

"What about boating? You said—"

"Boating, *My Alibi*, yeah." She giggled. "Maybe we'll shop for a boat."

"Are you okay?"

"It's *sooo* nice to be up here. Just what I needed."

"How's Ali?"

"She's great for feeling, *hic*, bad."

"That doesn't make sense, Susan. Those emotions are opposite."

Ice clinked in a glass on her end.

"Ali's good but upset," Susan explained. "She and Curtis were divorced for years. It's a shock, though. He drank too much." She snorted. "Like us."

"Does Ali suspect foul play?"

"Fouls? Are you watching baseball?"

"Are you drinking? When did you speak with the police?"

"An hour ago. We had strong coffee and were perfectly sober. Sang like canaries."

"Susan—"

"Gotta go. Love ya, Mel." She hung up.

I stared at my phone.

She spoke with the police?

Susan, I hope you didn't say anything you'll regret.

* * *

I WAITED for Cole on the deck. But then, as though the water had mystical powers, it pulled me from the patio, down the slope, and onto the pier.

Sticks and debris had washed up. The flotsam reminded me of the previous night's storm. I recalled Curtis Grey's *No Bullship* bucking and thrashing.

What happened to the businessman—was his death an accident or foul play? Susan had many friends and knew the dead man's ex. Had she said too much?

I wasn't a lawyer, but I knew a conversation with a police officer after a deadly incident was *not* a friendly chat.

Had Ali von Yaack spoken, too? Or had she let Susan do the talking? That was a clue if Ali was involved—perpetrators clam up.

It was ironic that Ali's boat was named *My Alibi*. Did the woman have one when her ex died?

I inhaled, savoring the pine scent floating on the air. It was *not* my place to quiz anyone about what happened. If a crime occurred, the authorities would reveal it soon enough.

But Susan was like a sister to me. I couldn't have opened my craft mall without her. She'd been a guiding light. From recruiting artists to sell their creations to helping refinish the floors, she'd been a godsend.

If she made a mistake speaking with the police, I'd help her. You don't abandon a friend when she's enduring difficulties, even if they're self-imposed. You do the opposite and fight for her.

You don't judge—you *help*.

Susan had been making awful decisions recently, but as her friend, I felt obligated to protect her.

CHAPTER 7

Saturday, Trail Ride

Cousin Lou raves about buttermilk. She uses it in recipes from fried chicken to pie crusts. I don't spend much time in the kitchen, so I leave scoop about ingredients to her. After today, when Lou hears about *my* experience with buttermilk, I will have gained stature in her expert-baker arena.

I stood at a corral fence, gazing at the most beautiful vanilla-and-black horse I'd ever seen. Buttermilk was a cream-colored stunner with ebony legs.

When I first saw her, my eyes popped. "Was she designed in Paris, Cole?"

He laughed. "Nebraska. Brought her back here as a yearling. I knew she was special."

Max and I had been at Cole's farm, a log cabin and barn on eighty acres, for ten minutes when I already sensed a problem. Max had jumped from the truck and raced about, embracing the land as his new frontier.

I owned a Federal-style fixer-upper on a city lot. Even though it had an expansive backyard, Max obviously preferred the farm. The dog loped to the corral, then flattened to his belly, studying the two horses within.

Buttermilk stared at him through kohl-rimmed eyes. The mare was a fashion model if I'd ever seen one. She was a blend of Bond Girl and dandelion puff.

Near her stood a stately gray gelding. The fellow had a chiseled head and rock-like shoulders. He could have been an ambassador or a Vegas high-roller if he had a tuxedo stashed in the barn.

I nodded toward him. "That horse has a Dean Martin vibe."

"Funny, that's his name," Cole said.

"Dean—really?"

He smiled. "No, it's Fred, as in Flintstone, but I like your suggestion."

The horse looked like he was made of stone. "I see that name, too."

Cole gave a tour of the barn, making Max feel at home, showing him the stalls, the tack room, and a bowl of water. Then he knelt to nose level and inquiries began: "Max, how old are you?"

I answered for the dog. Max can be shy. "The guess is about eight. We're not sure because he's a rescue."

"You've been on a farm before, Max?"

I nodded. "Yes, he's been to Fern Bubble's farm outside Cinnamon. She runs a public relations business and a horse rescue. He likes to visit."

Cole looked at me. "Does Max enjoy boating? Has he been on the water yet?"

"No, but he's enjoying walks down Lollygag. And he's working in the rental's fenced backyard, organizing the squirrels."

Cole scratched the dog's chest. "Collies like jobs. What's his skill set?"

"In his previous life, I believe he held an executive position in rodent control."

"Send me his resumé. This place is lacking in that department."

"He'll email it to you. His computer is back at the rental."

"Speaking of, Max was at your place—alone—when Curtis Grey was discovered on the pontoon?"

"Yes."

Cole frowned. "No alibi, Max. That's serious."

"He says he wants an attorney."

The dog barked, which was enough of a defense for Cole to clear him. I sensed a bromance. Cole continued speaking to the dog, giving him instructions for the horse ride: Don't get too close to the back legs. No running off. Chasing butterflies was allowed. Chasing deer was *not*.

"My property is fenced," Cole said. "And there's only one road along the south side. Very few cars on it. Max will be safe off leash."

Cole tacked up the horses. And me, as well. I learned there's "tact" that equines require. It's the manners humans should use while riding.

"Hold the reins, but not too tight," Cole instructed. "Don't hang on her mouth. Sit tall and follow her strides with your lower back. Breathe deep. She'll be more comfortable and move better."

I didn't want to interfere with Buttermilk's runway walk, so I followed orders.

I swung aboard and Cole adjusted my stirrups. "You have long legs," he said.

"Not like hers. This horse has million-dollar gams."

He climbed on Fred. The horse was a gray-haired mountain. The lawman tapped the behemoth with a heel, and the horse stepped sideways toward me.

Cole and I were inches apart. He smelled like leather and bacon (it's the breakfast special of the Northwoods, I hear). He put a hand on Buttermilk's rump. If I were a horse, I'd have bucked. But I'm a human, and my heart leaped at having him so close.

"One thing before we ride out," he said. "I'm smitten with you, Mel Tower."

Our lips met in the airspace between the horses. He tasted like leather ... and bacon.

Wowza.

We hadn't spent more than a few hours together. An appreciation of frozen custard appeared to be all we had in common. We also lived far, far apart. And I had an ex who—I looked at Cole.

We kissed again, and I smiled. Nothing else mattered at the moment.

I was on vacation, after all.

CHAPTER 8

Saturday, a Tale of Opposites

It was a tale of opposites, the best of vacations and the worst of vacations.

Cole's fields—how were they so green and lush? The sky above—how so blue? The lilacs—how so fragrant?

I marveled as we rode through fields and forests. Bald eagles flew over as if on cue. The majestic creatures played on the breeze like feathered kites, thrilling us with their skills. Then they flew off to entertain other lovebirds.

Pun intended.

As for the horses, Fred was a gentleman. He led the way over a creek, but allowed Buttermilk first dibs on grass. My girl was perfection on hooves. I barely used the reins as she walked, her first gear four cushiony beats.

Her second gear was a pitter-pat jog. Highly prized in quarter horses, according to Cole. And third gear was a rocking-chair lope.

Again, prized.

Buttermilk pricked her delicate ears as she glanced left and right, I saw the outline of her eyes, which appeared soulful and intelligent. It was rare to find such a lovely creature inside and out, equine status notwithstanding.

As someone who once worked among beautiful beings, it was not always so.

"Let's get off and walk," Cole said. "Your legs will be sore otherwise."

Did he think I cared? I'd have stayed in Buttermilk's saddle until a week from Tuesday.

We halted near the road that passed the farm. Cole helped me off. He kissed me again. It may have been the purpose of dismounting, but I wasn't complaining.

I leaned back into Buttermilk's warm shoulder, and Cole pressed into me. "Mel, I don't know how to say this. When I first saw you, I was ... I'm sorry, I can't describe it."

I felt like a teenager with a crush. "You shared custard on our first date. And the best horse in the world on our second. No need to say anything."

Max woofed.

Cole looked down. "I couldn't take my eyes off you, either, Max."

If someone had said I'd be standing by a super-model horse, kissing a Northwoods lawman, I'd have said I have a craft mall to sell you—which I was considering because I'd never met anyone like Cole Lawrence.

It was unlike yours truly to jump into anything, much less a relationship. I'd had an on-off thing with a pilot for years. I'd settled for it because it was my way of protecting my heart. Have a phone? Dial "1-800-Emotional Disconnect," and Mel Tower answers.

Once I realized that's what I was doing (it took me a while; I'm not the sharpest spur in the tack box), I ended it.

So, if Vegas bookies offered odds that a.) Mel Tower would fall for a lawman; or b.) Northwoods eagles were plaid, the bird bet would be the stronger one.

Cole kissed me again. An elixir cologne of fresh air, leather, and horse flesh made my mind race.

I lived five hours away. He was a busy sheriff with a county to run. Could we have a relationship?

Max barked. I looked to see an SUV stopped on the road.

Cole stared at it, narrowing his eyes. "Don't be alarmed, Mel. It appears that my ex is here. I'll handle it."

A blond woman emerged from the vehicle and marched toward us. She was Ericka Dimblé, the real estate agent I was haggling with to buy the rental! She was a tough cookie. Okay, so maybe I wouldn't sell my place just yet.

Maybe Cole and I would *not* figure this out.

* * *

AN EAGLE FLEW OVERHEAD and downloaded its breakfast on Ericka's car.

FYI, the bird's deposit was plaid.

Kidding.

Jokes were the only thing I had to think about while Cole and the woman argued.

He'd trudged toward her, leading Fred. The horse looked bored, like he'd experienced this drama before.

Fred rested a back hoof, and, I swear, rolled an eye at Buttermilk. She, being a lady, tried to distract me from the ugly scene by commenting about the weather.

Okay, so maybe not.

But I'd already tangled with Ericka. She was a shark, a stickler about rental contracts and offers-to-purchase. I hadn't been offended. It was due diligence. I was waiting on an inspection report from her. We'd haggled over who'd pay for it—should I hitch a ride with her back to town to discuss it?

Bad idea.

I studied her body language. She gave off not a horse-of-a-different-color vibe, more like rodeo-bronc-giving-eight-seconds-of-hell vibe. My career in modeling provided an ability to read body language. Humans speak through posture. Photographs are stories without words, after all.

Erika stabbed a finger at Cole while popping out word bubbles. I couldn't hear what she said, but she used bold font.

I felt for her. She was upset, and I didn't like to see anyone so distressed.

Cole remained stoic during the conversation. Like Fred, his horse, he cocked a hip and rested a foot. The more animated Ericka became, the more detached Cole behaved.

His relaxed vibe said he chewed a blade of grass in his mind, pondering life. It was like Cole listened to "The Old Gray Mare Ain't What She Used to Be" in his head while Ericka lost her marbles. By the end of their conversation, he appeared to be chillaxin' at the end of a pier. She looked ready to kill him.

Ericka looked past Cole's shoulder to glare at me.

Or, she was ready to kill me.

CHAPTER 9

Saturday, Later

On the ride back, I attempted to smooth things over. "I have an ex, too, Cole. He's a pilot. If you see a jumbo-jet tied to a hitching post in Copper Falls, it's probably him."

It was a joke, but it didn't go over. Buttermilk laid her ears back. Cole looked uncomfortable. We rode back to the barn as though under a gag order, then unsaddled.

Cole looked like he wanted to unsaddle feelings about what happened, but not to me.

I patted his arm. "I'll call an Uber to get back to town. Don't worry about me."

He shook his head. "Fred is the only Uber around here. Or, in winter, it's a snowmobile. I'll drive you."

I used the facilities in the house to wash up. The log home was open on the first floor—kitchen, dining, living. Neat as a pin. Also, I saw no "pins" during my brief visit inside. No pinned love notes from Ericka on the memo board by the door. No framed shot of them on the entry table.

One of her paintings was in the bathroom. I recognized the work because I'd seen pieces like it in her office. When I'd stopped to get keys for the rental, she'd shown off her watercolors.

In the bath, I studied the picture. It was black splotches interspersed with sharp lines of silver. It looked like a raven holding a knife. Or maybe a porcupine holding a spear?

The image hung in the bath, a location that added rich context.

I was overthinking, though. It wasn't my house, artwork, or relationship.

I went outside and hopped in the truck. Max was buckled in the back seat.

"It's okay, Cole," I said. "No harm, no foul. People our age have baggage and exes. Or, not-so-exes."

"It's not what you think, Mel."

"I'm not thinking at all. I enjoyed the ride. By the way, is Buttermilk for sale? I have a right arm I'd give for her. I'll even throw in a cousin named Lou—"

"Let's get back to town," Cole said.

* * *

WHILE WE DROVE BACK to Copper Falls, I felt the roll-splat, roll-splat of a flat tire.

Sure, I imagined the malfunction, but it was no less real. Cole and I had bonded over spaghetti, then shared a turtle sundae. We'd kissed and had a horse ride through heaven—then hell.

In the last hour, we'd detoured into Awkwardville, land of potholes, where exes pop up like cardboard ghouls in a funhouse.

Cole had retreated into his own world. He was embarrassed, I could tell. His eyes were blue crystals, clear as glass. Gorgeous, but that was the problem.

Glancing at him from across the seat, I could see straight into his mind. He was contemplating something, probably his relationship with Ericka, which appeared to be long-term and complicated.

Whatever was between them seemed to be a sinkhole—and filled with *sentiment*.

He pulled into the gravel drive at my cottage, then stopped. "Take care, Mel."

"Max says thanks." I smiled. "He had a great time. I enjoyed it, too."

The dog and I got out. Max whined as the truck drove away. His ears drooped when it disappeared around the corner. Poor pooch acted like he'd lost a friend.

Broke my heart.

I hugged him. "C'mon, Max. Let's get something to eat."

CHAPTER 10
Saturday Afternoon

On the deck, Max ate a bowl of Meaties while I ate a PB&J. The water glistened, still as a mirror. I recalled the song "Danger, Breakdown Dead Ahead," by Boz Scaggs had played in Cole's truck on the way home.

The song foreshadowed our date. Our day began with sunshine and horses, then finished with tension and uncertainty, the opposite of what I'd expected.

Opposite.

An intriguing word.

I'd always been fascinated by opposites. The fashion world thrived on them. From styling outfits in contrasting colors to staging high-fashion photoshoots in junkyards, themes of opposition filled magazines and advertisements. Fashion editors loved to present conflict and analyze its hidden connections.

Were Cole and I opposites?

All his life, he'd lived in the Northwoods. I'd lived in Skyscraper National Park, New York City, for much of mine. Cole had lifelong childhood friends. I had few. My cousin Lou, Susan Victory, and my business team.

But opposites don't have to be antagonistic—they attract, right?

I looked at my sandwich. Peanut butter and jelly. A perfect combo of salt and sweet. And in literature and film, I could name plenty of happy odd couples: Sheriff Andy and Barney Fife. Wile E. Coyote and Roadrunner. Romeo and Juliet.

Those two started out okay until—no, talk about a breakdown.

I'd ponder opposites another day.

Max and I finished lunch, then headed into Copper Falls. The sky was turquoise blue, and a breeze drifted off the water. Main Street buzzed with shoppers. The art-mall owner in my soul appreciated them. Artists and crafters need satisfied buyers. Smiles and shopping bags were the name of the game.

I walked to Ericka's real estate office and dropped a note about the inspection report in the mail slot. A sign on the door said, "Erika Dimblé: Buy the Northwoods and play!"

The catchphrase rhymed. Her last name "Dim-BLAY" and "play," I mean. Not "Erika," which apparently rhymed with "emotional baggage." I sympathized with her, whatever her story with Cole.

Relationships were challenging. At best, they were obstacle courses.

I looked in the window. Days ago, when I'd visited, I'd glimpsed a framed photo of her kissing a man. I hadn't paid attention to it.

She hadn't revealed his name, or that they had such difficulties they'd have a public confrontation.

Who would reveal such mischief? It would be like the coyote telling the roadrunner where the anvil would drop. Or Lady Macbeth warning King Duncan when the knife would pierce his heart.

Contrary to the Boz Scaggs "Breakdown" tune, one does not telegraph chaos, especially if one is its provocateur.

I strolled to the dime store to purchase a newspaper, *The Buck News*. Seventy-five cents bought a fat issue packed with articles about the Deliveree competition. A special section detailed the delivery-driver teams and event sites.

The front page headline announced "Death and Destruction in Copper Falls." There was a picture of the battered dock and a story about Curtis Grey's accident.

I parked on a bench and read about the police "chef"—oops, the newsie's copy editor must have had a long night—describing the storm and tragedy. The "chef" said his department would be the lead investigators into Gray's death.

There was no mention of murder or foul play, but the typo added a comedic element to the tragedy.

If I correctly recalled episodes of the British television show *Inspector Morse*, police departments weren't known for candid conversations to the press.

They didn't alert the bad guys (or girls) they were "on 'em like sprinkles to a frosted cupcake," as cousin Lou would say.

Learning more about the accident would be difficult. Internet service was sketchy. Finding a killer hiding among the locals and tourists of the Northwoods would rely on gumshoe work.

I flipped to the advertising insert. It was fatter than the paper. Seventy-five big ones was cheap. The discounts paid for my investment, and coupons cashed out like a slot machine.

A voucher for frozen custard fell to my lap. *No, thanks*. Been there, done that, and had the ruined dress to prove it.

My phone dinged.

A visitor was at my pier, the text read.

* * *

HILARIOUS WILDE TEXTED ASKING if Max and I wanted a boat cruise. I raced home faster than my "YES" reply dinged his phone.

My Northwoods getaway so far included a death, a violent thunderstorm, and an apparent fatal attraction between a man who claimed to adore me and his ex.

I needed relief.

I was in my suit within minutes. Before hopping into Hil's vintage pontoon, *The Wilde Ride,* I asked, "You don't have an angry ex who'll show up while we're on the water, do you?"

He shook his head. "My partner left years ago. No offense, Mel. You're beautiful, but you're not my type."

I climbed aboard. Hilarious had brought a life jacket for Max and a water dish. He jacketed the dog, set the water behind the driver's chair, then swung the pontoon north. "I'll show you my place. It's not far."

I loved the undeveloped side of Glass Lake with its rustic cottages. Other sections of the lake chain had giant homes, condos, and docks for parties. Fine for them, but I preferred the water experience from a half-century ago.

We cruised, enjoying the view. Boating calmed my mind and underscored my meditative habits. I'm a contemplative bird, like a blue heron that stands like a statue, analyzing what's before her.

My career reinforced this behavior. I was a mannequin back when models were seen, *never* heard—especially the B-list catalog and body-parts models like me.

While working among creatives, I had to be a blank slate, the least creative person in the room. Ironically, I gained a skill while doing nothing—I learned to read people and poses.

It's a superpower of sorts. It's how I survived in a crazy industry.

I may appear as a silhouette-like figure contemplating the middle distance, looking like a sculpture watching a cattail sway in the breeze, but like a heron, I'm reading what's happening below the surface. Being silent is how this tall bird catches her finned lunch.

Floating on the water felt great. Just what I needed.

"Mel, you look peaceful—and thirsty," Hilarious said. "How about a drink?"

"Friend, you read my mind," I replied.

CHAPTER 11
Saturday, Margaritaville

Hilarious Wilde's margaritas had superpowers—they turned bald eagles green. But that was because I peered at the birds through lime-colored drink glasses.

My cup was empty at the moment. How did that keep happening?

Hil shut off the motor to drift by his cottage. "I love my place. Got it from my folks. They raised three kids in it. My brother Harold, my sister Cherry, and me."

I reclined on a seat, contemplating his words. "So if I reverse those, your brother's name was Wilde Hare? And your sister's was Wilde Cherry?"

He laughed. "Most people don't get that so quick."

We bantered silly names for a few minutes. Then Hil said, "I'm sure we met each other in New York."

"Were you a professional margarita maker? If so, then I knew you."

He mixed another batch. "We must know the same people. I shot the runways of high fashion and *haute couture*." He squashed a lime.

"That's why we didn't cross paths. I worked in *haute obscurity*."

I did editorials and runway at age eighteen and a bit beyond that age. But as I got older, I became a working girl, the equivalent of a midlist author. I became a fit model, beetling up staircases in Lower Manhattan buildings to showrooms where I'd get poked and pinched by pins and needles.

After I turned 30—ancient in that career—I downshifted to body parts. "My legs and arms were booked more than my face," I said to Hil. "But I saved my pennies and retired before I got kicked out of the industry, and as social media changed it, but that's a tale for another day."

Hil handed me a drink. "When I'd had enough, I came home to photograph wildlife and work for county law enforcement."

I sipped. *Mmm.* "I deputize thee as sheriff of Margaritaville."

A boat flew past, rocking our little ship with waves. I read its name, *My Alibi.*

"Follow that pontoon!" I cried.

* * *

My Alibi, thirty feet of fiberglass and red paint, raced toward the Glass Bottom restaurant, its engines roaring. The pontoon's rooster tail made it look bigger, longer. It was a whale amidst dolphins compared with other boats.

I gripped binoculars as Hil buried the throttle to give chase, but the *Wilde* was a floating station wagon. We tried to keep up but barely passed a kid in a kayak.

My Alibi's driver was none other than Susan Victory. She was putting the "runner" in rum. Ali von Yaack was in the back, her long hair billowing behind her.

"Stop, Susan—*please.*" I prayed she'd slow before the no-wake zone.

She cut speed, but the downshift caused the *Alibi* to lurch, sending waves toward the boats tied to the restaurant's pier.

There were mega-pontoons, wakeboard boats, and glittery bass boats, all with splashy paint jobs, plush captain's chairs, and sound towers—and with wild names like *Hot Flash*, *Fin & Tonic*, and *Sotally Tober.*

I focused on the pilings where Curtis Grey's pontoon had been tethered. Cole had been correct. Damage was minimal, and the pier was still usable.

A group stood on the dock, waving at Susan and Ali, Ericka Dimblé among them. She held bottles of bubbly while a fellow grabbed a line, and then pulled the boat to the pier. Provisions and passengers were loaded like a cruise ship visiting a port of call.

The group planned an evening of fun, it appeared.

My alibi, indeed. I handed the binoculars to Hil. "What do you know about this group?"

He put the glasses to his eyes. "That's Curtis Grey's ex's boat. Ali is out every weekend in the summer. She knows everybody."

"She wouldn't take a day off after her ex passed tragically?"

He shook his head. "They've been divorced for years." He turned to look at the restaurant. "The Glass Bottom didn't close, either. Looks like people are arriving to pay their respects for Curtis. That's why it's so busy."

I studied the boats. "Was it foul play? What do you—"

"I should be asking *you* questions, Mel."

I held up my glass. "These margaritas are spectacular. What's in them?"

"I'll give you the recipe. Let's go somewhere quiet."

CHAPTER 12
Saturday Afternoon

Hilarious and I putt-putted to a cove. He cut the motor, and we drifted.

I watched the sky while the boat rocked gently. Shape-shifter clouds floated over, and I saw a hodag. This one was a giant, much bigger than the one I'd seen yesterday, all saber teeth and horns, the monster of a bad dream. It pursued a ... station wagon?

No, a pontoon.

I observed the slow-motion chase across the sky, feeling my muscles tense.

I'd traveled to the Northwoods for my first vacay in twenty years. But since arriving, I'd been stressed and worried about Susan, then frustrated with Ericka, the real estate agent. But I was excited to see Cole—then a dead body showed up.

How tragic for Curtis Grey, his family, and his ex, Ali. Had the businessman been murdered? Or was he the victim of an accident?

Hil sat across from me on a bench seat. Between us was a picnic basket with veggies and dip. I'd discovered a recipe box in the basket. It contained "From the Kitchen Of" cards decorated with little chef hats.

Hil had jotted the recipe for margaritas on one. Now, he held another, ready to jot down my recollection of yesterday's events at the Glass Bottom.

"Write my name on the hat," I said. "I wouldn't want my statement confused with anyone else's."

"They'll know which one is yours," he assured me.

"Place one fellow named Curtis Grey on the deck. Mix in the restaurant co-owner—what's his name?"

"Arthur Atkinson."

"What's his story?"

"He's day-to-day operations. Curtis is—was—the money man."

"Curtis assured us the cheese curds were free. Was that normal behavior for him? Did that generosity bother Art?"

Hilarious frowned. "No idea, but *I* ask the questions. How long was your group there?"

I sighed. What was the point of giving information if you couldn't get some back? Information sessions were negotiations. I'd worked in New York City for two decades. Nothing was ever free.

"What ingredient describes ex-wives?" I asked. "Ones who are hot and cold at the same time?"

Hilarious shook his head. "Don't know. It's your recipe."

I propped myself on an elbow. "Ali von Yaack was sweet but tart toward Curtis. Smiled, but then would make a rude comment about him. Not sure what that was about, do you?"

"I told you, they were divorced for years. I don't know anything else."

I continued, "Ali trailed Curtis to the bar and asked for free drinks. He gave them to her in those buckets."

"And?"

"She enjoyed them. Shared them with everyone at our table—"

"Who was at the table?"

"The three of us at first. Then friends of Ali and Ericka joined us. I didn't know them."

"What about Curtis?" Hil asked.

"He dropped off the platter of curds, chatted about the recipe, then returned to the bar. I was there for an hour, maybe. I went home to let Max out and get ready for the custard date with Cole."

"Got it."

"What's his and Erika's 'recipe,' by the way? Is it like sourdough? A bit fermented?"

Hil dropped his pencil. It could have been due to a wave. Or my question.

"You met Erika?" he asked.

"Sort of. I'd describe it as she left droppings in the road by Cole's place. Then he and I stepped in it."

"Oh, *geez.*"

"We went for a trail ride, and Erika confronted him."

I observed Hil's reaction.

One can learn a lot by watching.

He retrieved the pencil, then stared at the horizon. He shook his head. "Don't know much about their relationship."

Hil had to know about the relationship between Cole and Ms. Dimblé!

I resisted the impulse to act salty that he wouldn't reveal more, even though it went with the theme of my drink—you can't put the sour mix back in the bottle once you start.

A sailboat swooshed past, nearly swamping our little ship.

I read the vessel's name.

Yikes—it was *Headwind Erika*.

* * *

OKAY, that wasn't the ship's name.

The sailboat's name was *Passing Wind.* And its captain, Bill Hartland, and the first mate, Suko Jones, were a gas and a windbag.

Their words, not mine.

I don't make these things up—but I was feeling like an *l'enfant terrible* narrator. It's *l'tequila*. It's making me *dinghy.*

I'm sorry—it was Captain Bill's fault. He and Suko boarded our ship, then the puns began. Bill was a musician. Suko, an English professor. They lived on the quiet side of Glass Lake.

"We saw your boat and thought we'd come 'sea' what was goin' on," Bill said. He set out fenders and then tied our boats together.

Suko stepped aboard with a cooler of beer and cheese. They settled on a bench seat, and Max sniffed their knees. He wagged his tail and resumed his vacation behind the captain's chair.

"Glad you approve, Max." Bill looked at me. "Where do you tend bar, Mel?"

"My current position is the dog's valet. I make sure Max has a good life."

Suko smiled and raised her beer. "Must be 'ruff'."

"Is the Trio playing at the Sand Bar tomorrow, Bill?" Hilarious asked.

"Sure thing. You gotta come. Mel, you too."

I learned that the Trio was a band composed of about twenty members. Bill had formed the group in high school with two classmates. The Trio grew, but Bill disliked math and change. Twenty-five years later, the name remained "The Bill Hartland Trio."

"If it ain't baroque, don't fix it," I said.

Bill laughed. "You gotta show up tomorrow. Three o'clock sharp."

"Hilarious, what happened last night?" Suko asked. "Curtis Grey died? Was it because of the storm?"

Hil shook his head. "No one knows yet."

Bill cracked a beer. "Heard we lost an ambo. Tomorrow's gig is gonna be a fundraiser for another one. Ironic that I'm raisin' money for an accident involving the richest guy on the lake. Curtis was great, but wow, his son is tight."

Hil nodded. "I've heard."

"I was fishin' near their dock when that new pontoon got delivered. Curtis's son had a conniption about the cost. Good gawd, thought I'd see a murder. One of those father-son ones. What's it called in Shakespeare, Suko?"

"A patricide?"

"Yeah, one of those. Like a baby muskie goin' after his poppa fish. That son accused dad of squandering his inheritance."

CHAPTER 13

Saturday, Lake Time

Good things come in threes, according to Captain Bill—hot sun, boating, and meeting new friends.

I described this phenomenon in the cheese we were enjoying—colby, cheddar, and fresh, squeaky curds.

They laughed. Wisconsinites all speak dairy. Other states may be famous for technology or fashion, but we are known for superior coagulated milk.

Bill said blocks of prize-winning cheddar were prizes for the Deliveree. "I'm Master of Ceremonies. You wanna help, Mel? I can use volunteers."

"Sure, I'm an expert at receiving packages. I order tons of goodies for Max."

"You're qualified, then. We got great games this year. Theme is 'BO,' or Before Online. How'd stuff get delivered to the right place before we had mobile phones and GPS?"

I nodded. "Anything can get delivered. It doesn't mean the correct package is going to the right place, though."

As an example, Hil delivered us the wrong drinks. Bill and Suko got margaritas. I got water—what was up with that?

No, I asked for it. Hil encouraged me to drive *The Wilde Ride,* so I downshifted to H-Two-Oh.

With *Passing Wind* in tow, we winged around the lake at about one knot per seagull. I managed to stay ahead of a portly bird that looked as though he was a regular at the Glass Bottom.

"Take us past the camp," Suko said. "That's where the competition takes place."

I cruised under a footbridge opening to another lake. The trip took a while because the *Wilde* was an eye-catcher with its snazzy orange panels and fringed umbrella. It was like motoring in a famous vehicle like the Brady Bunch station wagon or the Mystery Machine.

"That boat is cute," a woman tourist called as we passed by. "It's like a vintage camper but on the water."

"I want one," her friend said, waving. "Smile for the 'gram, you guys!"

We gave thumbs up. Well, three of us did. Bill attempted to do something else—it rhymes with "loon"—but Suko stopped him.

We cruised for half an hour, perhaps more. The longer I was on the water, the more I realized that time was a suggestion, not a firm measurement.

We floated past a beach, and I watched children play in the water. They jumped on trampolines and rolled in the sand—such carefree moments and easy-looking friendships.

Friendships.

I adored the word. We can't pick our relatives. My cousin Lou is permanent. She's like a healed wound, which she embraces. "Love your scars. It means ya survived," she says.

Friendships were different. We choose them with purpose. Sift and winnow those we meet, making connections as volatile and vulnerable as waves. Lasting friendships depend upon timing, chemistry, and geography.

If we're fortunate enough to meet a true friend, it's a treasure, like finding gold in a miner's pan.

Susan Victory was that to me. I couldn't have established my art mall without her. I'd transformed a century-old building into a usable space. She'd been a gem during that long, rough work, for sure.

Driving a boat brought out the philosopher in me, it seemed.

"You're lost in thought, Mel," Hilarious said. "Everything okay?"

"Just pondering life ... and friendships."

He stood, then stepped over to rub my shoulders. "Here's to old friends who've just met. I feel like I've known you forever."

"Thanks, Hil. I appreciate that."

Bill and Suko were seated at the front of the boat. He pointed to a camp. I saw a log-cabin hotel with an enormous deck and cabins rising on the hill behind it. There was a tennis court, pool, and a beach with a swimming area.

"There it is, Camp Glass Eye," he said.

"Camp what?" I asked.

"Cool name, eh?" Bill answered. "Lake of Glass equals Camp of Glass ... Eye."

Suko explained: "Mel, it's really 'Camp Glass.' For years, Bill has been haunting campers with stories about a guy who leaves glass eyes in the woods, so Glass Eye is what everybody calls it now."

Bill winked. "Scares the heck out of the kids, but they love it. We have a lot of fun at Halloween."

* * *

I BEACHED *The Wilde Ride* on the sand.

Before stepping off, Bill cautioned, "Watch out for water hodags. Those things are like piranhas."

"Water hodags?" I asked.

He nodded. "Water hoes, yeah. We got regular hodags in the Northwoods. Heads like frogs, teeth like sharks. Fast as Tasmanian devils." He peered at the water. "But when the lakes thaw, water hoes come up from the bottom. Nobody's caught one, but they're down there. Every now and then someone gets a leg or an arm chewed off, and Dr. Suko here has to sew it back on."

Suko pressed her cup to her forehead.

I smiled at her. "Suko, is your doctorate in English Lit, or the fables of Captain Bill?"

"Both, and the second one, I may return to the institution that issued it ... and commit him there, too." She looked at Hil. "More sparkling water, please."

Bill hopped out, then tied the pontoon to a tree. "C'mon, hoes, let's tour the camp."

We climbed out, and I looked up at a flat, grassy area. Workers were setting up ropes for boxing rings.

"I heard about the Deliveree Games from my friend Steven," I said. "He's on his way up to compete. He's on the Cinnamon Shakers team."

Suko laughed. "Delivery drivers who call themselves 'shakers.' They're experts at rattling packages. Cheers to their sense of humor."

Steven had told me the games would be cutthroat fun. Four teams from the Midwest would compete in boxing, water skiing, and such, but with a delivery-angle twist.

In boxing, a natural fit for the genre, competitors had to wear a box. Or be a box. Points were awarded, but the punches would not be life-threatening. They would use foam-cheese boxing gloves, and Steven told me it was like getting hit with a stuffed animal.

Suko and I began walking toward the lodge.

"Bill is so excited," she said. "It's the fourth year the Northwoods has hosted the event, and he's like a kid. Well, no. He's always like a kid. And he just adores this camp."

"How did you and Bill get together?" I asked.

"You've heard of love at first sight? Or *Romeo and Juliet*? Our story was nothing like that. In fact, 'I Didn't Mean to Turn You On,' by Robert Palmer, is our unofficial song."

"There's a tale behind that."

"I was teaching at the community college and knew about Bill's band. I didn't take any notice, he was just a goofball wearing a Hawaiian shirt, always cracking jokes. One night about a year ago, his sister called me on stage to sing. I picked that Robert Palmer oldie. Bill loved it. He asked me out, and we've been together ever since."

"Do you two have an *official* song?"

"He says it's 'Addicted to Love,' but I prefer something more romantic."

Suko was absolutely lovely. She had skin the color of butterscotch, and her lilting voice reminded me of Natalie Cole.

"How about you, Mel?" she asked. "Anyone special in your life?"

"No."

"Ever been married?"

I shook my head. "Never. I worked a lot."

"You were a model in New York?"

I nodded. "Now I own an art mall. I run the place while the artists do the real work, all the creative effort."

Music blared. Loudspeakers hanging from the lodge roof blasted the ballad from *The Lone Ranger*.

Bill appeared on the deck and waved a cowboy hat at us.

"That's the theme song for the Games," Suko said. "A friend of ours named Cole suggested it." She studied me. "You need to meet him."

"I, ah—"

She grabbed my hand. "He's coming to our place for dinner tomorrow after the gig. He's a dreamboat. We're having brats on the grill, and I'm making potato salad." She hugged me. "You need to come, Mel. I'll send Cole to pick you up. I won't take 'no' for an answer."

CHAPTER 14

Saturday, Glass Lake Lodge

I attempted to reveal that I knew Cole, but it was impossible. Bill and Suko chattered excitedly about getting the two of us together.

The four of us and Max admired the high-ceiling lobby of the lodge at Camp Glass Eye. Bill paced alongside the check-in desk, a stunning piece of varnished wood about a mile long.

He pointed to a moose head on the wall. "Suko, did you say that's what Cole looks like?" He looked at me. "Nothin' to worry about, though. Cole's got a great personality."

I nodded. "I'm sure he does."

Hilarious kept his mouth shut. He'd donned a pair of invisible sunglasses and pondered the antler chandelier hanging from the cross-beam. He acted like he'd never met a man named Cole Lawrence in his life.

"Suko, we need to cook somethin' else with those brats," Bill schemed. "I ate nails on our first date to impress you. Maybe we should serve a plate of those to Cole?"

"Brats and potato salad are fine," I said. "What can I bring?"

"You got a horse? Or a rifle?" Bill asked. "If you and Cole get married, whichever one you *don't* bring will be your wedding gift from us."

Suko nodded. "He's been in such a terrible relationship, Mel. We can't wait to see him happy—"

"Ixnay, Suko," Bill interrupted. "Let's not discuss she-who-shall-not-be-named." Bill squeezed my bicep. "Ever taken self-defense classes, Mel? There are boxing rings out back. We can start tomorrow."

"I lived in New York City for twenty years. I'm good."

Bill slammed his hand on the check-in desk. "Great point! If you can survive the Big Apple, you can survive Erika." He looked at Suko. "This is gonna work, hon."

Max stood near Bill, pressing against the man's legs. The dog had taken sides.

Cousin Lou would have, too. I imagined her whispering in Suko's ear about a wedding dress and reception menu. My cousin claims I'm dysfunctional in relationships because my parents died in a car crash when I was seventeen, and I "bolted to New York like a mustang out of a corral."

There's more to my story. I took off because I had no money. My parents left me enough for a few months' rent, and that was it. I had no siblings or relatives to rely on other than Lou. My skill set was being tall and an ability to stand still.

I worked to survive. And I *did* have a dating history. I'd lived in New York, not a convent.

I smiled at my new friends.

I'd eat nails if they served them—especially for a guy like Cole.

* * *

WE ADMIRED the view from the lodge's deck. Even Max looked impressed at the pines and glittering lake. Bill said his sister owned the place and just finished improvements.

Log cabins dotted the landscape, their porch lamps flickering. Twinkly lightning bugs gave the grounds a magical vibe. In the distance was a meeting site with a campfire pit. Logs were built into the slope in rustic, stadium-type seating.

My gaze moved to the boxing rings. The workers had finished

setting them up, but boom trucks were parked on the grass with their long mechanical arms extended.

"What are those for?" I asked.

"The losers," Bill replied. "They don't go home. We hang 'em. This competition is the *Hunger Games* of the Northwoods. Stakes are high if you screw up on your team." He smiled. "I need a volunteer for that part. You got a strong stomach, Mel?"

I looked at Suko, who rolled her eyes. "The booms are for piñatas. The teams start the competition by hitting a box. They crack it open to get keys for their boats and maps for the scavenger hunt."

We watched the sun as it became a glowing orange ball, lowering itself into the lake. White pontoons floated like ice cubes, and a cherry-red ski boat zoomed across the edge of the scene as though it were a garnish on a glass.

"The sunset looks like a brandy old-fashioned," Hilarious observed.

"Ask, and ye shall receive," Bill replied.

He went downstairs, then reappeared quickly with drink fixings, plus water for those who declined alcohol drinks.

He poured, then announced, "The Openin' Night of the Deliveree is Tuesday, just a few days away. You're all invited." He lifted a glass. "Cheers to a great competition."

"And to Cole and Mel," Suko added.

"Woof," Hilarious said.

Okay, so he stole Max's line. I was going to do it, but Hil beat me to it.

Max looked up at me, panting and smiling as dogs do. If my dog spoke, his counsel would be profound, a Beatitude. Something like, "Blessed are those on vacation in the Northwoods—for they will need it."

Amen.

CHAPTER 15
Saturday Evening

We parted ways. Hil untied *Passing Wind*, then gave it a push. Blessed is the perfect crosswind because Bill and Suko zephyred off like a cork out of a wine bottle.

"Peace, love, and coconuts," Bill called out.

"See you tomorrow night, Mel," Suko singsonged from behind the wheel. "I can't wait for you to meet Cole!"

Hil and I putt-putted across the water, running lights on. He drove while I occupied a chair across from him. It was a perfect evening for cruising. The breeze swept away the day's heat, and the sea spray felt like mist from an outdoor spa.

Ski boats were docked, and lake traffic had calmed. I saw classic wooden boats and other vintage pontoons, their passengers enjoying a perfect summer evening.

Hil tooted at one of them. Its captain honked back.

A pontoon's horn, no matter the boat's size, is a merry chime that sounds like a toy saxophone. The sound prompted me to ask questions strategically, to use a boat Morse code, if you will.

"Hil, mind if I inquire about a few things?" I asked.

"Sure."

"They're about Cole."

He sighed.

"Beep once for yes, twice for no," I directed.

He beeped once. A sweet, short toot.

Perfect.

"My guess is that the relationship between Cole and Erika is long-term. Between five and ten years."

Beep.

"Cole wants out. But she keeps trying to make it work. He's become more determined to end it. She's gotten more determined to keep it going."

Beep.

"He's in a pickle. He doesn't want the law or the county judge involved. It's embarrassing and could impact his job. He doesn't want a restraining order against her, but she keeps pushing the limits."

Beep.

Hil waved at a mega-pontoon, and its captain doffed his cap.

I continued, "As Cole's friend, you've tried to help, but you can only suggest things. He has to solve this for himself."

Beeeep.

I shook my head. "The relationship sounds complicated. Coming between them may be above my pay grade."

Beep, beep.

"Keep an open mind, Mel," Hil said.

"Open like an abyss, you mean?" I replied. "A pit that I could fall into?"

"Cole's a great guy. He's nuts about you."

We floated to my pier. Max and I jumped off. To my surprise, my place was lit up like a Christmas tree

Someone was inside, and they'd thrown a party. I heard country music and could guess who it was.

Talk about nuts.

* * *

Cousin Lou accosted me as soon as I stepped in from the deck.

She wore jeans and a turquoise blouse. She held a plate of frosted cut-out cookies shaped like spurs. "I used your door code, Mel. It's always the same. Change it but gimme the new one. The police are here."

"*Excuse me*?"

Lou jerked her head toward the front door. My rental was the size of a shoebox, so the front door was visible from the patio slider.

A bright-eyed lawman wearing a gun, cowboy hat, and slightly crooked smile stood in the tiny foyer. He touched his hat. "Ma'am."

My heart leaped. "Sheriff Cole."

Lou marched toward him, the cookie plate extended. "Your Honor, my cousin Mel is single. She dated a pilot for a *long* time, but that was a missed connection." She pointed an elbow at Steven, who sat on the couch. "Mel and that guy are just friends. Everyone in Cinnamon thought they had a thing, but it was fake news."

She looked at Steven. "No offense, Steve-O, but you and Mel are like chocolate frostin' on a pickle. Not good."

"*Why is the sheriff here?*" I asked.

"It's a funny story," Lou said. "Is this the fella you had the date with?"

"*Why is he here?*"

"I take that as an affirmative. I approve."

"*Lou—*"

"Cool your britches." She set the spur cookies on a side table. "We decided to come up early. Jason drove, and I rode shotgun. Steven's in the back, writin'. How he can write a novel in a moving vehicle and not barf is beyond me. But the guy makes deliveries for a living—"

"*Lou!*"

"Okay, fast forward. We found your cottage. We're stayin' with you tonight cuz the place we rented isn't open until tomorrow. I break in, sorta—"

"You broke in?"

"I was goin' to." She pulled a folded knife out of her pocket. "Got my cowgirl toothpick. I can get in anywhere with it, but I tried your code first and it worked. We come inside, start unpackin'. Jason turns on George Strait." She smiled at Cole. "Officer, do you like King George?"

I stepped toward her. "Get on with it."

"We were mindin' our own business when this real estate gal showed up. Big hair, red lipstick, no cattle. Said she found your note about the inspection and came to say the deal was off for this little Ponderosa."

I frowned. "Erika canceled the purchase?"

Lou stamped her boot. "She tried, but I told her I'm your attorney and the deal is *on*. Said I'd be at her office in the morning with Muscle and Fang, here, to set her straight." She nodded at Jacob and Steven. "She wanted to call the authorities. Go ahead, I said, but she could call in her flyin' monkeys by stickin' her head out the window."

I glanced at Cole. He *did* look like George Strait, come to think of it.

Lou continued, "Then Sheriff Handsome showed up. The rest is history."

Cole shifted his weight. Holster leather creaked, and I smelled his sandalwood and pine cologne.

"Where'd you get your law degree, Louella?" Cole asked.

"Yellowstone."

"Good outfit, but as a representative of the law, I advise it would not be a good idea to appear at Ms. Dimblé's office."

"That's her last name?" Lou frowned. "Sounds like dimbulb."

"Do *not* go to her place of business," I warned.

"I won't. I promise."

"What else won't you do?"

She sighed. "I won't send her chocolate that's really poop medicine, or put Limburger cheese on her carburetor."

She blinked. That last promise was iffy. Maybe she'd already done it. Lou travels with a lot of weapons, including stinky cheese.

Cole looked at Jacob and Steven. "Muscle, Fang, anything to add to Miss Lou's claim?"

Both shook their heads.

"This sounds like a misunderstanding between parties. I won't be filing a report." He stared at me. "Ms. Tower, do you have any problem with these folks staying overnight?"

"No, she doesn't, your Honor," Lou said.

"Please allow the witness to speak, Miss Lou."

I nodded. "I'm fine with it."

"Your Honor, Mel said a guy got pontooned up here. If ya need assistance, she can help. Wait, as her attorney, I gotta ask: You didn't do it, did ya, Mel?"

"Of course not!"

"Just kiddin'. But put your right hand in the air, then repeat after me: I, Mel, take this sheriff to be my husband—"

"That's enough," I said.

"Oh, relax." She turned to Cole. "But sheriff, Mel *is* good at solvin' crimes. Solved one about eight months ago. Some weirdo took her hostage, and she went fist-city on him. As your attorney, Mel, I'd advise you to spill everything. Honesty is best in a relationship."

Before Cole could escape, Lou filled the backseat of his squad with Jingle's Kringle, her special-recipe Danish pastry. "For the night shift," she told him.

He thanked her. Then, with a tip of his cowboy hat, he was gone.

I watched the cruiser's taillights fade into the night. While I stood on the porch, a black SUV creeped by on the dark lane. Its driver was as Lou described—big hair, lipstick, no cattle.

No discretion, either.

Erika Dimblé was obvious about spying on me.

CHAPTER 16

Sunday Morning

In the morning, Steven, Max, and I took a walk. We strolled down the lane to the hole-in-the-wall breakfast place.

Steven eyed the hungry diners waiting to enter the tiny building. "If Lou saw this, she'd bring everybody to the cottage and feed 'em so they wouldn't have to wait."

I nodded. "She'd matchmake the single people, too."

Max trotted ahead of us, tail wagging.

"Your dog likes it in the Northwoods," Steven said.

"The cottage is for him. That's why I'm buying it."

"What's up with the real estate agent?"

"Not sure." I shook my head. "Ericka doesn't understand she's made a mistake."

"You mean because she'll encounter the wrath of Lou?"

I stopped to watch a bald eagle. "Yeah, that, too. Did you know birds of prey are mostly silent? It's easier to strike without warning."

Steven looked up at the dark-feathered bird. "Mel, what do you call a sick eagle?"

I pondered. "An *ill* eagle?"

"Yes, and I hope you won't do something illegal, something you'll regret."

I didn't answer. Steven is one of the few who can beat me in an argument, but that's because he's a novelist. Curious bunch, that crowd. They're psychologists, historians, and debaters rolled into one. Writers are freakishly creative. And FYI, never, ever peek at an author's computer search history.

Steven won a literary award with his debut thriller and was writing a second one.

"How's the sequel coming?" I asked. "It's titled *The Dead Room*, right? An ironic twist on 'living' rooms where tragedy befalls a real estate agent—"

"Not quite. But, speaking of tragedy, what do you think happened to the man in the pontoon accident?"

"Good question. No one seems to know what happened to Curtis Grey, but I fear for our mutual friend, Susan Victory."

"*Susan is involved?* No way."

"I'm hoping she didn't say too much, or the wrong thing, to the authorities."

"When?"

"Yesterday morning, after they found Grey's body." I sighed. "I'm positive Susan didn't hurt the man, but what if someone in the crowd she parties with did?"

Steven finished my thought. "And the perpetrator wants to cast doubt anywhere else, like toward Susan, so they let her talk too much and implicate herself."

I nodded. "I've been trying to reach her, but she hasn't responded to my calls or texts." I turned around to walk back to the rental. "If a murder occurred, that is. Let's hope I'm overreacting, and the guy had an accident and there wasn't foul play involved."

"I don't know about that, Mel. I'll tell you what I heard."

* * *

"THIS YEAR'S Deliveree competition almost didn't happen because we lost a major sponsor at the last minute," Steven said.

"Let me guess: The sponsor who pulled out was Curtis Grey."

He nodded. "I got emails explaining why entry fees increased, and some events were canceled. The organizers scrambled for last-minute funding."

"They managed to get it, though. The Deliveree is still on."

"Yeah, and you should know the new sponsor is—"

"Who was mad that Grey pulled out? Any idea?"

He stopped walking. "Good question. The favorites, the Bad Addresses, were really upset. Those guys win every year. They'd been counting on another trophy."

"Who are they?"

"There are four teams. Well, three, and the BAs. There's my team, the Cinnamon Shakers. The Boxer Shorts out of Omaha, and the Box Codes from Duluth." He winced. "Then the BAs from Chicago. No one messes with them."

"Would any of them be angry enough to hurt Curtis?"

"A guy on the team owns a place up here. He'd know Grey and his connection to the games." He pointed to a gargantuan pine. "He's built like that tree, and has the personality of a hodag on steroids. Not sure what he'd do."

We stopped to watch Max dash into the water. After a minute, Steven asked, "How's it going with Cole?"

I knew that was coming.

People at home had chattered about Steven and me being a couple, but we were like brother and sister. He was ten years younger than I, and had started dating a woman in Cinnamon. I couldn't be happier for them.

"Cole's a great guy," I said. "But his past relationship seems complicated, and I don't know if I fit into his life."

"It's Ericka, right?" Steven asked. "She's the person he's involved with?"

"Yep."

"It weighs on your mind, eh?"

I shook my head. "I'm just hungry. Let's get back—I'm starved."

I was so hungry I neglected to ask him about the new sponsor of the games.

CHAPTER 17

Sunday Morning, Later

Questions surrounding Curtis Grey's death—was it an accident or a murder?—took a backseat to breakfast.

Lou performed another one of her kitchen miracles. In the Bible, Jesus served thousands with just loaves and fish. In its reverse on Sunday morning, Lou cooked multitudes for the few. The four of us sat down to eggs, bacon, ham, potatoes, fruit, cinnamon rolls, muffins, and coffee.

When he'd finished, Jason pushed away his plate and exclaimed, "Fabulous meal, honey. Thank you."

She patted her husband's muscular arm. "You and Steve-O are headed to Camp Glass?"

"Yes," Steven answered, "We're meeting with the teams and checking out the place. We'll be there all day."

"I'm sendin' carrot muffins and homemade granola. Looks like good weather for you guys."

While Lou organized the food, I called my work group. My business manager, Inga, runs the craft mall. My public relations expert, Fern Bubble, handles social media.

I pay the bills and stay out of the way. All was well, according to my team. But Fern surprised me by saying she was driving north. "Summer is too short," she declared. "I'll run my agency from up there. I need a break."

"Who's taking care of the farm?" I asked. Fern has a horse rescue in addition to her PR biz.

"My niece and her husband. They'll feed the animals and watch the place while I'm gone."

Fern runs her PR agency out of a remodeled office in her barn. I sponsor a horse, a stunning old girl named Tulip. She's about the size of an aircraft carrier, but her lips are soft as a baby's cheek, and she uses them like precision instruments to take apples from my hand when I visit.

"Give Tulip a treat for me," I said.

"You betcha. See you soon. I can't wait to hear about the date with the sheriff."

"I'll tell you when you get here," I said.

An overflowing lunch basket and a trunkful of muffins later, the boys were ready to take off. Jason said he would check in at their rental.

"Watch out for hodags and 'water hoes.'" I warned. "And Steven, tell your team to *win*." I felt sure Captain Bill was joking about the *Hunger Games* element for the losers, but one can never be too careful.

I showered, then entered my room to find a tie-dye dress draped on the bed.

"We're headin' out for mimosas and girl talk," Lou announced. "As your fake attorney, I order you *not* to wear black for this appearance."

She was a vision in white flares and a cheetah-print blouse. Her hair stuck out in sassy blond spikes, and she wore fuchsia lipstick. She was a walking, talking middle-aged color spectrum. Perfect for a bar, just not the kind with a judge and rules of order.

Lou and I cruised to the Glass Bottom in my Saab. Lou being Lou, we secured the best seats at the bar. There's a gravitational pull about the woman, I admit. She found the owner and invited him to sit with us.

He had a mustache and curled hair, and wore a Hawaiian-print shirt.

Lou slapped a stool. "Mr. Selleck, sit. Tell me about yourself."

He extended a hand. "I'm Arthur Atkinson. King Arthur for short."

She laughed. "Restaurants gotta tell stories nowadays. Customers like a song and dance. I'm Lou Jingle. This is my cousin, Mel."

"How do you do," He looked at me. "Mel, I believe we met a few days ago."

Lou pinched my cheek. "Probably saw her on a magazine cover. Mel was a model. Then she bolted from New York like an ol' horse chased by a glue factory. That's what her agency said—she was *too old*. Now she runs a mall for artists. Some of 'em are off-plumb, but so what? People are who they are."

The man seemed enchanted by Lou—not the first time I'd witnessed the phenomenon.

"What do you do, Lou?" Atkinson asked.

"Bounty hunt, mostly. Cook a bit. What's your food like?"

He motioned to the bartender. "Menu, my good man. Provide whatever these ladies would like on ... ah, me."

Lou noticed his hesitation. "Mel's buyin'. She insists."

We all ordered drinks.

Lou refused my cash and put a large bill in the barkeep's hand. "That's for you. No change."

She studied the menu. I studied the customers approaching Atkinson. Folks of all ages expressed condolences about his business partner, Cutis Grey.

Atkinson took it well. His partner had just died, but he spoke of moving on. He even mentioned updating the restaurant.

* * *

SOME OF US are born cheese curds. Some of us strive to be cheese curds. Some of us have cheese curds thrust upon us.

I guessed that Ericka Dimblé didn't expect fried cheddar to land in her lap, but life is unpredictable. She was partying with friends on the deck. Lou saw her out there, too. She motioned to the bartender, pointed to the menu, then at Ericka's crowd.

Then, Lou turned toward Atkinson. "Where's the glass bottom in this place? I don't see it." She gestured toward the floor. "You need a looky hole to the water to entertain people. Mel's got an auger in her car. Want us to drill one for ya?"

Atkinson laughed, eyes sparkling at Lou's suggestions. He was like Noah getting tips to improve the Ark, or Wonka getting new chocolate recipes.

Lou continued, "We got a place in Cinnamon called the Tool & Rye. It's a combo hardware store and bakery. Pot-bellied stove and coffee station between 'em. Whole town shows up to chat and shop. It was my idea."

She looked around. "How about callin' this place the Glass & Bass? You could have a signature cocktail and specialize in fish dishes. I got great recipes." She waved toward wall. "That wall blockin' the view to the water has gotta go—want Mel to knock it down for ya?"

The bar had a limited view, with dusty decor cluttering the shelves. The building felt like it listed to its port side, unless my barstool had a short leg.

I recalled that Curtis Grey said he was updating the place—that must have been an expensive proposition.

"Do you have a business card, Lou?" Atkinson asked. "I'd like to chat."

"Don't need a card," she replied. "My motto is, 'If life gives ya a wrinkle, give Lou a jingle.'" She recited her phone number, and he tapped it into his cell. She added, "Sorry about your partner."

He held up his glass. "An unfortunate end to a fortunate life. Curtis was quite a man."

"What the heck happened?" she asked.

"The authorities are investigating. From what I understand, they are focusing on a female individual with whom he was last seen."

Lou's eyes widened. "A female what? Bear? Wild cat? You got lotsa females up here."

He sighed. "A woman who had too much to drink. An ugly situation, I'm afraid."

I saw, as if on cue, an ugly situation unfolding on the patio outside. A seagull-marauder had been pestering patrons, causing havoc in a quest for food. A guest—I glanced at Lou, who winked at me—had sent Ericka's group fried cheese curds.

The heaping basket arrived at her table, and Sir Seagull zoned in on it. The bird pestered, yellow eyes blazing. The beast was a mini pterodactyl flying toward fried, golden prey.

My jaw dropped watching the scene.

The bird clipped the goods with his beak, but gaining lift was a problem. The gull had no runway. He flapped madly toward one person —*Ericka Dimblé*.

The bird struggled, then gave up. He released the payload, splattering curds and grease all over Ericka's lap.

She pushed from the table and screamed. I heard her from my seat inside the bar.

Lou grinned. It was as if she'd planned the disaster. Not possible, but sometimes karma comes in the form of a seagull.

CHAPTER 18
Sunday Boat Parade

Hilarious texted me while we were at the restaurant:

Boat parade to the Sand Bar. Pick you up?

I replied with a thumbs-up emoji, and Lou and I zipped back to the cottage. I let Max out for a constitutional, then we met Hil at my pier.

Lou looked at the vintage pontoon. "Nice floatin' stagecoach. 'Knot' too shabby. Get it?"

Hil looked at me. "Does your cousin know Captain Bill?"

I smiled. "Twins from different mothers."

We pushed off. Max stayed home due to the heat. Lou took the first mate's spot, and I stretched out on a bench seat. The water and sky were hypnotizing. The sun felt hot on my skin, and the boat rocked gently.

Lou served drinks—sparkling water all around—then told Hil she'd become an attorney. "Started yesterday," she announced.

"What type of law?" Hil asked her.

"Haven't decided. Thinkin' about cattle rustlin'. Or, illegal search and *sea*-zure."

Hil laughed. "You'll enjoy Captain Bill. His trio starts in about an hour."

She looked at the boats around us. "Holy mackerel, look at them gorgeous things."

I saw a flotilla of wooden classics and vintage pontoons. It was like drifting back in time. The boats' polished sides and brass fixtures gleamed, and their names were a riot: *Wood Too* and *Wood Knot*. The *Deja Vroom* had an inboard engine that growled like a lion.

The pontoons were my favorite. I saw a flock—a sea?—of the boats. No, the mass noun for a group of pontoons was a *swell*.

I smiled at the variety of party ships. There was a double-decker with a diving board and a flamingo boat with pink panels. My favorite was the Hawaiian-themed barge with grass sides, green carpet, and lawn chairs for seats. Its name was *Glass Pu-Pu.*

When its captain saw *The Wilde Ride*, he tooted. Hil cut power, and the first mate of the *Pu-Pu* offered us mai-tais and egg rolls. We couldn't say no. The food and drink looked delicious.

Hilarious tethered a line to the other boat, and we drifted. The "Pu-Pus" were a delightful husband and wife from the area.

Lou made friends with them immediately. "Mel is buyin' a place, and we'll be here a lot," she said. "These drinks are great. How'd ya make 'em?"

Mrs. Pu Pu and Lou spoke recipes. Then, after Lou had jotted down a few of them, the *Pu-Pu* floated back to the parade, and we took a detour.

Hil wanted to stop by Curtis Grey's dock to deliver a sympathy note.

We cruised into a cold, dark bay.

* * *

I FELT CHILLED as we drifted around the shady bay. The spot looked like the Northwoods version of Cape Fear. There were five homes in the inlet. Four were dark colored, skinny structures built into a slope. It appeared their foundations had the droops. They could have been built by the firm of Edgar, Allan & Poe. Not a red geranium or colorful flag in sight.

There was one different-looking place—a gray, barn-shaped manse with black-trimmed windows. Its boathouse was shaped like a turret. It was a medieval castle meets a McMansion.

A man and a woman stood on the place's dock while boats approached in a receiving line. The couple would lean over and talk. They were then handed cards, flowers, or casseroles from the people in the boats.

We took our spot in the line. After about ten minutes, we drifted to the pier.

Hilarious looked up at the couple. "Greer, Dusty, I'm sorry about your loss. Curtis was a fine man."

Greer stared at his wife. "Hold their boat, Dusty."

"I have a bad back," she answered.

"But these shoes are new," Greer complained. "They're suede."

I grabbed a cleat on the pier. "Cut the motor, Hil. I'll hold us."

Hilarious handed Greer an envelope. "I'm happy to help with whatever you need. Taking out the dock, getting boats off the water. Call me."

"I appreciate that," he said.

"Quite a place your pop had," Lou said, standing up. "Sorry for your loss. My name's Lou. Gal holdin' your pier is Mel."

"It's a pleasure to meet you," Greer replied.

"I hate to ask in your time of need, but you got water problems in that house?" Lou asked.

He nodded. "It's a nightmare. I detest that monstrosity."

"My husband, Jason, is an excavator," Lou continued. "He's got a backhoe that can help."

"Does he have a business card?"

"Nope, I'll find ya. I'll bring over carrot muffins, too."

Dusty shook her head. "I don't eat muffins."

"How about carrots then?" Lou turned toward her. "Right from my garden. Organic and everything."

"That would be acceptable," Dusty agreed. "Thank you."

The current began to pull us away.

"This must be ... difficult." I stretched but had to let go of the cleat. "I'm ... sorry." Hil grabbed me, saving me from a dip in the drink.

Lou took the helm and tooted the horn. We waved good-bye to the couple.

Greer folded his hands and bowed in Namaste. Dusty glared at her husband.

I watched their dynamic. My impression of our interaction with the couple was twofold. First, he was strangely calm at the sudden loss of his father. Second, from the daggers she stared at her husband, Dusty was very angry with him.

* * *

LOU STEERED us around the gloomy inlet, shaking her head. "I see nothin' but water problems. They put these houses too close together."

"Let's get out of here," Hilarious said. "Hit it, Lou."

She buried the throttle, and we motored back to daylight. The sun and vintage boats reappeared. It was like emerging from the dark side of the moon.

Hil sat across from me; his legs stretched out like timbers. "Curtis insisted on developing that site. Greer disagreed. He wanted it to stay natural."

"It should've," Lou said. "People never think about drainage when they build."

"What's their story?" I asked.

"Not a happy one. Father and son always had conflicts."

"The stallion rejectin' his colt," Lou interjected. "I've seen it."

"Did you notice that brewhouse when you drove into Copper Falls?" Hil asked. "The one that's closed?"

Lou pounded the wheel. "Yeah, Greer & Dusty's—the place looks like the Old West. But the doors were locked, and the shades pulled down."

I nodded. "I saw it when I was searching through rental listings—"

"You should buy it, Mel. I'll cook." She looked at Hilarious. "Those two stiffs ran a western-themed brewhouse? Isn't that off-brand for them? Not to judge, but Greer and Dusty don't look the type."

Hilarious agreed. "Several people told them that, including me."

We passed by the Glass Bottom restaurant. Lou nodded toward the diners on the outdoor deck. "Can I do a *Top Gun* and buzz 'em like Maverick did to the tower? Spray 'em with water?"

"No," I said. "Absolutely not."

"C'mon, this cutie-patootie doesn't go fast."

"*No.*"

Hilarious pointed to the far end of the lake where boats circled like a pod of colorful whales. "We're headed down there. Concert starts in a bit. Keep it movin'."

CHAPTER 19

Sunday, Lake Time

Lou piloted us to a lagoon and dropped anchor about fifty yards offshore.

In front of us was a grassy park and bandshell jutting over the lake, with a pier below it. Up on the bandshell patio were Bill, guitarists, a drummer, and back-up singers. Below them on the pier were trumpet, trombone, and sax players.

More musicians stood on a pontoon.

They were college-age and wore school sweatshirts. If they had ties to the UW-Madison marching band, we were in for a high-energy show.

A percussionist section, including a steel drum and bongos, was on another pontoon.

On land, a sound guy was under a tent, and a video screen was strung between two pine trees.

"Welcome, everybody!" Bill said into his mic. "Ready to kick some *glass?*"

The drums began a gentle boom-whack. Bill picked a few notes on his guitar. "We're gonna kick things off with a video made by a guy who knows everyone—Sammy Sound!"

The sound guy stood up.

"Love ya, Sammy!" a group cried.

"Every penny we make today is going for a new ambulance," Bill said. "What the heck, maybe we'll raise enough for two."

More cheers.

He continued, "Speakin' of two, why do ambulance drivers always have a partner?" Bill put a hand to his ear. "Anybody know? Sammy, how 'bout you?"

The sound guy shook his head.

"'Cuz they're a pair-of-medics!" Bill cried.

The video screen flashed to life, showing first responders wearing uniforms of blue, white, and sooty fire coats. Every person stood near an ambulance, a fire truck, or a police car.

There were snowmobiles and plow trucks, too. It was the Northwoods, after all.

The band crashed the montage with a blast of horns. The sound zinged through my solar plexus like a knife.

Bill raked the strings on his guitar, then jumped in the air. The rest of the band followed him, powering full-tilt into Eric Clapton's classic "It's in the Way That You Use It."

Bill's baritone cut across the water. He sounded like Clapton, belting out "way" as though his voice was hung on a wire. The guy had serious pipes.

He powered through the verses, then tossed the song to the guitars, horns, and drums. They took over in a shake-the-lake moment that rocked water like a thunderstorm.

The musicians turned their instruments toward the sky, blasting away at the clouds for destroying the ambulance. The players strummed with such zest that I imagined everyone listening—even the vintage boats—felt young again.

The pontoons were untied from the pier. The musicians floated toward us. Sure enough, it was like watching the UW band at Camp Randall during a football game. They had shaka-laka dance moves, and the trumpets and saxes swapped solos with the drums.

They riffed while they moved among the boats. Then they threw it back to Bill. He called out, "*How ya gonna use it?*"

The horns powered out a final blast as if warning Thor, god of thunder, that he should think twice about messing up the Northwoods with his wind and lightning again.

"Toss your money in the hats coming around," Bill cried. "And keep it comin', folks."

The keyboard and tambourines started to jingle—*tink-tink-jang, tink-tink-jang.*

Suko strutted out in a print dress. Her hair circled her head like a halo. "Hi, everybody," she said into a mic, "keep those donations coming."

That was the band's cue. They throttled up, and the group morphed into "Suko and the Sunshine Band."

She swayed as the band launched into "Keep it Coming, Love." After that, she teed up a ten-minute medley of dance hits.

Her voice was like Aretha Franklin's, rich, with a smoky edge. Glass Lake was almost too small for her. Suko could have rocked a concert on Lake Michigan.

I looked at Lou. She'd grabbed Hil and taught him the Cowboy Hustle. Our boat wobbled as they heel-toed in a tight square.

"We're gonna buy that cottage and party up here all summer!" Lou cried. "Ericka Dimblé can kiss my grits!"

* * *

AFTER FORTY MINUTES, the Trio took a break.

"See ya in fifteen," Bill said from the patio. "Or, as Sammy Sound says, 'Audios, folks.'"

The Tijuana Brass's "Spanish Flea" started pipping from the speakers.

Hil, Lou, and I sat down after boot-scootin' and chicken-dancing during the entire set. We grabbed water bottles from the basket, then Hil pulled the anchor and putt-putted carefully through boats to *The Passing Wind*. The sailboat was tied to the dock at Billy Dan's Sand Bar, the tavern next to the park.

We found a spot near the *Wind* and tied up.

The Sand Bar pub was a two-story building with a restaurant up top and a casual place down below with a take-out window and picnic tables.

A woman wearing a swimsuit and long cover-up stumbled out a side door. She bumped into a man, nearly falling over. Then she bent over a railing and lost her lunch.

"Is that Susan Victory?" Lou asked.

"It is. Let's go."

I grabbed a towel. Lou, a water bottle. We jumped off the boat and trotted up the pier.

Susan hung over the wooden rail like a wet rag. I put my hand on her back. "Susan, it's Mel and Lou."

She turned around. "My friends ... it's cool ... to see you. Lou-Lou, when did you get here? Gimme a hug."

"No thanks, Suz. No offense, but ya look like mold on leather. Pretty green."

"I love you, Lou," Susan said.

"We love you, too, Susie-Q, but ya got monkey breath." Lou handed her the water bottle. "Take a sip."

She sipped, then spit.

I wiped her face with the towel. "It's okay, Susan. We're right here."

Lou asked, "You done, Susie, or still got some stomach chili in there?"

She puffed her cheeks, then back over the railing she went.

Lou patted her back. "You're a Bad-News Bear right now, Susie. We gotta get you some help."

* * *

IT'S one thing to offer help. It's another for the person to accept it.

Ali emerged from the restaurant, talked with Susan, and then loaded her onto *My Alibi* before we could make the case to get Susan onto our boat.

Lou and I stood on our pontoon, watching *My Alibi* pull away from the pier.

"Who's Ali von Yaack?" Lou asked.

"She's from Chicago," Hil answered. "Owns a condo on the other side of the lake. She's Curtis Grey's ex."

"Is she partying 'cuz he's gone?" Lou asked. "I've heard of that in Florida, not so much up here."

"They'd been apart for years," Hil answered. "She and her friends never miss a summer weekend on the water."

Susan was wrapped in a blanket and held an ice pack to her forehead. I watched her cruise away. The sky and water met in a sharp line on the horizon. If *My Alibi* kept going, it looked as though it would fall off the earth.

Lou patted my hand. "Let her go. She's gotta decide to get help on her own."

True, but I worried for my friend Susan.

* * *

SUKO SAW us and popped over. She radiated like an angel. The gold flecks in her eyes sparkled, and she was a red-carpet star in her flowing gown.

The woman didn't step on our boat so much as float on. Suko alighted on the seat next to me like a butterfly. It was like having a fairy godmother on board.

"Suko Jones, you look stunning," I said. "Meet my cousin, Lou."

She stuck out a hand. "Fabulous to meet ya. You're gonna give me a heart attack, but it's okay. I'll go happy."

"I'm glad you're enjoying the show." Suko said, turning to me. "Mel, are we still on for dinner? Cole said he'd love to come."

Lou gasped as if the matchmaker angel she'd prayed for had appeared. Cupid or Glinda—a partner to help Lou Solve a Problem Like Mel.

Lou briefed Suko on my dating history, turning it into a rap song. "Mel, she was orphaned at eighteen. Then the Big Apple called her name. A pretty woman, she became," Lou winked at Suko. "She worked hard for the money—"

"Lou, that was *not* my career," I said.

"Just kiddin'. But ya left home, and I couldn't get ya back."

"Was there a man?" Suko asked.

"Yep, a pilot. Washed him outta her hair after too many years. Beauty and the Bore, I called 'em. Mel was the boring one, hated travel."

"Mon Dieu!" Suko cried.

"Mon *dud*, ya mean."

There was more to their conversation, but I didn't need to rehash my life. I lived it.

Hil pushed off, and we cruised the water.

Suko and Lou sat up front. I sat on the chair opposite Hil, who did not acknowledge their conversation. He was the cheerful pilot of boaty-boaty bang-bang and hummed to himself.

By the time we dropped off Suko with the band, a wedding had been planned starring Mel and Cole.

I ignored the idea. Cole and I were getting to know each other and so far, nothing had gone as planned.

CHAPTER 20

Sunday, Late Afternoon

The Trio's encore song of "Lido Shuffle" had fans swinging so hard I feared we splashed the lake empty.

The synths and horns got into a battle, swapping lines while the drummers pumped furiously. It was a frenzy of sound, and we danced until we collapsed.

At the end, Bill reminded us to pony up for the rescue vehicle. "Go for broke!" he cried as the cymbals crashed and the lead guitar muscled out a final rip.

The song stopped like a train slamming into a mountain. I felt reverse resonance in my ears, airy silence like I was under a mattress.

"Wowza," Lou said, mopping her forehead. "Best concert I've ever been to, and it wasn't even in a country-western bar."

That's what I thought she said. It felt like pillows covered my ears.

Hilarious mouthed something.

"What?" I asked.

"TO HEAR THE TRIO IS TO BE EXHAUSTED BY THEM," he shouted.

Bill signed off from the patio, his voice booming through the speakers. "Thanks for coming, folks. Our next gig is at the camp. Peace, love, and coconuts, my friends. The Fire Department will tell you how much cool new stuff they're gonna buy."

Lou talked to Hil about my dinner date. She pretended to drive a steering wheel. I heard, "Cinderella ... big date with Cole."

I shook my head. "It's just dinner, Lou! I'm not wearing anything fancy!"

"Spinster ... die alone," Lou said, then added. "Ericka ... fatal attraction."

"Let Cole handle Ericka!" I replied.

"Limburger ... " Lou answered.

I let it go.

What will be, will be.

* * *

I DIDN'T HAVE cell service while we cruised home.

I sent texts anyway, hoping they'd swoosh to their recipients when we made land. I texted Susan, asking how she was, and said I'd call tomorrow, Monday.

I also checked in with Steven, inquiring about his day at Camp Glass.

Hil dropped us off. Lou trotted to the house while I had a convo with Hil. I looked at him to read his lips.

He mouthed, "Cole ... don't give up."

Loudly, I replied, "So I'm like the Apostle Peter? Supposed to walk on water and trust things will work out, and hope I won't drown?"

My elderly neighbors were out on their pier. They eyed me with concern because I yelled every sentence.

Hil looked at them and pointed to his ear. "She went to the concert today."

He floated off. I went inside and announced I was taking Max for a walk. My voice was so loud the poor dog drooped as though I'd scolded him.

"Hustle," Lou cautioned. "Cole is pickin' ya up. I'll get your outfit."

"Nothing fancy!" I said.

"Can't hear ya," she answered.

Max and I strolled the lane for about fifteen minutes. He did his business in the bushes—*I nearly got sideswiped by a speeding SUV!*

I didn't hear the vehicle. It whooshed by, spewing gravel, almost hitting me with a side mirror.

I jumped toward Max to protect him. I couldn't see the driver, and the SUV disappeared before I saw its plates.

The dark vehicle looked familiar, though.

* * *

I SHOWERED, then found a dress on my bed. Wide straps, soft cotton. *Not bad.*

I added a jean jacket, wedges, and a straw bag. Lou tied a red bandana around its handle. "In case a dust storm blows up," she said.

About twenty minutes later, Cole arrived bearing gifts. He offered a basket filled with frozen custard, pecans, hot fudge, and cherries. "My mother's recipe. It's been in our family for generations," he said.

"THANK YOU," I replied. "MY FAVORITE."

Lou took the goodies, then dragged me into the kitchen. "Play it cool. Lower your volume." She brushed my jacket. "You could be obsessing about him, ya know."

"*I'm* the one who's obsessing?"

She tugged an ear. "Don't talk too much tonight. Let other people into the conversation."

I thought about killing her, then blaming it on the fiend who did in Curtis Grey.

It might work.

I returned to Cole, who looked delicious in jeans and a Hawaiian shirt printed with police cars and donuts. I listened while Lou and Cole talked—*my choice.* I caught most of their conversation since my hearing was improving.

"How's the legal practice going, Lou?" Cole asked.

"Great." She held up a hand. "I may get sworn in this week, take the oath. Head, heart, eyes—and be sure your clients have alibis."

He smiled. "I always thought the legal pledge was Yabba-Dabba-Do."

"How's the Curtis Grey investigation goin'? You lookin' into those Beetlejuice folks?"

"Who?"

"You know, Greer and Dusty," Lou said. "The two sourpusses livin' in Amityville Cove."

"You met them?"

"Sure did. Gonna get Jason over there with his backhoe to fix their water problems. Hope he doesn't accidentally knock down those tombstones passin' for houses. Oops, you didn't hear that—"

"We should be going!" I announced. "Take care of Max!"

She handed Cole a pink box. "Take these brownies for Suko. You two kids have fun. I'll be on the porch with a shotgun."

She meant it, too.

CHAPTER 21
Sunday Evening

The drive up Highway 51 toward Bill and Suko's was uneventful. No storm, no radio squawking with bad news. No ambush by an ex-girlfriend.

Cole held my hand. I looked out the truck's window, feeling the strength of his fingers and the pulse of his heart in his palm.

He pulled off the road, stopping at an overlook. A sign said, "Fence Lake," and I saw a stunning body of crystal water surrounded by majestic pines.

"WHY ARE WE STOPPING," I asked.

Cole recoiled. I wondered if Bill and Suko were talking loudly, too. That would make Cole odd-man-out tonight. Good for me, but bad for him and any neighbors near their place.

Cole sighed. "Mel, I'm sorry about what happened yesterday at the end of our trail ride. You should know that I'm *not* in a relationship, despite what anyone else may be saying."

I lowered my voice before speaking. "Did you say, 'Don't let anyone intimidate me?' and, 'Let this relationship stand on its own?'"

He smiled. "That sums it up. I don't want my job to interfere with dating you. It will, though."

"It's okay, Cole. I don't need a lot of hand-holding. Except RIGHT NOW." I spoke loudly on purpose.

He laughed, and his eyes lit up like my own personal fireworks show. Leaning over to kiss him was the most natural thing in the world.

He kissed me back, too.

It felt *nice*.

He put his truck in gear, and we drove to Bill and Suko's.

* * *

COLE TURNED ONTO A GRAVEL ROAD, then stopped at a parking lot with a pier jutting into the water.

"If anyone asks, Mel, you don't know about this boat launch. I probably should have blindfolded you before we pulled in."

"I promise not to tell, but Buttermilk is mine now."

"Deal."

My hearing had recovered. I stepped out of the truck and breathed in the scent of the Northwoods—pine with notes of bark and moss.

I looked up and saw branches with tufts of green. I imagined our arrival awakened the Midsummer fairies asleep on the canopy. Oberon and Titania were up there. Puck, too. I wanted to see tiny lights cascade down, to believe Shakespeare's fairy army had arrived and was protecting us, promising an evening of magic.

Cole pulled a plaid satchel out of the truck, balanced Lou's brownies on it, and then took my hand as we walked to the pier. I saw a wooden boat tied to it, a charming two-seater runabout.

"It used to be my dad's," he said. "Welcome to the *Root Beer Float*. Would you like one? Make up for the custard disaster? "

"Love one. Dessert first is the best."

He escorted me to the boat. "After you, ma'am."

I pulled off my shoes and stepped aboard. Cole handed me the satchel and brownies. "That bag was my dad's, too. Open it."

I unzipped it and found a flask of root beer and mugs containing scoops of vanilla ice cream.

"Spoons are zipped into the lid ... I'll get a blanket." He pulled a plaid coverlet out of a compartment, then wrapped it around me. "Everything is plaid up here. Even Buttermilk is getting stripes in her coat."

"The good news is that no one gets gray hair in the Northwoods. We just turn plaid," I said.

"*We?* Does that mean you're moving here?"

I smiled. "Let's go, Buster. I want dessert."

Cole drove while I made root beer masterpieces. He said Bill's place was about a ten-minute boat ride across the bay.

We made it in thirty.

Good things take time.

CHAPTER 22
Sunday Surprise

It felt like time had ceased ticking. There was no wind. The water barely moved.

Cole cut the engine, and we floated to Bill and Suko's dock. She stood on the pier and blew kisses at us, posing in an animal print sheath that showed off her hourglass shape.

Something was up.

Suko glowed. Her dark eyes sparkled, and she beamed a thousand-watt smile. She placed a hand on her chest and fluttered her fingers.

She wore a ring that hadn't been there earlier in the day!

"Welcome, Mel and Cole," she said. "We're glad you're here to celebrate with us."

Bill strode down the dock. The fellow wore jeans, a tuxedo T-shirt, and a wide grin. "Suko's makin' me an honest man, Cole."

Cole looked at me. "I had no idea about this. Did you?"

"None," I said.

"You're gonna hit the pier!" Bill shouted. "Toss me a line!"

Cole steered, then grabbed a side-tie and pitched it. Bill grabbed the rope and pulled us in.

Cole helped me from the boat, then hugged Suko. "I'm happy for you. But I feel like we should be hosting." He pointed to our little ship. "Get in the *Root Beer Float*, and let's go to my place."

Suko laughed. "Nothing, doing. We've got brats, potato salad, and Champagne." She linked an arm to mine. "C'mon, let's start this party."

We strolled down the pier, our footsteps clanking on the boards. We followed a trail of glowing lanterns through the yard to a campfire.

"Careful, the ground is uneven," Suko warned. "'Bill's Island' needs a lot of work, but so do I. We match."

I chuckled. "If today's concert was an indication, you were made for each other."

"I hope so," she said. "Bill lost his first wife years ago. He still talks about her, but I think that's okay, you know? You can't erase your past."

"No, you can't."

She pointed to the house, flashing a hand under my nose. "Love the place, but it needs an update. Shag carpet throughout, avocado-green appliances—"

"And a *giant* rock. Talk about an appliance. Let me see the ring."

"He picked it out. I love it."

Her engagement bauble was an opal the size of a bird egg set in a gold band. The stone fit the size of her hand and her frame. In short, it was stunning.

"Suko, did you have any idea he was going to propose?"

"No, and I'm sorry for surprising you tonight, but Bill is private. One of the few people he'd share this news with is Cole." She steered me to a seat by the campfire. "Champagne or sparkling water? I have both."

"Champagne, please."

She poured two glasses, then handed me one. "Here's to new friends."

We clinked.

"And engagements," I said.

* * *

"WELCOME TO MY ISLAND, MEL," Bill said. "Used to belong to a guy named Moreau. Honey, did you show Mel my lab?"

I shook my head. "I worked in New York. Monsters don't scare me."

He laughed. He and Cole monitored the brats. Suko stood at the picnic table, scooping potato salad onto plates. I cut the brownies.

"These are done," Bill announced. "Put 'em in the crockpot, Cole. And cover those plates, my dear. Gather 'round the fire. I got somethin' to say."

"But we're ready to eat," Suko said.

"You know me, hon. Gotta talk when I have an idea. It'll disappear down the memory hole otherwise and get lost like socks in the dryer."

We stored the food and moved to the campfire. Suko directed Cole and me to a two-seater chair. She then perched on a log.

Bill disappeared into the house. After a few minutes, he emerged carrying a six-string and sat next to Suko.

"Know where we're havin' the ceremony, Cole?" he asked.

"Right here?"

"Nope." Bill glanced at me. "Mel, can you guess?"

"The camp?"

"Bingo. In one of the boxing rings. That okay with you, Suko?" She gently punched his bicep."Ouch—see? That's why it's gotta be a boxing ring."

"The food is getting cold," she said.

Bill ignored her, strumming while he talked. "But this is Wisconsin ... all we do is eat. Nobody is ever truly hungry in this state."

"Bill—"

"I got things to say ... to Cole. Might get down on one knee and give him a ring, too."

Cole looked at Suko. "Are you sure you want to marry this guy?"

"*Do not* angle in on my girl!" Bill exclaimed. "I sure as heck couldn't handle Mel. She's too 'Big City' for me." He winked. "Hey, I just thought of this ... Cole plus Mel. You guys are Cole-mel. The gooey stuff that goes on frozen custard. Say it fast. Kinda cool."

Suko said, "We need to have dinner."

"Honey, it takes me a while to warm up. You know I'm shy."

My ears—super sensitive after the day's concert—tuned in to music coming from my left. Drum beats, plus twangs from an electric guitar, floated across the air.

The garage door opened. Lights flipped on. I saw members of the Trio, along with a stunning blond who held a mic.

Suko gasped. "When did your sister get here?"

"Kristine's gonna play a few of your favorites, baby," he said. "Can't have a party without music." He handed the guitar to me. "Here, Mel. You take over."

"Ah—"

"Just kiddin'. Hit it, fellas—and Kristine."

The group launched into a sassy, sweet version of "Thing Called Love." Kristine had a rocker-angel voice and sang for Bill and Suko as though they were the only people in the Northwoods.

Bill stood and pulled Suko to his chest. The two gazed into each other's eyes and swayed to the music.

At the song's end, Kristine said, "Love you, brother. I'm happy for both of you."

Bill started clapping a beat and turned to us. "Get up, ya lazy bums. This one's for you. You guys are next. Gonna give the Northwoods somethin' to think about."

We stood, and Cole kicked a chair out of the way—*like a boss.* He extended his arms, posing like a Hawaiian-shirted matador. I placed my hands in his, and he pulled me toward him.

"One, two, three!" Kristine said. "You guys are ready to rock!"

The band launched into "Something to Talk About."

I felt Cole's body against mine.

Yes, I was ready to give the Northwoods something to talk about.

* * *

KRISTINE ENDED the mini-concert with a rousing "Rock Steady" that had Cole and me swinging around in a two-step.

The surprise concert made Suko weep happy tears. Bill dried her cheeks with a beach towel. When Hilarious Wilde showed up with a cake—frosted half in animal print, half tuxedo—Suko started weeping again.

Bill asked if anyone had a bedsheet.

Suko began laughing, which was the emotional state we all wanted her to maintain. She wiped her eyes. "Bill, you're the perfect guy for me. And Kristine is here. She should be on her honeymoon. I'm thrilled."

Food was served, cake was cut. The Trio crew ate first, then the band members. After that, Suko and Bill filled plates.

Cole and I skipped eating. We weren't hungry because we'd had root beer floats on the *Float.*

Plus, we still were dancing. The music stopped, but we hadn't. We stood by the fire and swayed to an invisible beat.

"What's your favorite song?" he asked.

I had my head on his shoulder. "The Lone Ranger."

"Favorite food?"

"Buttermilk."

"Color?"

"Hawaiian, with donuts and little cars."

"That's not a color. It's a pattern."

"Gunmetal, then. What's yours, Sheriff?"

"What's my ..."

"Favorite anything."

He touched my chin. I looked up. It felt like he peered into my soul.

"You," he said.

CHAPTER 23
Sunday Evening, Later

We wandered hand-in-hand to the dock. The sunset looked like melting sorbet. Orange, pink, and yellow hues reflected on the water and shimmered on the sides of *Float*, giving the boat a psychedelic vibe. The little ship wafted on its tethers, moving back and forth in the current.

"What's this lake called?" I asked. "Rainbow?"

"Stillwater," Cole replied. "But your name is better."

"Where are all the other boats? How did the band members and Hil get to this island?"

"They used the road."

"What road?"

"The one behind his house. Bill calls his place an island, but it's a peninsula. The highway is a couple miles east." He pointed to where we'd parked the truck.

"So we could have driven here?"

He nodded.

"Then why did we take the boat?"

"Because I wanted to be on a lake with you," Cole said. "I don't get to spend much time on the water anymore. I hope you liked it."

No question about that.

"Which one is your favorite lake, Cole?"

"That's a tough one. I grew up on these lakes with Bill and Hilarious. Lots of memories. Caught more than a few walleye and Trio concerts. My favorite would be ... the one with fish in it and a dock with a beautiful woman named Mel standing on it."

I heard footsteps on the pier. I turned to see Hilarious walking toward us.

"Mel, did you want something to eat?" he asked. "There are brats left, but you gotta get up there quick."

"No, thanks."

He cleared his throat.

I got the message.

He needed to speak to Cole.

"I'll help Suko clean up," I said.

I followed the path leading up to the food. Most of it had been devoured, even the brownies. Half the engagement cake was gone, too.

Bill was standing by the table, a plate in hand. "Tell your cousin her brownies put the 'G' in my string. They're great."

I nodded. "I'll tell her."

"I gotta meet her. Suko says she's like me."

"You are alike." I gestured toward Kristine, who sat by the fire. "It's great that your sister could be here."

He set down his plate. "You need to meet her. Hey, sis, stop tryin' to talk Suko out of it. She already said 'yes.' C'mere, I want ya to meet somebody."

Kristine stepped over. She was tall and trim, her only make-up being freckles across her nose and a suntan.

"Kristine, meet Mel," Bill said. "Arresting, isn't she? Cole thought so, too. He booked her in jail last week, and now here she is."

Kristine smiled. "I'm sorry for my brother. Sometimes, I think he should be the one who's 'booked.' It's nice to meet you, Mel."

"You have an incredible voice."

"I taught her all she knows," Bill interjected. "Kristine owns Glass Lake Camp. She and her new husband fixed it up and saved it from ruin."

"That's a story we don't have time for," Kristine said. "I have to go, Bill. I'm heading back to the airport to meet Jacques."

"He's her ball and chain. They just got married. I didn't like him at first. Almost offed him ice fishing ... and snowmobiling ... and bartending, but he survived."

"You almost killed him while he was bartending?" I asked.

"Yah, he couldn't make an ice cream drink. Guy doesn't have any Northwoods blood. But he's learnin'."

Kristine laughed. "Brother, you put him to the test."

"Had to. Couldn't let my only sister marry just anybody."

Kristine hugged Bill. "Congrats, brother. I'll say goodbye to Suko, and then I have to leave." She looked at me. "Great to meet you, Mel. We adore Cole. Take care of him."

I looked at the pier. He and Hilarious still were talking.

"I'll do my best," I said.

* * *

COLE and Hilarious stood on the dock, while Bill and I sat by the fire. Suko was in the garage speaking to the band members about a date for the wedding.

Night had cloaked the sky in black velvet, and embers drifted up like flaming crystals.

"Bill, if there's a hall of fame for fiancés throwing engagement parties, the backyard division, you've just been inducted in it," I said.

"Thanks," He belched quietly. "Cole won't go down as easy as I did, but we'll get him to the altar. I took time off from dating, like eighteen years. Lost my wife. Had to raise my daughter. She's travelin' right now, but she'll be back for the wedding."

He glanced at the dock. "Suko and I hit it off quick. But Cole is different. Never married. Got involved with she-who-won't-be-named and can't get rid of her."

"Can't? Or won't?"

He sucked in his breath. "She's a toughie. Like a wood tick that keeps diggin' in harder—no, Suko says I shouldn't talk about her. Forget I said that."

"It's Ericka, right? That's who you're talking about?"

"Can't confirm or deny."

"I think she has a fatal flaw."

"Yeah, she does—and they're on canvas. Have you seen her paintings? They're flawed. The Northwoods is beautiful, but her stuff makes it look like a swamp fire. I don't know how paintings can be that bad."

"I own an art mall. I've seen a lot of different 'art.'"

"They say it should make you feel something, like music. Ericka's pictures make me want to throw darts, but I gotta stop talkin'. Just know that if you need boxing lessons, I'm your trainer." He nodded toward the dock. "What's up with Cole and Hil? They don't look happy."

The two men walked from the pier up to the campfire. Hil had a deep line between his brows. Cole stared at the ground, looking as though he'd lost something. His keys? An eyeball? What was up?

Cole took a deep breath. "I'm sorry, but I have to leave."

"Sure, let's go," I said.

"Hilarious will take you home. Duty calls."

I had a terrible feeling. "You didn't find another person in a pontoon—"

"No, nothing like that."

"Gawd, it's not Ericka, is it?" Bill asked. "Did she pull somethin'?"

"Let's go, Mel," Hil said. "We'll talk in the car."

"I'll call you soon," Cole said.

I wanted to believe him, but he didn't sound convincing.

* * *

I TOLD Suko she would be a gorgeous bride.

"You'll help me plan the wedding?" she asked.

"Of course, whatever you need."

She glanced toward the dock. "Cole had to leave?"

I nodded. "Something came up with work, I guess."

"Cole never stops slayin' dragons ... him and I are alike that way." Bill hugged his fiancée. "Suko, take your hunk to bed or lose him forever."

Hil put his empty cake pan and cutting knife in a basket. We walked down the lane to his car. The moon was full, and the lake rippled where a wooden boat had departed for a distant shore.

He put the basket in the hatch, then climbed into the driver's seat. He had to fold in his limbs like a collapsible beach chair. "I should have myself hemmed. I need to be shorter to drive this car."

I clicked my seatbelt. "Hilarious, has Cole always had a problem with goodbyes?"

"What do you mean?"

"He doesn't like to leave people, does he?"

Hilarious sighed. "I think it's his job. It's stressful."

I suspected it was more than a job. My life was affected by tragedy at an early age—had something similar happened to Cole?

I didn't ask any more questions. I'd take it up with Cole.

Hilarious fired the car's engine. "How'd you like the cake? I bake in my spare time."

"Best animal-print, tuxedo-cake I've ever had."

"You didn't have a big piece."

"I'm saving my appetite for the wedding cake. You'll be making it, right?"

"I guess so."

"What do you suppose the halves will be? A sailboat and a lectern? A guitar and a tiara?"

He squinted through the windshield, eying the dark road. "Never know with Bill. He could ask for beach balls and grass huts with Gilligan and Ginger at the top. And the next day, he'd want something else. Always something different with him."

We motored down the dark lane, and then Hil pulled onto Highway 51. He drove as slowly, and I watched for deer.

When we passed a fire station, Hil said, "The department raised enough money from the concert to buy two vehicles. Cole says—"

"Did something happen to one of his horses tonight?"

"No, it's nothing like that .... department business." He sighed. "Sorry, Mel, but I can't reveal more than that."

"It's fine."

Hilarious must have felt guilty for not saying more. He launched into Cole's backstory, filling me in on his life. "Cole's mom passed away a few years ago. His dad is in senior-living near Rhinelander. They have individual cottages by a pond and do outdoor stuff. It's been good for him. I visit now and then."

"That's nice," I said.

"Cole's family was salt-of-the-earth. His mom stayed home and raised the two boys. His dad was a factory worker. Made lawn mowers. Worked his way up to foreman. Could have been promoted to management but stayed with the guys on the floor."

"Cole has a brother?"

"He did. Died young. Seventeen. Car accident."

Bingo. Early trauma that could affect Cole's ability to maintain a relationship.

After a few minutes, we pulled into the gravel drive of my rental.

I hopped out, and Hilarious seemed relieved.

He was nice to chat with, but I would have preferred to *Float* home.

CHAPTER 24

Monday Morning

My phone rumbled on the nightstand like an earthquake hitting the Northwoods.

I squinted at the device and saw a pair of spurs. "H-hello?"

"Mel, I found out why Cole had to leave last night," Lou said. "The sheriff threw Susan in the Hoosegow. I'm gettin' a posse together. We're gonna bust her out."

"What?"

"Just kiddin'. Jason went home to get the backhoe and 'dozer."

I rubbed my temples. "You'll bulldoze the jail? Then break her out?"

"No, silly. Gonna bulldoze that house at Amityville Cove and find the body, which will spring Susan loose."

"What body? Is she charged with murder?"

"No, drunk drivin'."

"How do you know?"

"Susan called Hank, her old BF, in Cinnamon. He called Fern Bubble to see if she was still comin' up here. Fern told Trudy—she's a baker, gets up at four." Lou took a breath. "That means Book Trout gals that meet at the Tool & Rye got the news at oh-six-hundred. I got texts from 'em. Add it up: It means Susan's in jail. *What are you gonna do about it?*"

"Max needs to go out."

"Call me back."

I stretched my arms over my head and wiggled my toes. I looked at the clock, six-thirty.

Did I just have a dream? Had Lou rambled about Susan and bulldozers?

It had to be a dream. It was too weird, even for Lou.

Max must have heard me rustling. I felt a cold nose on my cheek. "Hiya, Max. Time to go out?"

I put on a robe and slippers, then padded from the bedroom to the patio doors. The whole trip took ten steps. That's how small my place was.

I opened the slider, and Max trotted into the fenced yard. I followed him to stand on the deck, sucking in cold air. A strong wind blew, and I saw whitecaps.

A car sprayed gravel, then a door slammed.

Within seconds, Lou whipped around the corner, charging through the backyard gate like a bison.

She carried a cardboard box. "You need to call Hank. He says Susan's been depressed since they broke up last fall and was hittin' the hooch. We saw it yesterday at the concert. I told Hank that Susan was upchucking like an owl barfin' rat fur."

I pushed her shoulder.

She shoved me back. "What'd ya do that for?"

"Are you real or a dream?"

"I'm as real as a rear-end collision, which is what Ericka is gonna get if she keeps tailgatin' me. Wait, can we set her up for the murder of Curtis Grey?"

"She's tailgating you?"

"Sure is."

Lou placed the box on the table and opened it, displaying coffee, cinnamon rolls, and dog treats shaped like police badges.

She offered one to Max. "I deputize thee to help Susan and arrest Ericka Dimblé for being a dimwit."

I nodded. "Good idea. I think Max is smart enough to handle that assignment."

"Max? I'm talkin' about you."

* * *

I INVITED LOU INSIDE. "Have a seat. Let's talk about this with clear heads."

Famous last words.

"I left my purse in the car," she said. "Be right back."

She raced out and returned with cartoonish speed. I've always suspected that Tasmanian devil lurked in Lou's pedigree. I lassoed her and tied her to a dining table chair.

Not really—but I would if she didn't stop talking, I told her.

"It's not even seven o'clock," I said. "I need to wake up."

"But aren't you gonna rush the jail and help Susan?"

I smelled cinnamon. The rolls glistened with icing. "These rolls are still warm. Nice job."

"Call Cole. Order him to let Susan out."

I stepped to the 'fridge. "I'm not talking until you take a deep breath."

I poured cream into a pitcher and placed it on the table with plates, napkins, and forks for the gooey buns.

We both had a view of the water through the patio doors. It looked like a gray, boiling sea.

I squinted at the water. "The lake is rough today."

"That sounds like spy talk," Lou said. "Like a safe word."

"Okay, that's our safe word: 'The lake is rough today' means one of us is in trouble. Write it down."

"You don't write down a safe word. Ya memorize it."

"Done."

"Me, too. Now we're gettin' somewhere. What are you gonna do for Susan?"

"Is Patty still a member of your Tool & Rye group?"

"Doublemint Patty? She sure is. Used to call her 'Peppermint Schnapps Patty.' Now, she chews gum instead of drinking. Sober as a corporate slide show. Why?"

"When you knew she had a problem, what did you do?"

"Geez, we all tried to help Patty. I drove her to therapy. Trudy took her in to live with her. Opal paid her bills. But, eventually, we had to let that filly stand on her own legs, wobbly as they were."

"Then what happened?"

"She fell off the wagon good and hard. But we were behind her. She figured it out and got help. Hasn't had a problem since."

I tapped the table. "If Susan has been arrested, that's exactly why I'm not rushing to bail her out."

Lou raised her voice. "She's been arrested. She called Hank in the middle of the night. Then he called Fern, who told Trudy—"

"Why didn't Susan call me, or you? She saw us at the concert."

"Survivor's guilt?"

"No, that's if someone lives through an ordeal and others don't."

"Regular guilt?"

"You got it."

I stroked Max's head. He'd stepped over from the living room to do a quality check on the rolls. I gave him a nibble for his trouble.

Lou gulped coffee. "So what do we do?"

"I'm not sure yet, but what's Susan has done is serious. The good news is she didn't hurt someone, she's off the road, and she must sober up."

"Reentry is gonna be bumpy."

"I'll call Fern and Hank, too."

"Hank put up with a lot from Susan. He loaned her money, and then she had that affair on him. You gonna call Cole?"

I shook my head. "This isn't his problem, and I don't want favors."

"What will you do with Ericka?"

"*With* her? Do you have her in your trunk? It sounds like you kidnapped her and expect me to do something about it."

Lou looked at me with a gleam in her eye. "I hope she has a safe word."

I groaned.

My cousin reads too many spy novels.

* * *

I KICKED Lou out but first checked her trunk for real estate agents.

She roared off, heading to Greer and Dusty's manse to arrange an excavation consultation. Lou and her husband Jason were high school sweethearts, and they'd married at eighteen.

Like me, she couldn't afford college. For twenty years, she supported his business and the community of Cinnamon. She and her friends volunteer, and they bake goodies for every birth, wedding, and funeral.

She's my only cousin. Lou, Jacob, and Max are my immediate family. Steven, my favorite delivery driver, is family once-removed.

I was walking Max—safely off Lollygag Lane—when Steven drove up.

"Hey, good-looking," he said. "Need a ride?"

"Sure."

"I meant Max."

I laughed and tossed a pine cone at him. The dog hopped into the van for a ride home. I walked to my drive.

Steven parked, and we stepped inside.

"Did you hear about Susan?" I asked.

"Yeah, anything I can do?"

"No, I was about to call Hank Leigel."

He pulled a piece of paper from his pocket. "I stopped here earlier, looking for you, and found this note on your door. You may want to talk to Hank about it."

He placed an eviction notice from Ericka's office on the table. It declared I had to vacate in ten days.

I shook my head. "I contracted this cottage for a month. She has no legal right to evict me. I will exercise my option to buy the place, too. She has a wake-up call coming."

"Hank Leigel is your real estate attorney. He'll have advice."

I looked at Steven. *Uh, oh.* He was wearing his pensive look.

Steven was medium height, with the thick muscles and low center of gravity of a bull rider. Most of the time, he was a happy-go-lucky, but when he worries, his face contorts like he's riding Bodacious, the famous bull. Steven's brows draw together, and his green eyes glaze over.

"What's wrong?" I asked.

"When's the last time you talked to Rand?"

"My ex? A month, at least. Why?"

"Did he mention that he was coming up here?"

I frowned. "Rand lives in Chicago. He flies all the time. He has *zero* reasons to be here."

"His airline is a sponsor for the competition."

"There are other sponsors, too," I protested. "Are their employees here?"

"What if he's an ambassador for his airline and is an honored guest?"

"He's *not*."

"Okay. Just thought I'd ask."

"I need to make a call," I said.

CHAPTER 25

Monday Mid-Morning

Steven waited outside while I phoned Hank Leigel.

"Fern Bubble won't be up there until tomorrow," Hank said. "Would you post bond for Susan and assist her with regaining her vehicle?" He sighed. "It's been impounded by the sheriff's department. They said she can be released after three o'clock this afternoon."

"Does she have the money for this?" I asked.

"She does not. Please forward the funds on her behalf, and I will repay you."

I hesitated. "But—"

"I still care about her, Mel. I would come up to facilitate, but I fear seeing me would not be good for her."

"Leaving her car at the intake yard means Susan can't cause more problems, like hurting someone on the road," I reminded him.

"She will give her keys to a friend. She will seek help upon returning to Cinnamon, she said."

Hank revealed she had been to rehab previously, which was news to me. "She left the facility after a week, despite my encouragement to stay," he said.

I teared up for my beautiful, talented friend. Susan was a kind, encouraging soul, but it was like I didn't know her any longer.

Hank and I spoke for a few minutes. I had questions about the eviction notice and purchasing the cottage.

"You're good at this, Mel," he said. "Read the contract, write down a list of questions, and email them to me."

"I appreciate that, Hank. I'll do it by tomorrow, latest."

"You'll assist Susan?"

"I'll check on her later today. If I need anything, I'll let you know."

"Thank you. I'm praying for her. Please let her know that."

* * *

STEVEN TRIED to cheer me up. "C'mon," he said. "I've never vacationed in the Northwoods. How about seeing the sights?"

Copper Falls' downtown was only four blocks long. It had a row of western-facade buildings and wooden sidewalks. But hang a left off the main drag, and the Hoosegow was right there.

The jail looked like something from Deadwood or Tombstone, a two-story structure with an overhang and windows with bars. A large star with "Jail" written inside it hung on the front.

Naturally, it being a Monday, the prime day for Murphy to invoke his cruel law, Cole saw us creeping by.

He'd parked his truck at a hitching post—all of the parking stalls had hitching posts in front of them—and we drove right past.

I turned my head and pointed. "Is that Greer and Dusty's restaurant over there?"

"Yeah, want to drive by?"

"Please."

Steven pulled a U-turn in front of the jail—and promptly got ticketed. A patrol officer, jogging by on his horse, saw the illegal turn and followed us. When Steven realized the police horse was behind him, he pulled over and powered down the window.

All I saw from the passenger seat was the shoulder of a spotted equine and a cowboy boot in a stirrup.

"Howdy, sir," the officer said. "What's the rush? Strike gold somewhere?"

"My mistake, sir."

"We keep a slow pace in town to let folks enjoy their experience. There are no U-turns for vehicles. If you're on a horse, it's okay."

"Yes, sir."

"But a penalty isn't a good way to welcome you." I heard paper being ripped from a pad. "Here's your receipt."

"For what, officer?"

"See those hitching posts on the street? They're our version of parking meters. There's a coin slot in 'em. We don't charge for parking, but feel free to donate. The coins support local charities like the food pantry and the animal shelter. That paper is your receipt."

"Thank you, sir, I will."

"Rusty and I are much obliged." The officer patted the horse's shoulder. "This guy was a rescue. Loves his job."

Steven got out and dropped coins into a slot on a post. He waved to the officer who'd resumed his patrol, then returned to the van.

"Let's drive out to the camp," he said.

* * *

WE ZIPPED ALONG, the top-heavy van swaying on the winding route. There wasn't a straight road in Buck County, it seemed.

We emerged from thick woods to travel a hill overlooking the water.

In the door's side pocket, I saw a thick envelope with Steven's name on it. "What's this?"

Immediately, I knew I shouldn't have asked. Steven's quest for a publisher and literary agent had been frustrating for him. We were driving along a cliff—I should *not* have asked about it.

"I've revised that manuscript ten times. It just got another rejection from Rumple & Greed. They said it was too edgy."

I stared down at waves crashing against rocks. "I thought thrillers were supposed to be like that."

"Give it to me."

I handed it over.

He flung the packet out the window. The wind grabbed it, and pages burst out, wafting to the water like gulls. The toss caused Stephen to jerk the wheel. The van rocked toward the cliff—yikes!—and he pulled it back.

"Slow down!" I yelled. "I hope that wasn't the only copy of your manuscript."

"Oh, crap, it was. Let's go back and get it. Are sharks in that lake?"

The bay looked like a place where sharks would lurk. The calm water of yesterday had transformed into a frothy cauldron of white caps.

"There could be, but you'll need a boat," I said. "And someone else to go with you."

* * *

We waited at the camp's entrance while a six-person army marched across the road. The group stepped in formation and wore stern expressions. They could have been pallbearers.

I saw a tent in the distance near the lodge. "Is there a funeral here today?"

Steven watched the group. "This team is the Bad Addresses, the one to beat. They're as bad as you can get."

They looked like powerlifters, not package carriers.

"Do you have decent medical insurance, Steven? You should have taken out an injury rider for these games."

"The BAs win every year."

I studied the group passing by. "Remind me of the other competitors."

"My team, the Cinnamon Shakers, the Boxer Shorts out of Omaha, and the Box Codes from Duluth."

"And the Bad Addresses are from hell?"

"Chicago."

The last man stared down at us. He was taller than the van and looked like a statue with movable joints. I waved, and he grimaced. For a second, I wondered if the guy—or anyone on the scary-looking team—could have had something to do with Curtis Grey's death.

No, too weird.

We wound through pines to the lodge. A sign said, "Welcome to the Deliveree Games, the Package-Delivery World Cup Championships."

Steven drove through the parking lot, and then stopped at a van with lawn chairs around it. A charcoal grill wafted smoke, and I smelled burgers.

Fellows wearing rust-colored jerseys tossed a cardboard box. Laces had been drawn on it to resemble a football.

"There's my team," Steven said, rolling down the window. "Our motto is 'grill and chill.'"

"Really?"

"No, it's 'We Deliver the Fun.'"

A fellow walked over. "Hey, Steven. We're gonna hang here for a while, then check into the cottages. You're rooming with me."

"I snore, Ronnie."

"Yeah, I know. That's why the other guys put us together. Got a team shirt for ya. Hold on."

Ronnie walked to the van, then returned carrying a brownish-red jersey with "Cinnamon Shakers" written in neon yellow across the back. Steven's number was 007.

"I got you the spy one 'cause you write thrillers," Ronnie revealed.

Other numbers on the team were a mishmash of messages: 10-100, D3LVR, and FUN.

Steven tossed the jersey in the back, and then we drove toward the white tent.

What was bothering him?

Steven was the most laid-back person I knew. Give Steven a ticking time bomb, and he'd dismantle it while rescuing ducklings from a storm drain. The guy was unflappable.

That's why he was good at his job. I called him Santa with a CDL. He got a delivery job with an independent company after high school. For the next twenty years, he rode the wave of bar codes and on-time efficiencies to career success. His customers adored him, and he knew more about the delivery business than his boss.

"What's wrong?" I asked.

"Nothing." He braked at the tent. "The Opening Ceremony is in there tomorrow night. You have your ticket?"

"Yes, Lou, Jacob, and I will be here to cheer on the Shakers. Have you met Bill Hartland, the MC, yet?"

"No."

"You'll like him and the Trio, his band."

Steven acted like he hadn't heard me. "Huh?"

I sighed. "Rumple & Greed called. They want that manuscript back.'"

Steven ignored me. He stared at the tent for a few seconds, then put the van in gear, and we returned to town.

CHAPTER 26
Monday Afternoon

Steven said he'd go to the jail with me, but I could tell his heart wasn't in it.

Neither was mine, frankly.

He dropped me at the cottage and took off. I stepped inside with a load on my mind. Max tried to offload it by taking me for a walk. Then he supervised while I went on the county website to research springing Susan out of the Gulag.

My computer connection lolly-gagged, but I discovered what I needed.

I wheeled the Saab downtown and parked in front of a hitching post. The mounted officer was there again, and I walked over. "Hello, sir." I looked at his horse. "Hi, Rusty."

"Afternoon, ma'am," the officer replied.

"I'm here to help someone in the jail. Is there a person who can help?"

"Is this cowpoke one of our long-term guests? Or a tenderfoot, an overnight visitor?"

"She'd be a tenderfoot. With, ah, a lead foot."

He nodded. "You must be here for Miss Susan. I met her last evenin'. She got into the firewater." He pointed to the door next to the star on the building. "Venture inside and ask for Officer Jett McBride. She helps with our guests in the bunkhouse."

"Thank you."

He tipped his hat. "You betcha."

I didn't see Cole's vehicle, thank goodness. Our time together is better described as a rogues' gallery of unfortunate events rather than dates. He and I encountered death, a stalker ex-girlfriend, and cousin Lou "at law."

And today, it was a friend with a drinking problem. Meeting Cole at the jail would further pollute the tea leaves of our relationship, I feared.

I walked to the brig, crossed its wooden porch, then entered stage right. I expected the place to have swinging doors, but that's saloons, not jails, I guessed.

The room had a horseshoe-shaped bar in it. No, perhaps it's better described as a counter. The polished wood was a half-circle barrier between customers and officers.

A young woman wearing a uniform stood up. I guessed her age to be mid-twenties.

"Are you Officer McBride?" I asked. "I'm Mel Tower. I'm here for one of your tenderfoots."

"You must have been talking to Rusty."

I nodded. "The officer riding Rusty? Yes, I was."

The young woman had coal-black hair and a lovely face. "The human officer's name is Rusty, too. Guess what his last name is?"

"O'War?"

"It's 'Brown,' but yours is a good try." The officer smiled. "Nice to meet you, Ms. Tower. I'll get Ms. Susan's paperwork. She's a really nice person." McBride stepped through a side door.

The room I waited in was a small pen, only about thirty-by-thirty. But you know what they say—small lobby, big jail cells.

There were two desks behind the counter. Neither had a nameplate saying Sheriff Sparkle Eyes. Cole's office was in the room beyond, probably.

The bell on the front door clanged.

Ali von Yaack walked in wearing jeans and a sweatshirt. She had a cash pouch tucked under an arm. "Hey, Mel. Heck of a prob with Susan."

"I spoke with Hank, and—"

"I bailed her out."

I pointed to the bulging pouch. "With that?"

"No, this is the parking meter collections. I'm one of the volunteers that grabs it, then drops it here." She rolled her eyes. "Community-service thing I gotta work off."

Officer McBride returned through the door. "I have everything in order—oh, hi, Ms. von Yaack."

"Here's today's collection. Rusty watched me count it."

"Thank you."

"And, I bailed out Susan. Should I drive around back to pick her up?"

"I thought Ms. Tower was—"

"Just give me the paperwork, and I'll get going. Is the guy back there?"

"Yes, Officer Fyfe is in the jail." McBride looked at me. "Is this okay with you, Ms. Tower?"

"No, but I don't have a choice, it seems."

Ali took the packet and flip-flopped out the door.

"I hope your friend will be okay," McBride said. "I wish you were helping her."

"How is Susan?"

"She had a rough night, but she's doing better now. I gave her info about rehab places." She leaned over the counter. "You were the woman in Sheriff Cole's truck Friday night, right? When the storm hit, and the ambulance sank?"

"Yes, I was."

"Thanks for that video. I was the person who downloaded it and sent it to the officers checking out what happened."

"No problem."

"The whole thing is weird. It's hard for me to say this because I love this town, but watch out. Someone did something bad. He, or she, is still out there."

"Do you have a business card?"

"I do." She reached into a pocket and handed it to me. "Where are you staying?"

"The cottages on Lollygag Lane."

"I'll do extra patrols out there to be sure you're safe."

"Stop by for coffee, officer."

"Call me Jett, Ms. Tower."

"It's Mel, please." I smiled at her.

"Cool."

* * *

I SHUT my eyes and clicked my heels three times.

That's the short story of how I ended up at the Glass Bottom with Lou on Monday afternoon. I'll edit out driving back to the cottage, getting a call from her, and then arguing about my outfit for attending a memorial for Curtis Grey.

I won. Black. It's a memorial.

I'll skip describing the ten-minute race to the restaurant "to get good seats before the thing starts," as Lou demanded.

She operates on Lombardi time. For those living beyond the Cheddar Curtain, that edict is handed down by football coach Vince Lombardi. It means if you're not at least fifteen minutes early to an event, you're late.

I run by it, too. The fashion crowd in New York thought I was nuts —no one in that realm shows up early to meetings.

At the Glass Bottom, Lou and I sat at a table in a corner, spying on the front door, bar, and tables in between. The outdoor deck was closed due to windy weather. Our purview included all attendees, of which there were few but it was early.

Lou punched my bicep. "Mel, you need to figure out who sent Mr. Grey to the big pier in the sky."

"Ouch. Why should I figure it out?"

"Tell ya in a sec. Let's get plates."

A buffet was set up in a corner. We helped ourselves. Lou dropped a sympathy card in the basket, and I put a tip in the fishbowl on the bar.

We put our plates on our table and then visited the bartender, Pete. I remembered him from the few times I'd visited the place. We asked for Arnold Palmers, half lemonade, half tea.

"I'll bring 'em to your table," Pete said.

Lou and I ate, drank, and watched people wander in. Lou recognized faces from her short time volunteering at the camp.

"Mel, you gotta find out who killed Curtis," she ordered. "The police want help if they're worth their salt. Law enforcement can't solve murders on a lick and a promise."

I bit into a cheese curd. "They have way more tools than that. Why don't you solve it, Lou?"

"Great idea! We could work together. You got the looks. I got the brains. As your accountant, I advise you to go for it."

"I thought you were my attorney."

"After helpin' with the silent auction at the camp, I now identify as an accountant. Nobody suspects number-crunchers." She watched people enter, then line up to speak to Art Atkinson. "Got a joke for ya: Why did the accountant cross the road?"

"No idea."

"So she could count the chickens!" She nodded toward the door. "Look what's happenin' over there."

Greer and Dusty Grey walked in and stood near Art Atkinson. They acted like strangers—no hugs, no handshakes.

Dusty looked miserable wearing a washed-out expression that matched her pale dress. She crossed her arms while holding her purse—classic protectionist body language—and stood apart from the men. She didn't put a comforting arm around her husband nor speak much, if at all.

Greer, Curtis's son, worked a Gatsby vibe with a linen blazer, jeans, and spectacular driving mocs. Luscious, cognac-colored footwear—shoes for gods, really. He didn't make eye contact with Atkinson, but scanned the room instead.

"You went to Greer and Dusty's place today," I asked. "How did it go?"

"Good," Lou answered. "He liked the muffins. She liked the carrots."

I sighed. "Anything else?"

"I sold 'em a bunch of excavatin'. We may tip over those rental homes. Greer hates 'em. He wants the cove to be woods again. Kinda scary back in there, but whatever floats his boat."

"Speaking of boats, did he talk about his father's death on the pontoon? Or lead you to believe he doesn't trust the police to discover the truth?"

"Well, yeah, I asked Dusty about all that. That's why you should figure this out." She leaned toward me. "I think Greer-the-son did it."

That sentence was a lot to unpack.

I asked for another Palmer. Lou said she'd get us two more.

She got up and floated around the room, greeting people like a politician running for office. Eventually, she put down landing gear by Pete Bartender, and those two ended up in a conversation.

I surveyed the room, and again, it struck me that the place needed improvements. Its cartoonishly bright green walls were for a child's playroom, not a restaurant. The slick floor was a nightmare for people stepping off a boat.

Also, when I sat on one of the barstools earlier, it tipped precariously. Surely, they'd been supplied by the Barstool von Yaacks.

Replacing the stools would be expensive.

The Glass Bottom didn't add up. It had a fantastic location on the lake, a spectacular outdoor deck, and a decent menu. The staff seemed well-trained. It fell so short on aesthetics that the problems—which bordered on dangerous—appeared to outweigh its purpose of serving people.

I wondered how long Curtis had been a partner in the place.

My eyes turned to Art Atkinson, who stood near Greer and Dusty. None of the three made eye contact with one another.

Art Atkinson seemed a bit pompous but otherwise a decent guy. Loved his restaurant and looked to be grieving his dead business partner.

But how could the place become so neglected?

Maybe the problem was him.

CHAPTER 27

Monday Afternoon, Later

Lou returned with the drinks. "I had Pete add vitamins to yours, Mel. Pump ya up, get your detective brain firing."

"I didn't know I had a detective brain."

"Ya are what ya think."

I pushed my plate away. "I think I'm full."

Lou leaned forward. "Here's the scuttlebutt: The night he died, Curtis Grey took a boatload of people to that haunted mansion of his in Amityville Cove. He lit a bonfire, and folks partied outside. Curtis stayed by the water, showin' off his new pontoon—hold on, gotta wet the whistle."

She sipped her Palmer, then continued. "The storm hit. Folks skedaddled to the house. 'Where's Curt?' someone asked. Last anybody knew he'd been at the pier. Dusty said Greer went to look but couldn't find dear ol' dad in the dark."

I looked at Greer and Dusty, who still stood by the door. "They were at the house during the party?"

"Yeah, they lived with Curtis. Money problems. They sunk a fortune into that restaurant that tanked, and Daddy-o wouldn't loan 'em more cash. *That's why Greer did it.*"

I tapped the table. "Back to Friday night, the night Curtis was found. The police recovered the boat and called Greer?"

She nodded. "Yeah, cops said Curtis got hit on the head at his place, then the pontoon was untied. It floated away during the storm. Easy way for that son to get away with murder. Pops had a few drinks. Bop him on the head when no one's lookin'. Cut his boat loose to let wash away in a storm, make it look like an accident."

It still could have been an accident.

"There were no cameras in the house, yard, or boathouse?" I asked.

"Nope."

"Dusty told you this?"

"Yeah, her and I sat out back, ate carrots. Talked about stuff."

"She willingly gave you this info?"

Lou nodded. "Yeah."

I looked at the woman standing near the door. She appeared to be quietly weeping.

"Lou, why would Dusty tell that story to a stranger? It doesn't put her husband in the best light."

She pondered, her eyes shifting. "Oh, it could be the opposite of what I suspect. Dusty did it—*and she's settin' up her husband.*"

I nodded.

We both watched the group at the entry.

The door to the restaurant burst open—and everything changed.

* * *

It was like Art Atkinson rubbed the side of a genie lamp and three spirits vaporized through the front door.

Ali, Ericka, and Susan shimmered in wearing summer dresses. They giggled as though they'd come from cocktail hour.

Lou saw them, and I had to tie her by an imaginary leash to her chair. "Sit, Lou. Do *not* go over there."

"But—"

"*No.*"

Ali and Ericka linked arms and stepped to Greer, bypassing Dusty. She ignored them, looking away as the women crossed by.

Susan whooshed to Pete Bartender without her feet touching the floor, it seemed. She looked better than I expected. Tan, eyes highlighted with make-up. Pretty jewelry on her neck and wrists.

The last I'd seen her, she'd had her head in a bucket, and she'd spent the night in jail. I had no idea how a person should look after those experiences, but fifty-year-old Susan pulled it off.

She crooked a finger at Pete. They chatted, but he shook his head. Susan pointed to the drink menu. He again shook his head. She was oh-for-two on the count. The strikeout came when she stretched over the bar to grab a bottle of wine.

Pete nabbed her wrist.

"Stop!" Susan grabbed a stool for balance, but tipped backward.

The fall was like watching a trapeze artist drop from a wire, arms out, dress billowing. She crashed to the floor, landing *hard.*

The disaster struck so fast people watched in shock.

Time for an intervention.

Lou stood. "Susie got dunked like she was in a carnival tank—"

"Sit, Lou. I'll help her."

Before I could step in, Art Atkinson hustled over and lifted Susan to her feet like a puppeteer pulling up his marionette. He said something to her, then held her to his chest. He kissed the top of her head, and she began to sob.

I was not aware the two were close, but Susan had been coming to the Northwoods for years. Her friendships or lovers were her business.

I felt for Hank, who still cared for her and wanted to help.

As Atkinson and Susan embraced in the middle of the room, my gaze traveled to the giant clock behind them. For the life of me, I did not know why it hung in the restaurant. Time was a tyrant, and humans didn't have much of it. A huge clock was like a cemetery with ticking hands, a graveyard without tombstones.

"Lou, it's time to go," I said.

* * *

"SHOW'S JUST GETTIN' good," Lou protested. "I don't wanna leave."

"This place has filled up. Let's give someone else our table."

"I gotta use the bathroom."

I put my hand on her wrist. "Do not say a word to anyone. Use it and come back."

"Not even Susan? We can't just leave her like roadkill."

"Not a word. Go and come back."

"Why?"

"Because I'm assuming undercover detectives have arrived by now, and they're watching people. That's what they do to solve cases. Do *not* say or do anything to draw attention to yourself."

Her eyebrows shot up. "Ya think they're here?"

"I do."

"So they just witnessed Susan's meltdown."

"Correct."

"That's not good for her. Hysterics like that make ya look guilty."

Lou suddenly developed a stiff neck that needed stretching. She rotated her head side-to-side, scanning the room, her gaze moving from the door to the tables to the bar.

"Looks like Susan's gonna get operated on right there on that stool," she said.

Art Atkinson had helped Susan onto a new stool. Ali and Ericka swooped in like surgeons to a patient—Ali fixed Susan's twisted dress, Ericka dabbed Susan's cheeks with tissues, and Atkinson gave her a wine spritzer.

A horrible idea.

"Lou, do you still need to use the powder room?" I asked.

She shook her head. "Nope, I was lyin'. I just wanted to check on Susan, then poke Ericka with a stick."

"It's time to go."

Best laid plans.

The front door opened.

Hilarious Wilde strolled in. Cole followed, wearing his uniform. The guy possessed Cary Grant charisma that made you want to admit things, even if you weren't guilty.

He and I hadn't talked, and he seemed distant, not looking in my direction. The two men stood with their backs against the wall, two shadows skilled in silent observation.

Cole stared at Atkinson, the owner. Perhaps the sheriff and Hilarious had arrived to express condolences and nothing more, but they were by that abominable clock. The position foreshadowed that the proverbial bell tolled for someone in this room.

My gaze moved from Susan to Ali von Yaack, the dead man's ex-wife. Then to Greer, Curtis's son, and Dusty, his miserable-looking daughter-in-law.

I even eyeballed the owner to see his reaction when the sheriff entered.

I feared someone's freedom was nearing its end.

* * *

LOU SUGGESTED we slip out the door behind us, the one to the deck. The exit with the big sign saying, "Closed. No Admittance."

Before I could stop her, she'd flipped the lock and opened the door.

The restaurant might have been a wreck, but one thing that worked was the exit alarm to the outdoor patio.

The horn detonated like a blast from a Lake Michigan freighter. The screech sounded like a mating call for ships.

"Holy mackerel!" Lou cried. "Who set off the alarm? Is this place on fire?"

I jumped up and yanked the door closed, but my action made no difference. The shrieking continued.

Pete Bartender looked at us, but the area was so congested he couldn't get over to help. Cole opened the front door, escorting people out and away from the noise. People clutched their ears, and a woman at the buffet spilled her potato salad.

"Fire!" Lou yelled. "Get out!"

"No, it's the door—you tripped the safety alarm!" I cried.

Hilarious pushed his way over. He and I pawed the doorframe, hunting for wires or a trick to cut the connection. I finally threw up my hands and looked at Lou.

She'd been standing with her arms crossed, observing us. She marched over to a wall switch and flipped it.

The noise stopped.

"I got it, no problem," she said. "What's all the fuss about?"

* * *

Lou checked on the woman who dropped the potato salad. The gal was fine, and they trotted past me to stand near Art Atkinson. He was exceedingly polite that Lou almost blew down his restaurant like the Walls of Jericho.

Lou offered her husband's services to flatten the place if he desired. Atkinson said he had improvement plans in mind. Their conversation shifted to recipes for starches for a crowd because Ms. Potato Salad asked about a recipe.

For some insane reason, Ericka buzzed to Cole and loudly said, "Sheriff, arrest this woman for disorderly conduct!"

Lou was pumped on adrenaline—she lives on it anyway—and retorted, "Ericka, you should be arrested for disorderly sellin' of real estate. I hear ya sell two-story houses. Ya tell one story to sellers and another to buyers."

To make things worse, Potato Salad chimed in with a client-tale of her own. "I had a terrible experience when Ericka sold my house. Very unprofessional."

"Your place had zero square feet and wasn't on a lake," Ericka argued. "It was barely worth my time."

Cole stepped in before the argument got worse. "Ericka, take a seat by your friends at the bar."

"But—"

"Take a seat ... with your friends ... at the bar."

"Don't mansplain."

Lou held up her fists. "You want me to cowgirl-splain? How about Lefty and Righty—you and me—out back?"

"Let's go," I said.

"I can take her, no problem."

Ali and Susan jumped to action, surrounded Ericka, and pulled her out the door.

Cole and I glanced at each other. For a second, I saw the real person, the man under the uniform with its creaky leather and gadgets. I saw the guy I was getting to know, the fellow with broad shoulders and a dry sense of humor.

There was something about Cole that connected with my soul—*but could we make a relationship work?*

I'd avoided human connections and quashed feelings because my job required it. I'd been a mannequin, *seen,* not heard. As for a relationship, I'd had one with a man who flew away regularly. Opening my heart for a permanent connection wasn't necessary.

I feared Cole was like me. He had a job that required neutrality and distance. He had a relationship that worked once but was different now. He didn't know how to change it, feared changing it, or couldn't tell her goodbye.

He had no trouble telling Lou and me to scram, though.

To prevent a rumble in the parking lot, in case Ericka & Co. were hanging around, Cole and Hilarious escorted us to the car.

Cole ordered Lou to stay away from doors with "Closed" signs. Also, fights.

"That's missin' all the fun," she complained.

We climbed into the car and wheeled toward home. In the side mirror, I saw Cole speaking to Ericka.

Lou dropped me off. Soon after, Cole sent a text:

> Please stay safe, Mel.

That was about as neutral as could be. He may as well have added "kind regards." I replied:

> You, too.

I added a little flame emoji to lighten the mood, see if he'd thaw, so to speak.

He didn't respond.

Nothing was going right with Cole, it seemed.

CHAPTER 28

Tuesday Morning

Tuesday arrived bright and fresh, like clean sheets from the dryer.

I awoke feeling apprehensive, though.

The memorial at the Glass Bottom had been stressful. I felt distant from Cole. Worst of all, I worried for Susan. She was making poor decisions—and I sensed she was being set up in Curtis Grey's death.

A black nose appeared next to the bed. Max was recommending his version of therapy, a vigorous walk to recombobulate the mind.

I dressed, and we headed down Lollygag Lane.

The dog's perky steps reminded me to stop and smell the roses. Or, in Max's case, to sniff earthworms, tree trunks, and the leg of a bench placed in a shady spot overlooking Glass Lake.

He and I watched a boat drift along the shore, its trolling motor humming.

A fisherman dragged a line through the water while a woman with him peered through an impressive-looking camera. It looked like it could capture a bee on a daisy at a hundred paces.

She pointed at cottages along the water. Bald eagles whooshed over, and she aimed the lens skyward. After a series of clicks, the woman said, "They're so beautiful. Magnificent creatures."

The two appeared to be enjoying the lake before the frenzy of boats, skiers, and partiers began. It was a lovely way to spend a Northwoods morning.

Or, they were watching residences under the guise of fishing and taking pictures, the perfect way to monitor suspects and document behavior.

Were they working undercover? Had I seen them last evening at the Glass Bottom?

I pondered Greer, Curtis Grey's son. He wanted to improve his dad's home—the "monstrosity"—plus knock down the other places on the inlet. The chaos of a home reno would destroy evidence if there were any. It was an easy way to hide one's tracks.

I watched the couple in the boat, wondering if they had drifted past Greer and Dusty's place.

* * *

MAX and I returned to the cottage.

I checked my phone. No text from Cole. It pinged with a message from Fern Bubble, though. She'd arrived at her rental condo and wanted to have lunch.

I responded, saying I'd pick up salads and meet her there at one o'clock. Then Lou called with news about Steven and his quest to be published.

"He's in a funk," she said. "Another rejection. Agent-guy thinks his book was boring and needed more twists and turns. What's up with those New York types? They all got burrs under their saddles or what?"

"Not everyone is as calm and thoughtful as you, Lou," I said.

"We gotta cheer him up tonight at the Opening Ceremony. Games start tomorrow, and Steve-O is the Shakers' anchor. You're comin' tonight, right?"

"Yes, of course."

"Good, just checkin'. What are ya wearin'?"

"Are you telling me to look in my closet?"

"Put a tie-dye number in there for ya."

"Thanks."

"Say hi to Max for me."

She clicked off, and I told Max that his Aunt Louella thought he was the smartest dog in the world. He listened to my words with that unique border-collie intensity. Before I could say he was the most handsome, too, he cocked an ear toward the front door and woofed.

I heard a tap. "Ms. Tower? It's Jett McBride."

"Come in, it's unlocked."

She entered wearing a khaki uniform and a worried expression. Her brows knitted together over her beautiful eyes, shading them and making them look fearful.

"I thought I'd stop by," the officer said.

* * *

I MADE COFFEE, and a new friend.

McBride and I stayed inside the cottage, even though the deck called us out to enjoy the view. The officer perched on the edge of the couch and held her mug with both hands, which were shaking.

She'd spoken with Lou about me. "I'm working security at the games, and I met your cousin. She said you're smarter than you, ah, look."

"Oh?"

"That didn't come out right, sorry."

I smiled. "Lou has a unique way of putting things."

"I'm worried about your friend."

"Susan?"

"Y-yeah." Her voice broke.

Max noticed her distress. He padded to her and leaned against her legs. Jett abandoned her coffee on a side table and stroked the dog's fur.

"I read the statement she gave after Curtis Grey was found," she explained. "I also read the case the detectives are building. I'm not working on it, so I don't know everything, but it doesn't look good."

"What do you mean?"

"Ms. Susan admitted she was at Mr. Grey's house the night he died. She said she was with him on his pier."

I shook my head. "But other people must have been there."

"She thinks she blacked out. Basically, she admitted she could have done something to him."

"She said that to the police the next day? When she was with Ali at her condo?"

"Yeah."

"But isn't Ali her alibi? Weren't they together the whole time?"

"No, Ali didn't go to Mr. Grey's house that night. She claims she took her own boat back to her condo. Then she was gonna drive to Grey's place but didn't because of the storm."

"Other people could dispute who was around Curtis. It wasn't just Susan."

"Well, maybe. But the owner of the Glass Bottom, Art Atkinson, said Susan Victory was the last person seen near Curtis Grey before he died."

* * *

JETT GOT up and walked to the sliding doors. Max followed her, waving his tail.

"Can I let him out?" she asked.

"Sure."

The door was opened, and Max raced out. Jett watched the dog. Her posture straightened as she talked. "I grew up here. I've heard things. I can help solve this case—I know it."

"I believe you. What does Cole, er, Sheriff Lawrence, say?"

"He's cool, a great boss. I've only been on the force for a year, but he thinks I have good instincts. He said I should keep my eyes and ears open."

"Then do that."

"The police chief is sorta, well, your cousin would say he puts the 'sour' in 'puss.'"

I nodded. "That sounds like her."

"He's close to retirement, you know? He'd rather be on his boat than working a murder investigation. And the other detective is super-inexperienced. She's on loan from Madison. She's even younger than I am."

Jett turned toward me. "I can't take over, but I can do my part to figure it out. I don't believe Susan Victory did it. There's too much else to consider."

"Go for it, then. Be confident, Jett."

I stood by the patio door, smiling at the young officer, staying relaxed in my posture.

Posing 101: When Party A verbalizes anxieties, Party B listens, doesn't show impatience, and maintains a soft expression.

"Did you hear about Susan's meltdown at the Glass Bottom last night?" I asked.

"Sure did. I had a friend there. She told me everything."

"Good for you. You're working sources already."

"Would you be one? Will you help me?" She asked with such earnestness that I absolutely would *not* refuse.

I saw myself in Jett, the young woman I was before my parents died. The girl who wanted to attend college and become a teacher, but tragedy changed her destiny.

I will never complain about how my life turned out. My job was lonely and esteem-crushing at times, but it provided a decent income that allowed the life I have now.

I certainly would support someone seeking her life's purpose, learning a job she felt called to do.

"Yes, I'll help you, Jett," I said.

* * *

JETT LET MAX IN, then gave him a snack from the bowl on the counter. "You were a model once?"

"Are you asking me or Max?"

She smiled. "He could be, but I mean you, Mel."

"Yes, a long time ago, in a land far, far away."

"I'm glad you were in Cole's truck the other night. He needs to be with a nice person like you."

"I appreciate that."

Before she left, we made plans to communicate. She'd patrol my road, she said, but wouldn't stop for coffee. Too obvious, and I agreed.

A single visit like this could be seen as routine. More of them, and it would appear odd.

"I'm working the games," Jett said. "Will you be there?"

"Sure."

"Then I'll find you."

Before she left, I asked her about a place to purchase an engagement gift. She recommended a place that sold new and vintage treasures, and then she was gone.

Seeing Jett leave with a bounce in her step, a bit of a tail-wag, reminded me that my tail had the droops.

I had an offer-to-purchase that had transformed into an eviction notice courtesy of Ms. Dimblé. I needed to convince her I was *not* the enemy. We wouldn't be best friends, but the Northwoods was a big place with plenty to see and do beyond the purview of a specific person.

There was room for both of us in it, in other words.

I worked on my computer, then emailed ideas about real estate actions to Hank at Leigel, Leigel & Friendly.

I updated him about Susan, too, writing a summary of what happened. I told him I'd keep him posted. I did not say she faced imminent arrest for the murder of Mr. Curtis Grey.

I refused to acknowledge that yet.

I had faith in Jett. I believed that the young officer would discover the truth. She wasn't a knight in shining armor riding in on a horse, but she'd get there. It was obvious Jett had fire, a calling to help others and solve problems.

The thought of a horse reminded me of Buttermilk.

Then, of course, Cole.

Should I call him? Send another text? What was the right step in this situation where I saw nothing but problems?

Just then, my phone pinged.

CHAPTER 29
Tuesday Morning, Later

The text was from Suko.

> I need your fashion knowledge. Will you help me pick out a dress later this week?

I hesitated before responding.

I felt caught in an odd continuum, one of opposites. Suko was making a permanent commitment, stepping into a new phase of her life. I was thrilled for her. She and Bill seemed perfect for one another.

But my relationship with Cole was just beginning.

Or was it over, the victim of two people who had too much to learn about themselves before having a relationship?

Every relationship was its challenges, tests of patience and honesty. It's like experiencing Wisconsin's weather but in physical form—one minute, it's hot and sunny, and the next it's frigid and windy.

And don't get me started on the dealbreaker in any relationship: *timing*. Again, it's like Wisconsin's weather. In this state, if you don't like the forecast, wait ten minutes, and it will change.

Until meeting Cole, I'd never wanted to pursue a permanent commitment with someone. For years, I focused on my career in New

York. When I returned to Cinnamon, I opened a business. A serious relationship had never been on my radar.

Then I met Cole, and everything changed.

I stepped out onto the deck and re-read Suko's text.

I'd modeled wedding dresses but never shopped for them. My mother would have been so happy to see the pictures. She was gone, of course, and never got to see me in a wedding dress. She never saw any of my work.

Max followed me outside. Instead of racing off to chase squirrels, he leaned against my legs.

I knelt to rub his chest. He licked tears from my cheeks.

How do dogs know?

* * *

EMOTIONAL-SUPPORT MAX BOOSTED MY MOOD.

I replied to Suko saying I'd love to assist with a dress. Then Max and I swung by a shop to select an engagement gift. It was an amazing place off of Highway 51. A curated selection of one-of-a-kind vintage gifts and fun new goodies, many of them plaid, the color of the Northwoods.

I selected tuxedo can-cozies, and Max found fabulous animal-print napkins. The manager wrapped them, and he and I were on our way to Bill's place to drop off the items.

I sent Bill a text asking if he was around.

He replied:

> YES. ON PIER. GOING HALF-CRAZY.
> CHECK YES OR NO.

Hmmm.

I wasn't sure what to make of his message, but it sounded serious.

Max and I zipped out to the peninsula. I found Bill on the pier, dangling his legs in the water. He wore a flat fishing hat and looked like Huck Finn, not the kid adventurer, but a life-is-tough grown-up.

Bill had indulged in a few beers, and it was before noon. *Odd.* I hadn't seen him drink any alcohol, only root beer, plus one non-alcoholic brew on his engagement night.

"What's wrong?" I asked.

"Everything," he said. "Get in the boat. Let's go for a ride."

We got into *Just Passin' Through*, his pontoon.

I drove while he operated the radio. Max leaned against Bill's legs while we listened to "He Stopped Loving Her Today" and "Check Yes or No."

I cruised to the middle and stopped. We weren't on a leisurely ride. I had no interest in looking at homes, and I sensed Bill didn't want any neighbors to hear our conversation.

He reached into the cooler he'd stashed on board. "Want a beer?"

"No, thanks."

Max's nose twitched in what must have been an olfactory check for Bill's stress hormones. Bill had ignored the dog, but I knew Max wouldn't give up. He'd stay by the man's side until he comforted him somehow.

"Suko is packin' her apartment. She's movin' in later," Bill said.

"That's good, right?"

He rolled the cold beer over his cheeks and nose. I couldn't tell if the moisture from the can wet his face or if he was crying.

"Sorry, Mel, but if ya repeat any of what I'm gonna say, I'm gonna have to kill ya."

* * *

MAX GROWLED.

Well, no. *I* growled. On the inside. Only an hour prior, I'd been conversing with a police officer who believed a murderer lurked in the Northwoods.

Not exactly comedic discourse.

I watched Bill from the captain's chair and inhaled meditative breaths, focusing on the gentle waves. I wanted to throttle him for what he said, even if it was a joke.

I willed the lake to mellow me out. Clichés and quotes about lake life popped to mind. I imagined those goofy signs with sayings like, "No Swimming: Piranhas" and "Lake Life is a Load of Carp."

The problem with forced serenity is that it tends to have the opposite effect. "What's going on, Bill?" I demanded.

He swigged his beer. "I adore Suko. It's just that—"

"You're not thinking of killing her, *are you*?"

"Gawd no," Bill said. "What are you sayin'? I love Suko. I think I'm gonna marry her."

"You *think* you'll marry her?"

He wiped his eyes on his shirt sleeve. "Believe it or not, I was never a chick magnet, not in grade school or high school. Didn't go to college, so I didn't collect groupies like a rock star, not that I wanted that. Nobody pays attention to me unless I'm on stage. Even then, it's because I got a great band."

"You're selling yourself short, Bill, but go on."

"Hilarious was the guy with all the girlfriends. When him, Cole, and I were growin' up, girls flocked to Hil like gulls to the deck at the Glass Bottom. When he went to college and they knew he batted for the other team, gals loved him more."

Don't ask about Cole. Don't ask about Cole.

"What was Cole like in school?"

"He had girlfriends but nothin' serious. He was into huntin' and fishin'. Went to school in Superior, then came back and started police work."

"He never married?"

"Nope. But I did."

Bill abandoned his beer, dropping the can like it burned his fingers. He leaned forward, then gulped for air.

Droplets began sprinkling the deck, then rivered down, falling on Max. The dog pressed harder into the human's legs, his canine comfort instinct in overdrive.

I grabbed two towels from the basket on board, handing one to Bill, who buried his face in it, and used the other to soak up the spilled beverage.

I didn't say anything. To quote the ancient proverb: What soap is for the body, tears are for the soul.

Sometimes, it's best to have a good cry.

* * *

LATER, Bill sat on a bench seat, discussing his wife, Becky. "We met in eighth grade. She knocked off my feet by throwin' a spitball. We got our first detentions together for talkin' in class. We were together every day after that."

Bill patted Max. The dog had worked his magic. "Becks and I married at eighteen. She could shoot a squirrel out of a tree at a hundred yards. Walleye would throw themselves into the boat. Becks didn't even need a pole. She was a keeper."

"She sounds special, Bill."

"She gave me the best thing ever—our daughter, Billy. We laughed that the stork delivered the kid to the wrong address. Billy doesn't take after her mom or me." He sighed. "She always wanted to leave this place. She's a kid that needs to travel around the next bend. She'll be home for the weddin'. She wants to see her old man happy again."

I moved to the cooler. "Bill, would you like water?"

"Nah, hand me that beer, that one in the gold can."

I handed it over. He opened it and poured the liquid over the side. "That's for Becks. She hated this beer. The night she died, I came out and dumped all we had left, except for that one can."

"I'm sure she's looking down and appreciates that."

"Yeah, if she took the upstairs elevator." He looked at the sky. "Just kiddin', hon. Of course, you're up there. Who else would tie the angels' shoelaces together when they're not lookin', or put a chocolate-bar floater in the punchbowl up there?"

"Was she a singer, too?"

"Gawd no, had a voice like a buffalo stampede." He sighed. "I loved every minute of being married to my wife."

"What happened?"

"Breast cancer. Got her after we'd been married fifteen years. I thought for sure she'd beat it. Docs radiated the snot out of her. Tried every treatment you could imagine. I took her to Canada for experiments, too. Couldn't get her to turn the corner."

"I'm *so* sorry."

"You shoulda seen Cole. Both him and Hilarious were the best friends a guy could want. They loved Becks." He rubbed Max's fur. "I never thought I could date someone like Suko. Complete opposite of my wife. She sings like a bird, smart as a professor, probably 'cuz she is one. I can't believe she fell for me."

"Suko is crazy about you, Bill."

"Maybe just crazy. I'm not sure I'm doin' the right thing. How can a guy like me keep a woman like her happy?"

I shook my head. "It's not about keeping Suko happy. It's about being content with yourselves first, then making one another happy."

"You ever been married?"

"Not even close."

"Then what the heck do ya know about it?"

I laughed. "Excellent question."

"Just kiddin'. Startin' to get my sense of humor back. Gotta test it on someone. Cole's never been married, and his advice is pretty good."

"Oh?"

"Heck, *no*. He's great, but his advice stinks. I think it's 'cause he never dated much, so he has horrible taste in women."

"*Huh*."

"Oops, not you, you're an okay chick—and you got a great dog." He patted Max. "Cole had no experience in dating. I called him Cole 'Gump' in high school. He got twisted up with a fatal attraction about five years ago."

Bill stopped to replace his hat. It had fallen off earlier. "Cole finally told Ericka they were over, but she won't listen. I told him we could try radiatin' the snot out of her. Put a wall of fire at the front gate of his place to keep her out, but he says there's a reasonable solution to moving on."

Being reasonable didn't sound like bad advice, but I was biased in Cole's favor.

I started the boat, and we cruised the lake. Gorgeous. Nothing but dark blue water, a few cottages, and coves with tall grasses and water lilies. All I heard were loons and an occasional splash from a fish.

"Been here all my life," Bill said. "I'll die on this water. Never gonna live anywhere else. I hope Suko is okay with that."

He reminded me, "Ya can't tell Suko what I said, or I'll have to do somethin' harsh. Cut your brake lines—"

"Let's not go that far. If I squeal, how about just tying my shoelaces together?"

"That's a good one, too."

I steered toward home. "I won't say a word, but at some point you need to tell Suko."

"She'll never understand. Women remember stuff. Becks never let me forget that I was late for our wedding. I got caught at the *one* stop-light in Buck County, and it made me late. That's why I had to be on my toes around her when we were huntin'. She aimed at me a few times."

"Are you sure it wasn't for something else? Do you snore?"

He smiled. "Nope, but she did."

We listened to Becky's favorite songs on the ride back. One was "Danger, Breakdown Dead Ahead."

Not sure how I felt about that given the most recent time I'd heard it.

I docked, and gave Bill the engagement gifts. He and Suko would open them after she'd arrived with boxes from her apartment. He seemed stronger, less stressed.

When I left, he asked, "Can I call ya if I have another meltdown? Bring Max, too. That dog is a great therapist."

CHAPTER 30

Tuesday Lunchtime

I picked up take-out salads with a side of chicken for Max, then zipped to Fern Bubble's condo.

She'd rented a place in Ali's and Susan's development.

No, forest, to be accurate.

The development was made of unique buildings. A-frames of all sizes, scattered about as though grown on the land, not built there. Minimalist, straight-line shapes painted green and brown to look like pine trees and not distract from the shoreline.

It was Frank Lloyd Wright meets the Northwoods.

As I walked the path to the Treehouse, Fern's rental on the far end of the property, Susan Victory stepped off the porch of a towering place, Throwing Shade.

She walked toward me, and Max strained at his leash, wagging his tail. He recognized Aunt Susan immediately. He adored her like I did.

She down her insulated bag, bottles clanking inside, and stretched out her arms. "Max, come here, handsome. It's *sooo* good to see you."

He hustled straight to her.

"Max thinks it's nice to see you, Susan," I said. "I do, too."

She kept her eyes on the dog. "Have you been enjoying yourself, Max?"

"Yes, and he's inviting you to lunch." I lifted the basket. "He brought enough for us to share with Fern, you, and me."

She hugged him. "You're so sweet, Maxie. I'd share dog food with you any day."

"Great, let's go. Fern just arrived. Her place is—"

Susan finally looked at me. "Fern Bubble is here?"

I nodded. "She'd love to chat."

Susan brushed her hair back, showing brilliant turquoise earrings. Hand-crafted by her, no doubt.

She stared at the water, patting Max, her face relaxing, the creases of her forehead softening, aging her backward in seconds. For a second, I saw the Guardian Angel who'd welcomed me when I'd returned to Wisconsin from New York City.

She waved at a pontoon arriving at the pier. "Sorry, Mel, but I've got a date."

I looked to see Art Atkinson piloting a boat.

Yikes.

The pontoon was in rough shape. Its name, *The Glass Bottom*, had worn away, and the remaining letters said *The —ass Bott—*. But the off-color moniker was the least of its problems. One of the pontoons had a large crease, making the boat lean starboard, and the engine puffed blue smoke.

I couldn't tell if the thing was painted rust color or if it *was* rust. The seats were shredded, too.

Had an angry bear been on board?

Susan picked up the insulated bag and started walking toward the pier.

I trailed her. "Susan, wait."

She stopped abruptly, and I bumped her. "Susan, you're in trouble. You were just in jail. You need an attorney, and a therapist."

She looked around, eyes wide. "I won't discuss this in *public*."

"Will you come to Fern's condo?"

"Art and I are going on the water. I think he could be the one, Mel."

What did she mean?

"Wait!" I bumped her again. It was a Mel-in-a-China-shop move that made her angry.

"Melanie Tower, stop! What I need *now* is a friend who doesn't knock me over."

"I have business cards of people who can help you."

She ignored me, bag clanked as she hustled toward the pier.

"Susan, call me!" I cried out.

She didn't turn around, but Art Atkinson saw me and waved.

* * *

I STOOD on Fern's porch, shaking my head. "Fern, that pontoon made the *S.S. Minnow* look seaworthy." I felt like a pontoon stalker as I peered through binoculars searching for *The —ass Bott—*.

"See anything?" Fern asked.

"Boats. Lots of them."

"I've got the salads ready. Let's sit."

I parked in a chair, grumbling. "I plowed into Susan like a Percheron. Not my best moment. Even Max was embarrassed."

Fern shook her head, her gray hair flowing like silk. "I'm sure it wasn't that bad, Mel."

"I was relieved to see Susan. But I blurted out that she needed an attorney *and* a therapist. No one wants to be confronted like that."

"Do you believe you are Susan's biggest problem?"

"I feel like it."

"You're not."

"Why is she making this so difficult? She needs help. Why won't she accept it?"

We ate our salads. Fern nibbled while I chomped and stared at the sky. An eagle swooped down, perched on the deck railing, and began a lecture about the shovel of butter I'd smeared on a roll.

Okay, maybe not, but point taken—*nobody wants to be lectured.*

"Susan is resisting help," Fern said. "You could have bribed or threatened her, but you can't force her. She's an adult and makes her own choices."

"Sounds like you have experience."

She sighed. "I'm in the public relations business. I can't reveal confidences, but I've dealt with this issue too often to count." She patted my hand. "Mel, the good news is that Susan is strong and smart. She has a good jewelry business, and people who won't give up on her. At some point, she'll come to us."

I looked at the water. "If Art Atkinson is truly concerned for Susan, they'd be having sparkling water and chatting about healthy behaviors."

"Life doesn't work that way sometimes, sadly."

I changed the subject. "You heard about the fellow who died up here Friday?"

"Yes, I heard it at the Tool & Rye, your cousin Lou told her reading group, the Book Trout gals, who told—"

"Susan is in trouble," I blurted.

Fern's brows shot up. "Are you inferring *that she killed him?*"

"I will never believe that, but she may have said too much to the police."

CHAPTER 31

Tuesday, Lake Time

I had to tell Fern about what happened, but the condo came with a an ancient rental pontoon.

Why sit on land and talk when we could float?

The boat looked like it was delivered via Time Machine—seventies-style, avocado-green fiberglass panels and harvest-gold cushions. Cute as a button but named *Outlaw*, which was painted on the stern in a Wild West typeface.

Fern, Max, and I climbed aboard. Instructions for *Outlaw*'s operation included priming its engine before starting and checking for oars.

Fern read the manual. "The booklet says to make sure two are on board, just in case."

I lifted a cushion and looked inside its storage hold. "Check, two collapsible oars. But in case of what, pirates?"

She laughed. "You packin' heat?"

"I put spicy turkey sausages in the cooler if that counts."

"Good enough."

She drove. Max settled on a cushion. I sat in the co-pilot's seat. The weather was perfect. Hot sun, and a refreshing breeze.

I guided us to the first stop on the tour, the Glass Bottom restaurant.

Fern cut *Outlaw's* engine to idle, it growled like a mini Bobcat, and we floated near it.

I pointed to the deck. "That's where Susan, her friends, and I had cheese curds before Curtis Grey was killed on Friday night."

"Wasn't she with you? Isn't that her alibi?"

"No, I left early and drove home for my date. Susan went with Curtis Grey's house on his boat."

Speaking of alibis, *My Alib*i was docked at the restaurant. *The —ass Bott—* was next to it. No passengers on either.

I told Fern about Ali von Yaack, "She's Grey's ex, divorced long ago." I pointed. "That's her pontoon."

Fern looked at the two vessels, then the restaurant. "Susan must be inside."

"It appears so."

"Want me to wait out here while you go in and bump into her again?"

I smiled, sort of. PR folks take no prisoners when it comes to sarcasm.

"What's Ali like?" Fern asked.

"From Chicago. Barstool manufacturing royalty. Petite. The stools her family's company makes are bigger than she is. Likes to party."

"Does she need money? Own a life insurance policy on her ex?"

"I have no idea."

"The police are checking into that motive, I hope. What was Ali's relationship like with Curtis?"

"She was hot and cold on Friday. Nice one minute, sneering at him the next."

"And Susan? How was she behaving?"

"Flirty. But she'd been drinking. And, it wasn't toward Curtis, it was toward Art Atkinson. I'm surprised Susan didn't stay with him at the restaurant."

"Where did Grey live?"

"I'll show you. Let's cruise."

* * *

WE PUTT-PUTTED TOWARD AMITYVILLE COVE.

The *Outlaw* was a sterling little ship. A bit dated on its exterior but powered by a feisty engine. It held its own in the waves caused by larger vessels.

"Take a left into that bay," I directed. "Amityville is Lou's name for it, but it fits."

We cruised into the cove. It was like be-bopping into a black hole. Giant pines blocked the sun, and temps dropped.

My skin prickled.

Max came over and pressed against my legs, keeping them warm.

There was no activity at Curtis Grey's house. No boat tethered to its dock. Not a flower nor a flag displayed in Grey's honor. No one wandered the pier or the home's back porch.

"Did we just enter the *Twilight Zone*?" Fern asked. "That's his place?"

"Yes, and the other houses are rentals. Seems like they're empty."

"Wow, I'd never rent back here."

I kept my voice low. "This is where it happened. Curtis was hit on the head, then his new pontoon, *No Bullship*, cut loose. The current took him into the lake, and the storm hit."

"How awful."

"There was an informal memorial for him at the Glass Bottom yesterday. From what I heard, the family is having a private service and a burial."

"Who's his family?"

"Appears to be just one son, Greer, and his wife, Dusty. I'm not sure if he had siblings."

Fern stared at the house, staying silent.

She was a psychologist, lawyer, and parent-figure for her clients, who she was selective about taking on these days. She wouldn't work with just anyone.

Thankfully, she tolerated me and my business.

Finally, she spoke up. "Susan had a meltdown at that informal memorial, I heard."

"She was refused a drink," I said. "And, Susan told me she 'sang like a canary' when an officer spoke to her the morning after Grey died."

"Had she been drinking?"

"I doubt during the interview, but she was making Bloody Marys afterward. It gets worse. Art Atkinson told the authorities that Susan was the last person seen with Curtis on the pier that night. Susan told the police she blacked out and remembers nothing."

"Oh, *no*," Fern said.

* * *

I DIDN'T SPEAK to Fern during the buzz back to the condo. When a public relations expert utters, "Oh, no," one allows space.

Though *Outlaw* wasn't large, God's sky was above, and His waters below. That provided plenty of square footage for Fern to contemplate Susan's predicament.

We arrived at her dock about four o'clock. The sun shone brightly, and gentle waves rocked our little ship.

Max stepped to Fern, and she stroked his glossy coat. After a minute, she said, "Lou told me you're working on Susan's behalf."

I nodded. "She's encouraging it, yes."

"Solving a mystery isn't easy."

"Neither are friendships, but Susan would do the same for me." I blinked. A bug flew in my eye, I swear.

Fern saw it. "I love Susan, too. She's a wonderful person going through an awful time." She patted my hand. "You're a good friend, someone who stays and prays even when a friendship seems over."

"Stays and prays. Yes, I like that."

"A poet once wrote, 'Rare as true love, a true friendship is even rarer.'"

"Foghorn Leghorn?"

"Close. It was Jean de La Fontaine." Fern gazed at the water. "Why is Susan with a man implicating her in Curtis Grey's demise?"

"My guess is she isn't aware of it. Art Atkinson probably doesn't understand he made an off-hand comment, and now the police are developing a case on it."

"Or it's the opposite. He's throwing suspicion on someone else."

"I hope that's not true. As you said, Ali von Yaack could have a life insurance policy on Curtis. Maybe she's broke and needs cash."

"Any other suspects?"

"Curtis's son, Greer, or his wife, Dusty."

Her eyes widened. "Oh?"

I described the unhappiness I'd witnessed between Greer and Dusty. "She could have set up her husband in anger. Also, Greer allegedly was stressed about his inheritance."

"Most murders are committed by someone the victim knows."

"Or, it could be none of those people and a games competitor is involved. The man wants another trophy and became upset that Curtis withdrew his donation last-minute." I threw up my hands. "Who knows?"

She grimaced. "May as well blame a hodag, it sounds like. Have the authorities said anything?"

"There was an article in the newspaper about the damaged ambulance and pier. The Copper Falls police 'chef' said—"

"The police *chef*?"

"It was a typo. The copy editor must have had a long night. The 'chef' said his department was investigating. That's the last I've heard."

Fern nodded. "They're working the case, observing suspects, and doing background checks. In the early days of my career, criminal defense lawyers hired me after departments began questioning suspects. I'm glad I no longer accept that work."

She paused, and I knew what she was thinking—investigating a murder in the Northwoods put me at odds with Cole.

In a preemptive strike, I said, "Cole's not handling this case. The 'chef' is. So, ah, Cole should be fine that I'm nosing around, helping my friend. He'll respect my loyalty to her."

Fern rubbed the bridge of her nose. "That's what you're telling yourself?"

"What's the PR term for 'no comment?'"

She pulled a notebook from the bag she'd brought on board. Fern never travels without her red book, it's how she stays on task.

She jotted ideas. "I subscribe to a service for background checks and financial records. I'm good at digging for intel. Tell me what you need, Mel."

"I appreciate that."

"I'd love to hear about your date with Cole when you'd like to talk about it."

"We've had three dates," I began, "all ending poorly. The first ended by discovering a dead man on his boat. The others by having an ex show up, and then Cole had to leave on a call. I can't say our time together has been successful." I nodded toward Max. "But he approves if that helps."

"Max is an excellent judge of character." She scratched the dog's chest, then looked at me. "You'll be at the Opening Ceremony tonight?"

"Yes, look for the woman wearing a Sherlock Holmes cap and gazing through a spyglass."

"I'll be podcasting for my blog, *Bubbles & Fiber*. Stop by my booth."

CHAPTER 32

Tuesday Evening, Opening Ceremony

Move over, New York. There's a new party scene: Camp Glass, in the Wisconsin Northwoods.

Instead of skyscrapers and limos, there are trees and pontoons. Instead of celebrities in designer clothes, there are delivery drivers in team shirts.

Rather than a red carpet, there's a path of pine needles leading to a white tent near a log cabin resort.

I waited in line, standing near Hilarious. He looked splendid in a plaid jacket and jeans, with sun-streaked hair. He was a Northwoods surfer dude.

"Feeling okay, Mel?" he asked.

"Yeah, sure," I lied. I was uncomfortable, probably because the pine needles pierced my sandals. Yes, that was it—it was *not* because my ex, Captain Rand Cunningham could be in attendance. Curses to Lake Time, I'd been so busy I'd forgotten he could be a sponsorship ambassador for The Deliveree Games.

His airline, Viking Ship, was based in Minneapolis, only a few hours from Copper Falls. In the years we'd been together, Rand had attended an event as a company representative exactly once.

I did *not* anticipate seeing him. My luck wasn't that bad. My karma played above par, but it wasn't disastrous.

Sure, the airline gave money to this event. Its name on the step-and-repeat by the tent entrance, but there were other patrons. Bigger ones, including a corporation that made cardboard and one that made strong tape.

I looked around to see cardboard sculptures painted like pine trees. The sky was an ombre wash from blue to black. Volunteers wearing white cardboard signs wandered about, and their boards glowed in the fading light.

Hilarious patted my arm. "Your dress is lovely. It goes well with plaid."

I grinned despite my worries. "What doesn't?"

Lou had left the dress in my closet. For once, she'd hit the mark. The frock was a wrap-around style. Perfect for twirling away from uncomfortable situations ... *if* they happened.

Hil and I approached the photo-op. Two knights in cardboard "armor" posed with attendees.

One of the knights stepped to my side. "Welcome to the party, Mel."

I peered into the slats of the soldier's cardboard helmet. "Officer Jett?"

"Yep, hidin' in plain sight," she whispered. "Hey, do you know that pilot guy?"

"Huh? Where—"

"Smile!"

A strobe flashed. A teenage photographer was snapping before his subjects were ready.

I began, "What pilot—"

"Smile, lady!"

Another flash. *My pose would look awful.* I dropped Hilarious's arm, trying not to glare at the teen photog, or stare at the men standing behind kid.

Captain Rand Cunningham was right there, at the tent entrance. He was impossible to miss—tall and striking in his dark uniform. Beyond the captain, to make the scene more bizarre, was Sheriff Cole Lawrence. He wore a denim shirt with a cardboard badge and observed the area with his usual intense gaze.

I wished to be cardboard. Then I wouldn't have to walk between the two men who stirred my heart.

Speaking of stirring, Lou arrived. She was one to mix the pot.

* * *

LOU SWOOPED in like an eagle diving on prey. "I'm gonna steal Mel. See ya inside, Hil."

She hooked my elbow and towed me through a side door of the lodge. We hustled inside, and I glimpsed an office where volunteers were working.

Lou rushed me into the resort lobby. The space had been transformed into a silent auction gallery. Tables with bid sheets were positioned near artwork.

"You gotta see Ericka's stuff," Lou said. "Looks like it was crapped out by a goose." She pointed toward huge doors. "Them are gonna open, and Rand's walkin' in. I saw his name on the VIP list yesterday but didn't say anything cuz I thought you wouldn't show."

Feigning nonchalance is the best defense sometimes. "I saw Rand outside. It's fine."

"Then why'd you look like a goof in that photo you just took?"

I smoothed my hair. "Looking surprised is a trend. All the stars are doing it."

"You've never done what the 'stars' do."

Lou was correct, but I'd made the claim. Never jump a crevasse in two bounds, as mountaineers say.

"It's called the shocked-face pose," I said. "Try it. Have some fun."

"Sheriff Cole is here, too."

"It's a big tent. All are welcome."

"You may be partnered with him or Rand to play a game later."

"*What?*"

"How are ya at Pass-the-Orange?"

"Never, Lou, not in a million years!"

"The game they got planned is like musical chairs but with boxes. No idea if you'll get picked."

I studied Lou's face. Years of playing Sheepshead meant she could control her facial muscles better than I could, a former professional model.

She was a five-foot-three dynamo with a good heart, and a rotten habit of pulling strings behind the scenes.

"What does 'silly' mean, exactly?" I asked.

She smiled. "Tonight won't be *card-boring*. Get it? Card*board*?"

"What did you do?"

"Got a joke: How do ya load a cardboard gun?"

"Lou—"

"With paper *clips.*"

"What have you set me up for?"

"Nothin', but do the shocked-face pose when they call your name."

Just then, the doors to the lodge opened. Patrons flooded in like it was high tide and they'd crashed a seawall.

Whatever privacy Lou and I had disappeared as though swept away by a tsunami.

* * *

WE BACKED up to the check-in desk. The stretch of polished wood had been transformed into a serving station with finger foods and punch bowls. As the crowd got closer, we rushed away further. Never stand between a Wisconsin crowd and appetizers.

Hilarious spotted us. He carried drinks and split the humanity like Moses parting the sea. "Sparkling water, or Brandy Old-Fashioned Slushies, ladies?"

"Water," Lou said. "I'm on duty with the silent auction." She nodded toward a display. "Your cupcakes look outstanding, Hil. I was your first bidder."

He handed me the slushie. We moved past photos of the Northwoods in high summer toward a stand of baked treats, tiers of vanilla, chocolate, and key lime spongy goodness topped by creamy frosting.

A card beside the tower read, "Summer of Cupcakes: Chef's Choice. Delivered Locally by Vintage Pontoon."

"If I win 'em, you can float 'em to Mel's place on Lollygag," Lou said. "As her accountant—her 'Lou-P-A,'—I'm makin' sure she buys that cottage."

"Is there trouble with the purchase?" Hilarious asked.

"Nothin' that a cream pie to the realtor's face won't solve. You make pies, Hil?"

"Ericka returned my earnest money," I said. "She's claiming the deal was rejected." I sipped my drink.

"Anything I can do?" he asked.

"How's your pitchin' arm?" Lou wondered. "First, we'll get cream pies. Then—"

I stopped her. "I'm letting my attorney review legal options."

"A pie and the element of surprise is the way to go. Lawyers cost money." She changed the subject. "You guys seen Ericka's art? She must've painted 'em under a blood moon."

We stepped toward a collection of easels. It was like being sucked into a portal of doom and getting smacked with negative energy instead of banana cream.

I swear my slushie melted.

A framed description was on a stand, its border charred as though set afire. Ericka wrote:

Double, double, toil and trouble.
In a mirror, eat an apple.
See your mate.
Time beguiles others,
But not me.
Seasons change,
But not me.
You and I will be.

"Wow, she's gone off the deep end," Hilarious said.

"If anyone needs desserts to cheer herself up, it's Ericka," Lou said. "If I win the auction for your cakes, I'm donatin' 'em to her." She pointed to a black canvas with mustard-colored lines and dark smears.

"It looks like a goose with the runs painted this stuff. I'm gonna start calling her 'Ericka Allan Poe.'"

The art was macabre, like seeing Poe's words on canvas.

I shivered. It was due to the cold slushie and *not* the evil energy from the images, I hoped.

CHAPTER 33
The Opening Ceremony

When in doubt, converse with someone astute like a writer. Writers are keen. They mix psychology, research, and human behavior into tales for public consumption.

Steven was the only writer I knew. He was part shrink, part comedian, part Labrador puppy. His skill set included small talk—he meets new people every day—and expert hand-eye coordination.

I bid on Hil's cupcakes, then dashed to the tent to find my favorite courier-novelist. He was at the bar.

I slid next to him. "Steven, great to see you. I wish you'd warned me about Rand. No hard feelings, though."

The best offense is denial, one knows.

Steven studied my face, then looked at the bartender. "A shot of Fireball for the lady."

I shook my head. "*No*, thank you."

He leaned toward me. "It's for appearances, Mel. You're surrounded by two lovers and a romantic rival."

He nodded toward the tent entrance. "Ericka and her friends are headed inside. Also, a murderer could be skulking around. You need to disarm all of them, especially the bad guy. Act stressed and gulping a shot fits the character you should project."

I disagreed. Steven-the-astute was having an off night. I chalked it up to nervousness about the competition.

Bill Hartland, the emcee, stepped on the raised dais. Captain Rand was up there with other sponsor-ambassadors.

Bill spoke into a mic, "Welcome to the Deliveree, where we honor those cats the world can't do without—delivery kings and queens. We're gonna kick off by deliverin' *fun*. We got musical boxes comin' up. Contestants, get into your pairs!"

Steven patted my back. "That's us."

"No, the competition is for you professionals."

"This one's a pro-am. That's you and me. Lou said you'd do it."

He dragged me to the dance floor. Box "chairs" were set out, and I heard notes of the Beer Barrel Polka.

Steven was right about physical activity and stress. Before I knew it, I *was* the Fireball.

* * *

THE MUSIC STOPPED.

I dragged Steven to a box.

I wanted to win, by golly.

Our wrists were tied together, which had caused exciting clashes during the opening rounds.

"Ugh," Steven groaned as we crashed to a seat. "You ever play rugby, Mel?"

"Buck up," I said. "There's no whining in parlor games."

"Another one bites the dust!" Bill Hartland cried. "Good show, Blood, Sweat, and Boxes. That's a bronze medal. Collect your prize and boot-scoot off the dance floor. Let's give 'em a hand, folks."

The crowd cheered, and Bill continued, "We're into sudden death. We've got the Box-nadoes vs. the Box & Chain to compete for the gold."

Steven and I were Box & Chain, a name we came up with on the fly.

A helper removed a seat from the floor.

Steven rubbed his wrist. "Mel, it's like you're possessed or something. What got into you?"

"It was the slushie. Liquid courage."

For the record, Steven wasn't dead weight, but he could be lighter on his tootsies. Playing bumper cars to music was exactly what I'd needed. Nothing like exercise to reduce stress.

"We're uppin' the ante for the final round," Bill said. "It'll be scored for style, too. Teams gotta get the last box with dance moves for bonus points. Judges, get your cards ready. Teams, hit it!"

An accordion bellowed, then the bebop melody of the "Chicken Dance" tooted through the speakers.

Steven gripped my hand. He'd become energized, finally.

"Follow me," he ordered.

I eyed the other team. The Box-nadoes had come to win. The female duo had attended more than a few Wisconsin weddings. They swished through the state's favorite dance like professional chickens.

Steven and I did a two-step, pausing only to flap, wiggle, then clap.

He interacted with the crowd and got them in on the moves. Then, he twirled me away from the precious box—a risk—and then dipped me.

I found myself eye-to-heel with a pair of familiar cowboy boots that tapped in rhythm. It appeared Cole was enjoying himself. Tough to do as a cop with murder on his mind, I presumed.

The tempo increased. We swirled faster, a full stride away from the lone chair, while the other dancers stuck close to it.

Judges wrote scores. On what, I had no idea. Bill seemed to make up rules as the game progressed.

"Hold on, Mel!" Steven shouted.

In perfect timing, he spun me around, then guided me in backward in an offensive gambit. We screened the 'Nadoes from the seat like the Green Bay Packers running a sweep.

The music quit, and our rear ends connected with the coveted chair.

Gold medalists Steven and I were named. We hugged, and the crowd cheered.

If the game was like what the delivery teams would compete in, it would be a wild couple of days.

* * *

IT TURNED out a gold medal offered privileges.

Steven and I became king and queen of the evening and were awarded seats on the dias near the sponsorship ambassadors.

Promoted to First Class, if you will.

Rand pulled out the chair next to him. "It's lovely to see you, Mel."

"Wow, I did not have this seat assignment on my bingo card."

"You were really 'winging' it out there." He kissed me on the cheek. "Why didn't we ever enter a dance competition?"

I inhaled, still breathless from the competition. "We had our head in the clouds?"

"If you ask me, it was a missed connection." He smiled, and the room lit up like a runway.

Rand was a heartthrob, dashing in his uniform. He'd been wearing his official duds when we'd met. It had been October, almost Halloween, a downpour in New York City, one of the few times I'd hailed a cab.

Rand had flagged the same one. I offered the ride to him. In a battle of "Midwest Nice," we argued about who should take it.

The cabbie eventually tore off to find another fare. Rand asked me to lunch, and we went to a place known for its green-and-gold decor.

After burgers, he asked for my phone number. I asked for his flight number. (Halloween was nigh—what if his "uniform" was a costume?)

He'd shown me his credentials, then called me the next day. We'd been together ever since, until I'd broken it off last year. We'd had an up-and-down relationship affected by weather delays and jet lag. Plus, one of us had commitment issues due to losing her parents at a young age.

I wasn't sure which of us suffered that affliction, but I could guess.

Rand studied the medal hanging around my neck. "Is that real gold?"

I tapped it. "It's real gold paint over cardboard. Worth at least one-fifty, maybe two bucks."

He laughed. "I've missed your humor, Mel."

I looked at the dance floor. "They're introducing the teams. The Bad Addresses are the ones to beat. They're the ones who look like Boeing Triple Sevens while everybody else is light aircraft."

Rand patted my hand. "Remember when we talked about buying a house up here and retiring on a lake?"

I shook my head. "Pilots don't retire, they just fly away."

"Not this one, Mel. I want to talk." He leaned close. "You and I once discussed a ring."

He wasn't talking about one of those boxing rings outside, I guessed.

I looked toward the bar where Cole stood among a group. They chatted. He faced the crowd, watching people, always alert. He glanced at me, then Rand. I wanted to speak to him—but I heard a scream. There was a ruckus outside the tent. Was it a fight?

Another scream!

I saw Cole bolt for the entrance.

CHAPTER 34
The Twilight Zone

I stood at the tent entrance and watched the melee. Three choices about the fight that ensued:

One, Lou argued with Ali von Yaack about missing donation funds.

Two, Lou argued with Ali von Yaack about barstools.

Three, Lou argued with Ali von Yaack about her ex-husband's death.

Jett McBride, cardboard knight, had gotten involved, but didn't blow her cover by removing her helmet. It was like watching the Tin Man mediate a quarrel.

Ali von Yaack clutched a zipper pouch, the same one she'd carried the day she posted Susan's bail. "It's my community service," Ali protested. "I collect donation money and turn it in at the police station."

Lou scoffed. "Collect or pocket it?" She pointed to the resort. "I watched ya in the lobby. Ya went to the donation box, put cash in that bag, then stuffed some in your pocket."

"*I did not—*"

"Why didn't tell us you were takin' donations?"

Cole stood with his arms crossed, listening to the women argue.

Ali glared at him. "Sheriff, arrest this woman for harassment."

"Arrest this gal for making crappy barstools," Lou countered. "You ever think about making 'em from cardboard, Ali? They'd be sturdier."

Ali gasped.

Lou went for the jugular: "By the way—*where were you when your ex was killed*?"

Onlookers murmured. Cole stepped to Ali and spoke with her. She stood in a posture of pure defiance.

Had Ali been pilfering cash from community donations? It could be hundreds, thousands, of dollars a month. Did she have money problems, or a life insurance policy on her ex?

Curtis's demise could pay her well.

I backed away, seeking the person who could discover the answer.

* * *

LOU, Fern, and I jammed into a room off the resort lobby.

Lou tapped the microphone in front of her. "This thing on?" She lowered her voice, "Hi, folks. Ali von Yuck did it on the pontoon boat, with a lead pipe. Call the sheriff's office. Put pressure on 'em to arrest her. Ericka Dimblé, too."

I stared at Fern. "The mic isn't on, is it?"

"It's off," she assured me.

Fern had been podcasting about the games. She had a lively over-60 group who enjoyed her Bubbles & Fiber broadcasts.

Lou tapped the mic again. "Crank her up. Let's crowdsource this murder investigation. I'm startin' a betting pool. Ali's in first. Dusty, the daughter-in-law, is runnin' second. Who's third, Mel?"

I ignored the question and quizzed her. "You're *sure* Ali took money?"

Lou nodded. "She came in, looked around, then opened the donation case. Started stuffing cash into that pouch. Made it seem official, but then she dropped bills 'accidentally' and tucked twenties into her purse."

Fern narrowed her eyes. "Any cameras?"

"One, which I was watchin'. But when Ali bent down, she was hidden. I snuck out and watched her doin' the dirty with my own eyes."

"The bills aren't marked," Fern said. "If Ali hid them with other cash in that donation bag, there's no way to prove anything."

"I did the math after confrontin' her," Lou said. "Ali could be pocketin' buckets of donation cash every week. That's a lot of moolah for parties on *Big Gassy*, that boat of hers."

"No, it's *My Alibi*," I corrected.

"Then I did more math and—"

I looked at Fern. "Lou identifies as a CPA now."

Lou rapped the console with a fist. "No, I'm a Lou-P-A. And your fake attorney, Mel. As such, I sentence you to not interrupt me. *Capeesh*?"

I nodded. "Sorry. *Sí*."

"Here's how the murder went down: Ali's got money problems. Her bar stools are doll furniture, basically. Her company is circlin' the drain. Boats, drain—get it?" She smiled. "Barstool von Yaack gets sued. So in the dead of night, under a full moon, in a land far away—Chicago, where people can get away with it—she rides her broom to a mortician's office and sneak-writes an insurance policy on Big Sexy, her ex."

I didn't translate for Fern. She'd get it.

Lou continued, "People do it all the time." She jerked her head toward me. "I got a policy on Mel, even."

"*What?*" I said.

"Just kiddin', but I should. Folks like takin' shots at you, Mel. Could pay out big."

"What do you think, Fern?" I asked.

"I'll check out Ali's financials and let you know."

"Do not say *one word* about your theory to anyone," I ordered Lou. "Whoever did it, killed once. They easily could do it again."

* * *

LOU RETURNED to the volunteer office. I remained at the podcast booth for a command-performance interview with the gold medalists. Steven stood next to me. Bill Hartland was next to him.

"Bill, tell me about establishing the Deliveree Games," Fern asked.

"Delivery folks are knights on the road," he said. "Heck, one driver I know delivered a kid." He grinned. "Now that driver's nickname is 'MedEx.'"

We laughed.

"My band and I wanted to celebrate delivery folks," Bill continued. "A sax player knew a middle-management guy, who knew a bigwig. They got talkin' and darned if they didn't get sponsors for this shindig. This is our fourth year."

Fern looked at Steven and me. "And these two are the first gold medalists of this year's games?"

"Exhibitionists," Bill corrected. "They're exhibitionist dancers, *hehe*. Thought we'd have entertainment—"

Fern interrupted, "Listening audience, for the record, the 'exhibitionists' had clothes on."

Bill rapped the console like Lou had done earlier. "Yah, this event is family-friendly."

He sounded and acted so similar to Lou that it was like I'd entered a different dimension. All he had to do was mention carrot muffins and a merge with Lou would be complete.

My phone buzzed. A text from Rand asked:

Where'd you go?

I tapped:

The Twilight Zone. BRB.

The interview ended when Bill added, "Tomorrow's kick-off will be a smashin' of piñatas, followed by a waterski race on cardboard skis," he said.

I was headed back to the tent when Bill stopped me. "Your cousin is excavatin' at Curtis Grey's place, right?"

"Last I heard."

Bill scratched his head. "Doesn't it seem strange for Dusty and Greer to get on the job so fast?"

"What are you saying?"

"The rumor is Greer and Dusty are reopenin' that restaurant they had, too. Sink another bundle of money into that pit." He leaned in. "Tell your cousin to get paid *up front*. People are sayin' Greer expects a Paul Bunyon-sized inheritance, and he's spendin' the money like crap oozin' from a goose. Make sure your cousin doesn't end up doin' the work for free. *Capeesh*?"

I nodded. "*Sí.*"

CHAPTER 35

The Opening Ceremony, Later

The Bill Hartland Trio took over the tent. About twenty band members stood on the stage, including a percussionist with a massive drum kit.

Bill pointed at Steven and me. "Hey, Wisconsin version of Astaire and Rogers, get on the floor and show this gang how to two-step."

Steven grabbed my hand. With a "one-and-a-two!" shout, we were off, cutting up the floor to a cover of "One More Last Chance.'

The music was lively, the wagon-wheel chandeliers twinkled, and a breeze blew in.

The floor quickly filled with boot-scooters, and I relaxed. Smiled, even, as thoughts of storms, murder, inheritance, and barstools floated away from my mind.

Cole stood on the sidelines, watching the crowd. While quick-quick-slowing past him, I noticed a change in his posture. His shoulders appeared stiff, and he eyed party-goers with a clenched jaw.

The conversation with Ali probably stressed him—was her behavior a clue in the demise of Curtis Grey?

A hand tapped Steven's shoulder.

"Mind if I cut in?" Rand asked.

Steven wiped his brow. "Sure, I gotta reserve my energy. I'm heading out, Mel, but the team needs you to drive the boat tomorrow. Call me."

He ditched, and Rand took me in his arms. "I'd like another chance, Mel, shall we?"

We took off. Rand was in great shape and moved like a panther wearing a uniform.

We swooshed past the bar, where Ericka stood with her friends. Her eyes lit up when she spotted me with Rand. He and I lapped the floor, and when we swooshed past a second time, she nudged Ali von Barstool and pointed at us.

I recognized her actions. Watching her rival dance with another man was manna from heaven, pilot style. I recalled the poem she'd written and the loosey-goosey artwork.

Whatever Ericka was scheming wasn't good.

* * *

I SIGNALED FOR A TIMEOUT.

Rand guided me toward the bar. "May I buy you a drink? They serve cocktails, soda products, and coffee or tea. Duty-free."

"Time for crew rest. I've got a walk with Max early in the morning." I spied a knight standing near the exit—Jett McBride. "I'm heading out."

Rand clasped my hand. "You're like Cinderella dashing off before the clock strikes midnight."

I smiled. "If you find a slipper made of cardboard, it's mine."

He kissed my cheek. "I'll call tomorrow."

I didn't beeline to McBride. *Too obvious.* I drifted among partiers and listed to gossip: "Yah, the Behemoths will win. They got a ringer." And, "Curtis and Greer never got along. Where was Sonny when Daddy was killed?" Then, "The police are gonna arrest a gal from outa town, I heard."

Please don't let it be Susan Victory.

I needed to speak with Jett.

* * *

JETT STOOD at the entrance posing for pictures. It was like partiers were on a shore excursion, and she was a tourist-trap photo op.

She saw me. "Folks, by Order of the Northwoods Round Table, this knight is taking a break." A few people groaned. "Sorry, back in a jif."

She nodded toward a path and disappeared into the darkness, moving quickly for wearing a bulky costume. I followed the sound of her cardboard "armor," a clunky swish-scrape.

It was after ten, and a storm rumbled in the distance.

My eyes widened like saucers.

Walking into a forest while a killer lurked in the community—and while Ericka skulked, too—wasn't a great idea.

That cardboard sword I'd seen on Jett's chest wasn't much of a weapon.

A voice floated out to me, "C'mon, Mel. I don't have much time."

I shuddered, suddenly feeling cold. The tent had been stuffy, and I'd been dancing. The cool air made me shiver, or maybe it was goosebumps.

I looked for a weapon—a chunk of firewood, a sharp stick, anything.

"Ouch!" I found a rock with my toe. "*Where are you, Jett?*"

"Back here. Behind the tree."

"Is it safe—"

Oof!

* * *

I RUBBED MY NOGGIN, thinking I should have done the opposite of wandering into the woods.

I should have gone home.

I'd taken a tumble after tripping on a tree root, and then collided with Jett.

She sat next to me on a log by the campfire pit, where a blaze crackled. A large cooler sat open on the grass. It held bottles of electrolyte water for partiers returning to their cabins.

I made a fist and knocked her thigh. "Are you sure this costume isn't armor? It sure felt like it."

"No, tin foil over cardboard." The outfit crunched and crinkled while she talked; it was like speaking to a wrapped gift. "Sorry I bumped ya. Need water?"

I sighed. "Yes, please."

She lumbered to the cooler. If I'd had less of a headache, if circumstances had been less of a hornet's nest, I'd have guffawed at watching her try to bend for bottles. The costume offered the flexibility of a school bus.

"Don't get close to the fire," I cautioned. "Unless that costume is flame retardant, you'll go up like a Christmas tree."

She took the long way around, then showed me two bottles. "Watermelon flavor or cherry?"

"Whichever one will make me smarter and provide answers about what's going on."

"That's watermelon, for sure." She sat as best she could and removed the helmet.

We sipped while staring at the fire.

Jett began, "I wanna give you an update, but first, who's that pilot guy? The older ladies were saying he's handsome as Robert Redford. Who's that?"

"The Brad Pitt of our generation."

"Who's he?"

"You're kidding."

She giggled. "Just trying to make you smile, you look stressed. Anyway, Curtis Grey's toxicology tests aren't complete yet, and the medical examiner's report isn't finished. The death happened over the weekend, so it slows it down."

"Will the police chef announce it was a murder?"

"OMG, that typo in the *Buck News*—man, he got ribbed for that." She lowered her voice. "Between you and me, he's not sharp, not like Sheriff Cole. I wish *he* was running the investigation."

Branches snapped nearby.

"Someone's coming," I said.

Jett scrambled up. Well, as fast as the cardboard would allow. "Mel, my gut says Susan should get a lawyer." She grabbed the helmet. "Don't go back by yourself, especially with a killer on the loose."

She took off.

I heard her *galumph* through the woods. I'd think the racket was a hodag if I didn't know better.

Black sky, trees tall as monsters, and a tiny campfire as the only light surrounded me.

I was alone in the Northwoods.

* * *

JETT LEFT me alone while telling me *not* to be alone.

Ironic, but I was used to it. I'd worked in fashion. That scene was just as illogical and dangerous as being stranded in the woods with a bad guy, girl, or fanged creature lurking about.

Footsteps approached, and looked for a stone, a log, anything I could use as a weapon.

"*Oh WEEE oh, we'll win, oh!*

The tune was a riff on the guard chant from *The Wizard of Oz*. Given the weight of the footfalls, it had to be the Bad Addresses.

Sir T-Rex and his Merry Band of Behemoths jogged into the clearing. I quick-stepped to the cooler and grabbed bottles, hoping they'd see them as a peace offering.

I held them up. "Water, fellas? Be safe. Hydrate."

The T-Rex snatched one, and his followers did the same.

The last guy said, "You're Steven Delavan's friend, the gold medalist. What are you doin' out here?"

The medal still hung from my neck. "I needed water after all that dancing."

"You're alone? Want me to walk you back?"

"No, I'm fine." I nodded toward the path they'd traveled. "Is that the quickest way to the tent?"

"Yeah, but don't go alone—"

I kicked off my sandals. "Great, thanks. Enjoy the water." I sprinted down the path as fast as my tootsies would carry me.

Not my wisest decision, but you know what they say. In a world of poor choices, pick the best one.

CHAPTER 36

Wednesday Morning

The day began with dawn's rosy fingers ... gripping a baseball bat.

I stood on the soccer field at Camp Glass, watching the T-Rex —Hercules in a black T-shirt—whomp a piñata. Contents burst from the box, then ran. I swear the map, a scavenger-hunt list, and boat keys fell to the ground, sprouted legs, and fled for the pines.

Lou stared through binoculars. "Put that fella in the Curtis Grey bettin' pool to Show, or Place, even. He's a monster."

I squinted at the players swinging at boxes hung from booms. Max rested behind us in the shade. We mingled with Steven and the Cinnamon Shakers.

Wisconsin being Wisconsin, the breaking of the piñatas had turned into a tailgate party. Teams and their supporters grilled brats on the sidelines, spectators cheered, and music played on loudspeakers. Once a box had been clunked and its contents gathered, new ones were put up.

Teams offered guest whomps as a fundraiser for the local mental health organization. It gave spectators a chance to offload aggression if they felt the need.

Lou continued staring into the spy glasses. "I'm seein' lots of folks who coulda done the dirty to Curtis Grey. Hey, there's Art Atkinson, his business partner." She paused to watch him swing at a box. "Naw, forget him. Arm like a wet noodle. Musta quarterbacked for the Bears."

She handed the glasses to me. "You gonna take a turn? Pretend it's Ericka?"

"I'll pass."

"Yah, you'll kill her with kindness. That's your style, but I'd smash it."

"Shh, loose lips sink ships. No one should overhear—"

Her eyes widened. "You're gonna sink her pontoon? No, you'll sink *My Alibi*." She winked. "Solvin' mysteries is fun, a free pass to cause trouble. While everybody's here, let's skedaddle to town and break into Ali's condo."

"Let's not, Lou."

"But I got my cowgirl toothpick. I could jimmy the lock."

"No."

"Why?"

"Think about it."

"Cameras, yeah." She slapped her knee. "We could do it tonight! Rent grizzly costumes, dress up, and rummage in her garbage cans."

Max woofed.

Lou glanced around. "Shh, Rand's comin'. Stop talking about this stuff, Mel. He shouldn't hear your crazy ideas."

"Good morning, ladies." He kissed my cheek, his cologne smelling of cedar and vanilla.

"Gimme your jacket, Rand-O," Lou said. "Take a whomp. Pretend it's an empty suit from corporate, or a big-mouth passenger."

He smiled. "Fortunately, I don't encounter many of those folks, Louella."

"Yeah, sure." She winked. "How many pilots does it take to change a lightbulb?"

"No idea."

"None, silly. You guys are unionized. Bulbs are maintenance's job, *hehe*."

"I've missed your humor, Lou."

"Everyone does eventually. You hear Mel's solvin' another murder?"

He shook his head. "I had not."

"I'm talkin' her out of it. Ordered her to stay in her lane. Run the craft mall and her new bookstore back home. Buy some property up here." She nudged me. "But you know how she is. Don't be surprised if ya hear she's involved in shenanigans. Just ignore it."

"We should chat." Rand looked at me. "How about dinner tonight?"

"Mel would love to!" Lou answered. She scanned the shoreline across the lake. "Glass Bottom's closed for now. Owner's cleanin' out junk, I heard. How about Once Upon a Pond? Hole-in-the-wall outside of town. You guys can talk alone."

Rand smiled. "Is it okay with you, Mel?"

"Darn tootin' it is," Lou continued. "Wheels up at seven. No, six. Gotta plan for weather delays, *hehe*. I'll have Mel ready and watch Max while she's out."

"Is that okay, Mel?" Rand repeated.

I nodded. "Sure."

"Whatever you do, cousin, do *not* quiz Rand," Lou cautioned. "Don't ask what he's heard about Curtis Grey's murder from the sponsors he's hangin' with. Don't nag if he knows weird stuff about the teams, the players—or even killer hodags lurkin' around."

Rand hugged me. "Mel can quiz me all she wants. I look forward to our evening together."

* * *

"HIT IT!" Steven yelled from the dock.

I pushed the *Wilde Ride*'s throttle, glancing over my shoulder. Steven wobbled but stayed up on flimsy cardboard skis—*which were similar to flimsy alibis.*

I couldn't help but make the connection. *My Alibi* and Ali von Barstool were on my left, engines roaring.

Ali pulled the Behemoths, the favorites, but they kept face-planting because she was overpowering her skiers—*where had Ali been when Curtis Grey was dunked, no pun intended?*

"Steady, Mel!" Steven yelled. "I'm gonna pass the third buoy this time!"

The "race" was a fifty-yard putt-putt. Few skiers could stay up on the skis, two pieces of thick, painted cardboard. The trick was a light hand on the gas and greyhound-like skiers.

This competition was producing the opposite of expectations. The favorites, the Behemoths were off to a horrible start. Despite their strength and giant tow boat, they'd failed to reach the first buoy and hadn't earned a single point.

Lou, my spotter, gave a thumbs up. "Great job, Steve-O!"

There were only two of us aboard because that's all the *Wilde's* engine could tolerate while towing.

"Is Ali tryin' to drown her skiers?" Lou asked. "She's a murderer in plain sight, if ya ask me. She's drivin' that boat like she stole it."

Lou's words resonated with me. "Lou, when you saw Ali taking money—"

"Watch out!" she cried.

The *Alibi* veered, swells rolled toward our little ship.

I yanked the wheel. "Hold on!"

"Waves comin', Steven!" Lou called. "Ride 'em out"

He curled his body, preparing for the hit.

Lou and I grabbed the sides of the pontoon as it tipped.

"That woman's a menace!" Lou screamed. "She's tryin' to kill us, Mel!"

* * *

THE WILDE RIDE tipped like a toy in a bathtub.

The *Alibi* powered around, causing havoc. Waves crashed our bow, but the *Wilde* handled the chop. We see-sawed and rode the swells, the craft's advantage was its maneuverability.

If the Alibi was a draft horse, the Wilde was a handy mustang.

A boat stunt driver I was not, but overcoming the mini-squall gave me confidence in my skills.

We escaped the worst of it, and the water calmed.

I spied Susan, the spotter on the big boat. She appeared shocked at the near-accident her boat almost caused. Perhaps she recognized the same metaphor I did. Her friends—friend*ships?*—were sinking due to reckless behaviors and poor choices, some of them her own.

Lou patted the *Wilde's* console. "This baby should be named *Lionheart!*" She looked behind us. "You okay, Steve-O?"

He floated, just his head visible, the skis and rope abandoned. He gave a thumbs-up.

Lou offered one in return. Then, she stood on her seat and gave *My Alibi* a sign, too.

Not a thumbs-up.

They didn't see it, fortunately.

"Call me!" I yelled to Susan as they powered off.

* * *

THE SUN GLINTED off the leaderboard high above the resort's deck. The sign looked like an old-fashioned baseball scoreboard with hooks to hang numbers on. A fellow, wearing pinstripes and a ball cap, was in charge of the official record.

Steven and I read the scores. The Cinnamon Shakers led after the first round.

The Behemoths lagged in last place.

Steven smiled. "That wasn't predicted, eh?"

I raised my glass of iced tea. "Here's to the opposite of what's predicted."

He'd changed into dry clothes, and his T-shirt said, "Shaken, but not Stirred." An excellent mantra for staying calm during a competition.

"Mel, if we ever hit another pothole in the water, I want you driving," he said.

"The *Wilde* did all the work. I just steered."

He took my elbow and guided me to a corner of the deck. Quietly, he asked, "You're solving the Curtis Grey murder because the police chief is a chef of some sort? That's what Lou told me. Is that true?"

I grimaced. "It's not been announced that his death is a murder. And your intel is coming from Lou. Take that with a barrel of salt."

"What about Sheriff Cole?"

I shook my head. "He didn't do it."

"That's not what I meant."

"He's law enforcement, the least likely suspect."

Steven looked up, suddenly entranced by the pines swaying in the breeze. He inhaled, and then released it like he was counting beats.

Square breathing, it's called, and I've done it in the presence of foolishness, too.

In short, S. knows when his good friend M. is playing dumb. This was not our first time at the game. M. (that's me) thinks independently and detests arguing, so feigns ignorance at times.

Steven nodded toward Cole, who stood on the deck, mingling but not. Always aware, like law enforcement officers must be.

The hunk, er, Cole, wore his team colors again—cargoes, denim shirt, cowboy hat, and badge. Accessorized by a suntan and crystal eyes that changed from green to blue, depending upon the light.

Fifty Shades of Sheriff, a senior-aged law enforcement stallion.

Steven nudged me. "Mel, did you hear what I said?"

"No, yes—what?"

"By meddling in a murder, you're messing up a new relationship." He nodded toward Cole. "He's cool. And believe me, I know how guys can be. What if Cole interfered in your profession and told you how to model?"

I shook my head. "I'm retired from that. Besides, look at him. He's a human cologne ad. Cole's a better model right now than I ever was."

"What if he told you how to run your art mall?"

The best defense is an immediate change of subject.

"You've told me to investigate murders before," I said.

"*One* murder. Last November. Do you understand you're tracking a killer? Instead of *you* getting him—"

"The perpetrator could be a woman. Ali von Yaack and Greer Grey, the daughter-in-law, are suspects. Susan Victory, too."

He frowned. "Susan Victory could be involved?"

"She is, and I fear the real killer is setting her up. I've told her to call an attorney, but she ignores me."

"What about Hank Leigel? He's a lawyer. She won't consult him?"

"Not yet. I'm working on it." I stepped closer. "Fern Bubble is digging into financial info. Would you keep an eye on the teams? Murders usually are committed by someone the victim knows."

I nodded toward Hercules Behemoth, who stood on the grass

bench-pressing pine trees. No, kidding. He was chatting with his teammates, but he could lift trees if he wanted to.

"I will because you're my best friend. If something happened to you, I'd forget addresses, ruin my career." He hugged me. "Be careful."

"Don't worry," I tapped my temple. "Foolishness wonders. Wisdom finds answers."

CHAPTER 37

Wednesday Evening

I was wise enough to play a fool. That's my answer to anyone wondering why I agreed to dinner with an ex-boyfriend and had another conversation in the woods with a killer lurking about.

The night did not go as planned, but then I didn't have a plan, so there was that.

Lou sent me out of the cottage in a white dress with narrow metallic stripes. "Lakeside glam," she'd called it. "Showin' off the gal you are beneath all those black outfits. Outdoorsy and casual, with a hint of sass."

It was plaid, but elevated for evening. I liked it. The Northwoods was working its magic on me.

I met Rand at Once Upon a Pond at six-fifteen, slightly late, but he was in the airline business. Late arrivals don't count.

Rand looked great, a silver fox in a gray sweater, wool so fine it looked like silk. He ordered the filet stuffed with blue cheese and grilled asparagus with sea salt.

He ate his meal with the fork tines down, the knife gently moving the food onto the back of the utensil.

For dessert, we moved to the bar. He ordered a cappuccino, not an ice cream drink like everyone else. "Would you like a turtle sundae—"

"No," I answered quickly.

We sat near a window overlooking a mirror-like pond. Pines surrounded the water, and an eagle sat on a branch, silhouetted by the orange-pink sky.

"You've seen the Aurora Borealis?" I asked. "In Wisconsin, we call it the Wis-rora Borealis."

He sipped coffee. "It's delightful to chat about the weather, Mel. And Max, who's received stellar reports from the vet."

I nodded. "We've had good rain. And the staff at the clinic says Max is their best patient."

He sighed.

I sensed what was coming.

"I don't want to pry, but a little bird told me you met someone." He covered my hand with his. "Can we talk about it?"

I'd bet the dang bird wore sequins, boots, and was named Lou. "There's not much to say," I answered. "He's tall, lived here all his life."

"Oh?"

"The problem is he has a pet. She's gigantic and blue, and she puts Max off."

Rand smiled. "Let me guess, she's an ox named Babe, and his name is Paul."

"You got it."

I gently punched his arm.

"Ouch, careful, that's the one I use for steering the airplane. Hurt that, and it's a federal offense."

I didn't want to end up on the no-fly list, so I rubbed his bicep. "Sorry."

"Are you sure you don't want a sundae? It's not like you to pass those up."

"I'm fine, thanks."

He finished his coffee. "Do you recall the time we went to Singapore?"

"Ah, no."

"Norway?"

I shook my head. "We could never *a-fjord* it."

"Greece?"

"God, no."

"London?"

I paused. "We watched *International Velvet* during a snowstorm when your flight out of JFK was canceled. So, yes, I remember."

"Paris?"

"Not exactly, but we both love French fries."

"There's something I need to say—"

"I'll have that sundae."

He leaned toward me. The man had a commanding presence. He exuded a captain's energy, even in a sweater and slacks.

"Mel, we met at the wrong time. We were working and didn't have time to travel and relax." He smiled. "I'd like to try. And I may know someone who can get us reasonably priced tickets."

Across the bar, movement caught my eye.

Suko Jones, wearing an animal print dress, sat alone with a drink —*was she crying?*

I looked at Rand. "A friend is over there, and she's upset. I have to speak to her. Thanks for dinner." I kissed his cheek, remembering I hadn't asked a single question about Curtis Grey or the games' sponsors. "We'll talk later."

Then, like Cinderella leaving the ball, I spun off my stool and swooshed to my friend.

* * *

SUKO WANTED to keep our convo private, so we moved outside to a bench by the pond.

It was after nine, and the forest looked dark and moody.

An owl hooted, *hoot d'hoot, hoot d'hoot.*

Suko blew her nose into a tissue.

If hodags lurked in the woods, I hoped the honk sent them scurrying back to their lairs.

She dabbed her eyes. "Bill has been distant since I moved in."

"In what way?" I asked.

"He's barely picked up a guitar since our engagement party. He hasn't said one joke, not even a pun. Earlier, I asked him what day was best to be on a boat, an easy one, and he missed it."

I pondered. "Ah—"

"It's *Sunday*, Mel."

I patted her back. "I noticed you weren't at the Opening Ceremony last night."

"I wanted to give him space, but I don't know if Bill and I will get past this." She stared wide-eyed at the pond, like she suspected a monster lurked in its depths.

"Before you jump to conclusions, remember Bill was married to his high school sweetheart and—"

"I left credit card statements on the counter," Suko interrupted. "He probably saw the past-due notices, but I'm catching up. My car needed repairs, and professors don't make much money." She looked at the ring on her finger. "I hope Bill doesn't think I'm irresponsible. Maybe we moved too fast, Mel."

I patted her hand. "Are you and Bill friends?"

She nodded. "We're in love, yes."

"I didn't ask that. You can love someone you don't like, families do it all the time. Love is an emotion that can feel like an obligation. Friendship is an action."

She smiled. *Good to see.*

"Do you and Bill have mutual interests? Do you respect one another?"

"Yes, of course."

"Can you share a secret and trust he won't use it against you in an argument?"

"Yes, except about money, apparently." She rolled her eyes.

"You're not worried about a bar bunny flirting with Bill?"

"He doesn't know how to flirt." She sighed. "Bill's like a twelve-year-old. He thinks passing gas is funny, but I love that about him."

"Does he make you smile when you think of him?"

"Bill makes me laugh when I think of him. He's adorable."

"Then talk to him."

"But I'm *so* embarrassed. I'm a responsible person. I don't want this to be how we begin our marriage." Tears welled again. "I shouldn't be buying an expensive wedding dress, and I won't ask him to pay for it."

She shook her head. "I asked you to help me pick one out, Mel, but I'm canceling."

"Make the appointment at the bridal shop in town, and we'll go."

"But—"

"It will be okay, I promise, but talk to Bill."

"What do I say?"

"You'll figure it out." I smiled. "Do it when you're rested on a *Sun*day. He could have things to talk about, too."

The owl sounded off again—*hoot d'hoot, hoot d'hoot*—was it agreeing with my wisdom or warning about disaster? The birds were known for both.

Suko stood and smoothed her dress. "Thanks, Mel. I need to freshen up before going home. I don't want Bill to see I was upset." She glanced toward the dark trees. "Don't stay out here. There's a dangerous person haunting the Northwoods."

She dashed up the path before I could say goodbye.

I was alone again in the forest.

* * *

I SKEDADDLED to the Saab and hopped in. As I left the restaurant's parking lot, a set of headlights pulled in and trailed behind me.

The driver flashed the car's lights, unnerving me.

I glanced in the rearview and recognized Rand and his white Volvo.

He must have waited while I spoke with Suko and made sure I got back to my car.

He followed me to Lollygag Lane, idling in the driveway until I was safely at the cottage's front door.

Lou yanked open the portal. She saw Rand's SUV, waved, then hauled me inside. "What'd he say about the sponsors? Does he think one of those buckaroos clobbered Curtis Grey? Spill the beans, girl." She pointed to the wall phone, a retro-style oldie with a long cord. "Erika Dimblé called. She wants to talk to you. But we gotta strategize first."

I was exhausted and kicked Lou out without strategizing about Ms. Dimblé. The real estate agent could wait.

CHAPTER 38
Thursday Morning

At seven-thirty, Lou kicked on my door. She held a basket and knocked with her western bootie. "I brought coffee, muffins, and biscuits for Max. Why are you still in jammies? Something's goin' down. Turn on the TV."

We parked in the living room, the squawk box tuned to a local station. Murphy's Law, Northwoods edition, said on the morning Mel Tower slept in, H-E-double toothpicks would break loose.

The presser was held in a green space by the jail. It looked to be Rusty-the-horse's corral.

Unfortunately for the police chef, chief, the cameras showed the "Greer & Dusty's" restaurant" sign over his shoulder. Chief Luke Howard did *not* inspire confidence.

He was medium build, medium voice, medium hair. If they handed out prizes for middle-of-the-pack energy, he'd be at the center of the group receiving the top award, if that made sense.

He read from a script. "Mr. Curtis Grey, businessmen, age five-eight, was discovered dead on his pontoon, *No Bullship*, last Friday. Days ago. Six ago. *Days*, that is."

The fellow must have been nervous due to the cameras.

"This guy's a bore," Lou said. "He puts the 'sour' in 'dough.' I'd rather watch bread rise."

"We are treating this as a homicide," the chief continued. "We have identified a person of interest. She, er, the individual, is large—*at large.* We have a citizen hotline, for tips from ... citizens."

Lou slapped the couch. "Holy Friesian slip, he just admitted the suspect is a 'her'—and she's large!"

"He said it's a woman, not that she's large."

"Susan is off the hook!" Lou cried. "She's probably one-thirty soakin' wet. But none of the gal-suspects are large, not Susan, Dusty, or Ali. Heck, Ali von Barstool is the biggest one, but just cuz of her ego." She rubbed her temple. "He gave us a clue, a Friesian slip."

She meant Freudian. I let it go.

A Friesian was a horse breed, one of the most gorgeous animals ever created.

I did a photoshoot with one of the horses. If Coco Chanel and Farrah Fawcett teamed up to design the perfect equine, a Friesian would be it. A jet-black hair model of a creature as majestic as Pegasus but without wings.

Lou's malaprop wasn't wholly wrong. If humanity thought of horses while under stress, there would be a lot less sadness and tragedy in the world, I believed.

* * *

LOU WALKED Max while I showered and dressed.

We had to be at Camp Glass for the second day of the competition. Today was the Pony Express Relay Race. Competitors raced with a package, transferred it to one another, and then delivered it to an address near the camp—all via stick horses, sans GPS or electronic devices.

It was a challenge that favored the light and the quick. Good news for Steven and the Cinnamon Shakers.

Lou returned with Max. "You won't have to worry about Ericka anymore. My favorite collie and I"—she gave Max a belly rub—"were walkin' when she drove past. Then the wind ginned up and plopped a house down on her. All that was left of her was a pair of red shoes."

"Let Mother Nature handle it," I said. "That's one way to deal with a problem."

Lou rummaged in the pantry, then began packing an insulated bag. "Call Ericka and say we're puttin' excavating machines around this place as a blockade. Jason's got plenty more machines to drag up here to park on the lawn."

I yawned, still feeling sleepy. "Ericka can wait."

"She's driving past this place like a stalker. Let's get a dust-up goin'."

"Who will Ericka call if I don't vacate the premises?"

Lou pondered. "Sheriff Hottie, Buck County law enforcement, and senior fox. She will *not* want that. Hey, have you heard about the Silver Foxtrotters? They're like Chippendales but older, better."

I held up a hand. "I don't want to hear it, Lou."

"But they're dancin' at the casino. We should go."

"*No.*"

"What will we do about Ericka and the notice to buck off?"

"I have a contract to rent this for thirty days. I signed an offer to purchase and provided earnest money. I'm not in violation of what I agreed to do."

Lou frowned. "You won't hire an expensive attorney to fight this battle. That's not your style. The Mel Tower I know is tight. She didn't retire in her forties and buy a money-pit art mall and bookstore by throwin' cash around."

My cousin was correct. I did save my pennies. My three-story mall and bookstore in Cinnamon *were* money pits, but I employed great people, and the businesses broke even, plus a bit more.

"If I was you, I'd be backing up the truck and dumpin' cow chips on Ericka's front lawn."

I wasn't sure what to do about Ericka, but Lou gave me ideas.

* * *

I BUCKLED Max in the back seat of Lou's dually pickup, then I squeezed next to tins of frozen treats for the competition.

She'd lassoed me into riding with her against my better judgment. Being strapped inside her truck, harnessed like a bag of provisions, made me uncomfortable.

Lou began driving in the opposite direction of the camp.

"Why are we headed to town?" I asked.

"I need to zip past Greer & Dusty's. Gotta check the foundation of the restaurant. It may have drainage problems, and Jason wants the job."

We rolled down Main Street, turning by the jail. Officers Rusty, equine and human, were absent, probably on patrol.

Cole's truck was parked at a hitching post.

I hadn't heard from him—why he'd disappeared, I wasn't sure, but there were legitimate reasons, I imagined. They all began with the letter "E." Cole was investigating an *egregious* death, he was *exasperatingly* bad at goodbyes, and he had a girlfriend named *Ericka*.

The reasons caused me to think I'd made an *error* in judgment by hoping Cole and I had a future.

Lou pulled into the parking lot of G & Ds. The building was solidly built with log siding, a metal roof, and a large deck. It had lovely landscaping, and the ground sloped away from its foundation.

I doubted it had water problems. The drainage issue was an excuse to get me to look at it. I knew I shouldn't have ridden with her.

Lou shut down the engine. "You should buy this place, Mel. The way you spend cash, what's another money-pit business investment?"

"I'll wait in the truck with Max, thanks."

"Let's take a peek. This could be the best burger joint east of Hayward."

"I thought Greer and Dusty wanted to reopen."

She shook her head. "That'd be as successful as the Chicago Bears tryin' to beat a Pop Warner club. Those two need somethin' less stressful."

"Why is that door open?" I asked.

Lou peered at the front doors, two stunning panels carved to look like pine trees. Then she craned her neck to view the side entrance for servers—*it was open.*

She gasped. "When's a door not a door, Mel?"

"When it's a-jar."

"Who the heck broke into our new restaurant?" Lou groped in the back to rip the lid off a tin. "Grab a roll of frozen cookie dough. My molasses crackles are hard as baseball bats. *We'll clobber the bad guy, and he'll be down for a week!*" She yanked off her seatbelt. "We're headin' in, partner. You first, I'll cover ya."

* * *

IT WOULD HAVE BEEN WISER to wait for the authorities. They were two blocks away. Investigations were their thing, not mine. Plus, a killer was on the loose. I had a decent argument against going in the restaurant.

We'd gotten out of the truck. Lou was behind me.

She gave a gentle shove. "We're not waitin' for Chief Luke Warm. Go in, Mel."

I crouched, gripping the frozen dough, eighteen inches of sugar and flour, hard as stone. "Is the truck locked?" Max was still in the backseat.

"Yeah."

"Get your phone out."

"Done. Number's set for Jason."

I stopped creeping toward the open door. "No, get ready to dial nine-one-one."

"What's that number?"

"Not a time for jokes, Lou."

Dough-bat in front of me, I pushed the door, careful not to touch anything. The lights weren't on, but it was mid-morning and daylight streamed in the dirty windows.

Inside, I saw tables, shelves with booze, and a wooden bar with stools in front of it.

To my right was the kitchen. I smelled something funky.

Grease? Damp linens?

Lou was a few steps behind me. "What stinks? This place needs a scrub down. Whew, they shoulda called it Greer and Musty's."

Someone moaned.

My gaze cut to the floor. A lump—*a body!*—sprawled out next to a tipped-over barstool.

"Call nine-one-one!"

"But—"

"Call them!" I cried.

CHAPTER 39

Thursday Morning, Later

Clippity-clops clattered down the street before sirens shrilled. Officer Rusty, riding Rusty, arrived before anyone else.

Lou went to speak with him outside.

I waited, kneeling near Dusty Grey, careful not to touch anything. She was unconscious, the victim of a bump on her head.

I looked around. The barstool she'd been sitting on—perhaps, I could only guess—lay broken on the floor, its legs splintered.

I heard a snort by the open door, then a metal-shod hoof scraping pavement.

"You got trouble, ma'am?" Rusty asked.

Lou answered loudly, "I ... we, found Dusty inside the place. She's with my cousin, Mel Tower. We're guessin' the perp came up behind and whacked her."

"What are you holding, ma'am?"

"A frozen roll of my molasses crackles. Hard as rock. Hit someone with this and—"

"Put the weapon down, please."

Uh, oh.

Rusty's voice became stern: "Put the weapon on the ground, ma'am. Then back up and keep your hands where I can see 'em."

"I didn't do it!" Lou protested.

"On the ground, ma'am. Keep your hands in front of you. *That's an order.*"

* * *

OH, what a tangled web we weave, when from law enforcement two trespassers seek reprieve.

In the parking lot, Officer Rusty and the police chief questioned Lou and me.

Cole had arrived, too. He leaned against his truck and watched the interrogation.

The officers looked skeptical. Heck, even Rusty-the-Police-Horse gave us a side-eye.

The ambulance had loaded up Dusty and taken her to hospital. She was alive, thank goodness, but unconscious.

Lou explained what happened, "I spied her, then told Mel to do nothin,' even though the place smelled ripe as rotten melons. 'Don't clean, wipe, or take out the garbage.' We left everything alone. Then, I called you guys." She held up her phone.

"Is that true, Ms. Tower?" the chief asked.

"More or less ... Lou dialed for help." I tried not to glance at Cole while speaking. "I walked inside and knelt by Dusty to check her pulse. We didn't touch or affect what could be a crime scene." I motioned to the side door. "Dusty must have used a key to enter. The lock isn't broken, nor is the door dented or marred."

"Hmm," the chief said.

I pointed to the rolls of dough on the ground. "The victim had a bloody gash on her head. We couldn't have used these to hurt her. They're not sharp and wouldn't cause that type of wound."

"Yeah, right," Lou agreed.

"Have them tested, chief," I said. "You won't find blood or Dusty's DNA on them."

"Nope, just molasses, sugar, eggs, flour, vanilla, and secret ingredients," Lou said. "I always add—"

"Why were you here?" Rusty interrupted.

"Mel's interested in buyin' the building," Lou answered. "I was showin' it to her."

"Are you a real estate agent, ma'am?"

"Not yet. I'm leanin' toward CPA. No, law enforcement." Lou looked at the horse. "Especially with a cool partner like that."

I stole a glance at Cole. His face appeared impassive, like he and I were strangers. Surprisingly, he came to our defense.

"I'll vouch for these ladies," he said. "They have no history with the victim or a motive. They were only providing assistance." He nodded at Max, who sat in the driver's seat of Lou's vehicle. "They wouldn't bring their dog to commit a crime."

Lou agreed. "The sheriff is correct. Max is innocent." She put an arm over my shoulder. "We're just a couple of Good Rotarians. Always willin' to help those in distress in the community."

"Let 'em go, chief." Rusty pointed at the dough thawing on the pavement where a ring of moisture formed. "We got bigger fish to fry. Or, in this case, bigger cookies to bake."

* * *

FIFTEEN MINUTES LATER, Hilarious Wilde showed up with a camera. He waved and disappeared into the building.

Lou, Cole, and I spoke near his truck. He wore a blue denim shirt, Wrangler jeans, and a grim expression. His eyes looked gray, like looking a mountain on a gloomy day.

"Sheriff, we're persons of interest in this investigation," Lou said. "Especially now that I, *we,* discovered a victim. How can we help?"

Cole shook his head. "No, a person of interest is a suspect—"

"We're PIs—Interested Persons—it's the same," she insisted. "Would a license help? Mel could apply online."

"Will Dusty be okay?" I asked. "Is there anything we can do for her?"

Lou slugged me—*ouch!*

"Mel, the sheriff can't talk about the case *here*." She smiled at Cole. "Come for supper tonight at Mel's place. I'll make olive burgers. We'll tell what we know, and you give the inside scoop."

"That's not possible," he said.

"Sure it is." She jerked a thumb toward the chief's cruiser. "We're gonna solve it before Chief Lukewarm does. Is that guy's crockpot always set on 'Low?'"

Cole looked at the pavement, pursing his lips. "That's an interesting way to put it, Louella."

"On TV this mornin', he said the suspect was a 'large female.' We got doubts, especially after finding Dusty on the floor lookin' like a calf bowled over by a team roper."

"Oh?"

"Come for supper to hear my theory," Lou ordered. "As for now, we're droppin' food off at the camp. Then we'll haul casseroles to that haunted mansion Greer calls a house. We'll have a chat. Play 'Good Lou, Bad Mel' with him. See how he responds."

I shook my head. "We won't be doing that."

"Don't you two get what's goin' on?" Lou huffed. "Have either of you seen a soap opera?"

"I can't say as I have," he said.

"We got a love triangle as part of this mystery. Greer Grey and Ali Barstool are havin' an affair. One of 'em clobbered Old Man Grey cuz they want a future together and need money. They get rid of Dusty, and the coast is cleared for those two cheaters to go legit."

Just then, a familiar SUV drove past. Ericka Dimblé cruised slowly, staring at the police vehicles, the restaurant, and the three of us.

Lou rolled her eyes. "Cole, I'm no psychologist, but you got a fatal attraction. Ever seen *that* movie?"

"Please don't interfere—" I began.

"That gal is a few rum shots short of my pecan pie." Lou jerked a thumb toward the SUV. "Do somethin', Cole. Put on your Sunday plaid and give her the heave-ho, like David ditchin' Goliath. Mind you, don't pelt her with a slingshot, *but send a clear message.*"

"Lou, no—" I began.

She pointed at me. "Mel's not gettin' younger, but she can still attract a fella. Her old boyfriend is in town—"

"Enough!" I interrupted. "Cole and I need to talk. Wait in the truck."

She harrumphed off. Cole looked surprised, like he did *not* want to talk.

It didn't matter. I had things to say.

* * *

THIS WASN'T the time or place to have a long conversation, so I got to the point. "I miss you, Cole, and I wish we could see each other. Communicate, at least."

A cloud passed over, shading his face. "Me, too, but things are ... complicated right now."

"I think about you a lot."

He smiled but looked down, avoiding eye contact. "In a good way, I hope."

"Sure, mostly."

He winced. *Wrong answer.* I said it as a joke, but it didn't land.

"Sorry," I said. "I didn't mean to—"

"I have work to do, Mel. If you're headed to the camp, be safe."

He brushed past me, walking toward the restaurant, boots scraping the pavement. He didn't look back, didn't acknowledge me, it was like I was a stranger.

Wrong place, wrong choice of words, poor timing. All on me, my fault —but Cole was awful at goodbyes.

CHAPTER 40
Thursday Afternoon

At the camp, the phenomenon of opposites continued. Life is *not* a bowl of cherries. It's mixed fruit, at best. It's clashes of colors and flavors as different as humans' thoughts and behaviors.

Lou and I stood on the lodge's deck, reading the leaderboard, the results opposite of expectations.

"Talk about David beatin' Goliath!" she exclaimed. "The Cinnamon Shakers are further ahead. The Bad Addresses should be called the Slow A—"

"There's Steven," I interrupted. "He looks tired."

Steven climbed the steps to the deck. Max pulled against the leash, and I let him go. Steven greeted the dog and gulped water from a bottle.

He gave the scuttlebutt. Many competitors went off course without the assistance of electronics and GPS.

Lou elbowed him. "Why don't bears get lost in the woods? Cuz they never lose their *bearings*."

Steven smiled weakly. "It was humid for chasing through the wilderness. We've been out since five this morning. Some guys collapsed. The big monster from the BAs went AWOL. That's why they finished last."

Lou slapped her thigh. "Steve-O, what are you sayin'?"

Steven placed the bottle to his forehead. "What do you mean?"

She pointed toward town, ten miles as the crow flies. "You were in charge of eyeballin' the teams. Where was the big guy?"

"I can't monitor him while I'm competing." He looked between us. "You guys look like you saw a hodag."

"Nope, just a cowgirl that looked like she got trampled by a bull." Lou stared at me. "I did *not* have the monster from the BAs hurtin' Dusty on my bingo card. Did you, Mel?"

"We shouldn't jump to conclusions."

"Are you kiddin'? Besides polka music, they're the best thing to jump to. People are always doin' the opposite of what ya think."

"Steven, could that BA have driven into town?" I asked.

"I have no idea, but that sounds crazy."

Lou grabbed my arm. "We need to find out where he was."

* * *

I HAD to act before the police got involved, before they threw the BA in a stock trailer—he'd barely fit in a squad—and haul him in for questioning.

If they did.

Lou and I may have been the only ones to suspect the man.

I turned toward her. "Do you need to unload your truck?"

"Yeah, gotta move the frozen bakery into the freezers in the kitchen." She gestured toward the lodge. "I need a pack mule to help. Then we'll scatter to find the big guy."

"Freezer, you say?" Steven asked. "I could use cold air."

"Will you help Lou?"

"Sure thing."

"Take Max, please. It's too hot for him out here."

Steven reached for the leash. "C'mon, fella. Let's watch Aunt Lou carry boxes while we relax in the AC."

I dashed from the deck before Lou could protest, trotting across the lawn, searching for the path to the campfire, the route I'd taken after speaking to Jett McBride during the Opening Ceremony.

From what I recalled, the Bad Addresses's cabin was near the campfire pit. I'd sneak to the BA's cottage and listen to discover if the big fellow had a defense for disappearing for hours.

He probably had nothing to do with the attack on Dusty, but any intel I gathered could absolve my friend Susan from suspicion.

I stopped and tapped out a text:

> Checking in on you, Susan. I'm worried. Can we talk? Please call me!

I looked around, scanning the wall of evergreens for the path not more than a deer trail—*there it was*!

I slipped between the trees and stepped onto pine needles. The cabins were somewhere in the forest.

* * *

I CREPT THROUGH THE WOODS, grateful for wearing walking shoes, lightweight cargoes, and a T-shirt that said, "I'm Not Sleuthing Around."

Kidding. My shirt was blank as my operating plan—what would I say to a granite-jawed fellow as big as Hercules who may have hurt a woman?

I recalled the man's body language. His erect posture and intense eyes showed confidence, almost arrogance, but that could mean the opposite. The guy was insecure and used bravado to intimidate people.

A breeze blew through the pines. The air felt steamy, and sweat dripped from my temples. Ahead, I saw the spot with the campfire, the log seating, and the cooler with bottles of water.

I grabbed a few to look legit, like I'd been "tapped" as VP of Hydration for the day.

I spied a log cottage, plus tents around it.

I heard voices and zipped behind a tree, squinting through branches. Behemoth talked to his teammates. They looked dejected, their shoulders drooping like a stone mason had chiseled away their deltoids.

The smallest fellow pounded on a picnic table. "We need to act like a team!"

Behemoth responded, but I couldn't hear him. What struck me was that he looked insecure, dejected. He'd lost the intense stare and furrowed brow. He appeared confused and embarrassed—had he simply gotten lost in the woods and *not* masterminded a way to sneak off, hurt Dusty, and return undetected?

Perhaps the man was brawn, less brain, and lacked navigation skills.

His not-so-merry band drifted into the cabin, leaving their leader alone.

I moved—*snap!*

He heard the noise and looked up the hill.

I was busted.

He charged toward me, his arms seeming to grow longer and his thighs bigger. "Are you spyin' on us?" he bellowed.

I held up the bottles. "Water for your troubles?"

* * *

BEHEMOTH STEPPED CLOSER, his scowl intense.

He seemed different, less frightening, though. There was more to the brawny behemoth than I understood.

There was a cheerful jingle behind me. I turned to see ... an ice cream truck?

Bill Hartland drove a white ATV toward us. The path was just wide enough for the little vehicle. Sure enough, the off-road unit had a refrigerated box on the back with a pink logo.

Bill stopped and got out. He must have sensed a problem because he immediately stepped in front of Behemoth.

"Why the long face, fella?" Bill asked. "Step back, Secretariat. Give the nice lady some room."

"She's spying for the Shakers," the big man said.

"Mel's with me. Official beverage delivery for the games." Bill pointed to the cart. "I'm motorized, she's on foot. We aim for personal service, you know?"

"She's here for another reason," Behemoth protested.

"Get back to your cabin, ya big stallion," Bill said. "Go jump in the lake, cool your hooves. The lodge has floaties bigger than pontoon boats. Use one. Have fun, but don't splash the water out of the lagoon."

"She's up to something—"

"She's *not.*" Bill brushed the man's shirt. "There's a bake-off tomorrow. You gotta make cookies and deliver 'em. No broken ones or you'll get points off for those."

"Keep her away from our campsite," he ordered.

Bill took the bottles from me and handed them over. "Seriously, dude? You won't get water. Then you'll dehydrate and crash over like a ginormous pine, and no one will put you back together again." He pointed to the cabin. "Don't be a grumpty-dumpty. Turn that frown upside down."

The giant turned and marched down the steep bank to his cabin.

Bill looked at me. "Nate's a bit of a Neanderthal, but he's human, too."

"Yeah, like three humans combined," I said.

"Maps are Nate's kryptonite. He's awful with 'em, then his team gets bound up like they're on a diet of bananas and cheese."

"How'd you know I was out here?"

He stepped to the merry little truck. "I saw you sneak into the woods. Hop on. Let's go see what other trouble we can get into."

* * *

BILL DROVE THROUGH THE FOREST, traveling farther from the resort.

He patted the dash. "For Halloween, I dress this thing up like a ghost and blast a spooky soundtrack. Looks like a UFO floatin' through the woods. The kids freak out. I love it."

We delivered water to remote stations. After stopping at the last spot, he rummaged in the cooler. "Let's have popsicles. Lemonade vodka or cheddar cheese?"

"A cheese popsicle? Never heard of it."

"Me, neither. Lemonade vodka it is." He popped back to the driver's seat and handed one to me. "Cheers."

We drove to an overlook, then parked. The glittering lake was below, the crystal sky above. A loon sang its distinctive call.

"Why do loons swim by themselves?" Bill asked.

I pondered. "They have to, or they wouldn't be *a-loon.*"

"I knew you were smart." He lapped his popsicle, then said, "I heard you found Dusty Grey."

"I figured the word would get out. What are your thoughts?"

"*My* thoughts? I don't have 'em. I'm a Northwoods guy. Up here, men are from fishing boats, and women are from Pluto. That's the money god, right? Pluto?"

I studied his expression. "What's wrong?"

"Nothin.'" He bit his treat. "Okay, it's Suko. I said stuff about money. Like, my utility bills will double now that she's moved in. And, in winter we'll use the furnace instead of a campfire, and that costs extra. And, we'll use the washer and dryer instead of beatin' my undies on rocks."

"That bothered her?"

"They were *jokes.* Now, she doesn't want to buy a weddin' dress and wants to cancel everything because it's too expensive."

"No, I'm sure she doesn't want to cancel the wedding."

"I don't make a ton, but I got money and nothin' to spend it on. My truck's only fifteen years old. I got more Hawaiian shirts than I can wear. I got flip-flops, huntin' gear, and two boats. I live like a king. Suko is welcome to all of it."

"You'll work it out, Bill."

"I heard your old boyfriend's back, and you and Cole broke up."

"*That's not true—*"

"Yeah, see? That's the same reaction Suko gave when I joked about money."

"I'll walk back from here."

He grabbed my arm. "No way, Hansel, we're in the middle of nowhere, and there's no trail of breadcrumbs. The hodags will eat ya."

I shook my head. "I want to be a-loon."

* * *

On the ride back, Bill and I argued about *Hansel and Gretel*.

"Hansel was the brainy one with short hair," he insisted. "She wore glasses and solved the mysteries."

"Are you sure that wasn't Velma from *Scooby Doo?*"

He shook his head. "You're confusing her with that getaway movie, *Velma and Louise*."

"How many of those popsicles did you have, Bill?"

"Just one. Why?"

"No reason."

We beetled toward the lodge. The cart zoomed like the little spaceship from *The Jetsons*, speaking of TV shows. We wound around the soccer field, drove past the beach, and parked in a garage below the resort's kitchen.

Bill said, "I'm sorry about sayin' you and Cole broke up. He's got his mental attraction, and you got the pilot. You kids have to deal with it."

"*Mental* attraction?"

"Yeah, didn't you see that movie? You grow up in a little house on a prairie somewhere?"

I sighed. "I'm not dating my old boyfriend. Please don't spread that rumor."

"I won't."

"Thank you."

"Wait, don't leave." He looked around. "I hear you're askin' questions about what happened to Curtis and Dusty. Is that true?"

I nodded. "A friend may be involved. I want to protect her."

"Gotcha. You're a *Charlie's Angel*. You look like one of 'em, Linda Carter." He squeezed my bicep. "Are you bionic?"

"No, but you have your TV shows mixed up. Did you ever watch *The Moronic Man*?"

He chuckled. "Good one. But, Mel, you should know that Cole's nose is out of joint. If you snoop around, it's gonna make him more upset, so please don't. Have you talked to him?"

I nodded. "Yes, earlier today."

"Yeah, at the restaurant, the scene of the crime—you didn't do it, did ya?"

"*Of course not.*"

"Cole's cranky because he screwed up and dumped the ambulance in the lake. The police chief blames him. Those two have always been like the Road Runner and Lay Z. Coyote."

"That's an interesting description of the chief."

"He's a different animal. Folks around here say Sheriff Cole graduated from the Green Bay Police Academy, and Chief Luke graduated from the Gan*grene* Academy."

I shook my head. "Too bad."

"I've tried to light a fire under Luke, get him involved. I invited him to play the triangle in the Trio, but he won't." He flexed an arm. "Just shows that not everyone can be as fun and cool and rich as me."

* * *

BILL WOULDN'T LET me leave until I agreed to take Suko wedding dress shopping.

"You lived in New York, and Suko likes that," he said. "I don't, no offense, but I'll give ya money—"

"Suko wants to pay for it herself."

"But—"

"Let me handle it, Bill. In the Northwoods, men are from fishing boats, and women are from the Land of Emotional Maturity. Suko and I will figure it out."

"Cliché, Mel. Cliché."

"*Touché*, you mean?"

"If that's the French word for 'you won't *touché* the Curtis Grey murder investigation." He shook his head. "Do *not* make things worse for Cole. He's my buddy. You solve the mystery, and Cole won't live it down with the chief." Bill smiled, but there were worry lines between his brows, and the grin didn't reach his eyes.

I'd seen the expression when models were tired or fearful but still had to do their job for the camera.

I'd done it, too.

"Thanks for the warning," I said.

"It stinks for Cole if you are gettin' back with your old boyfriend.

He finally finds a halfway decent gal, and she goes back to her pilot BF who looks like a Norse god." He frowned. "Careful he doesn't go Howard Hughes on ya. That guy went off-plumb at the end."

"I'm not back with anyone."

He slapped the dash. "Darn it, Cole is in a tough spot, and I don't want him hurt or losin' his job. He's the best guy I know. He's Pink Floyd, and the rest of us are from the dark side of the moon."

The dark side.

Yes, somebody in the Northwoods was showing their true colors.

I got the message, dark and clear.

CHAPTER 41
Thursday Afternoon, Later

In a service bay at the lodge, I disembarked the ice cream truck, then yanked open a door that led upstairs to the kitchen.

I assumed it did. The staircase was narrow, and the hallway at the top had several doors. It reminded me of the set of a British farce. I trudged up the steps, unsure of which door—

One banged open. "Susan's missin'," Lou announced, hauling me into the kitchen. "She took off for the Dells."

"The Wisconsin Dells? How do you know?"

Lou marched along a row of refrigerators, pressing against their paneled fronts, checking if they were shut. "That's where people go when they need a vacay. Axe throwin', old-time photos, duck tours. Way better than that overpriced mouse place."

I waved to get her attention. "Why does Susan need a vacation from her vacation here?"

Lou sighed. "Because she's in the clear. She's not 'large'"—finger quotes—"and wouldn't hurt Dusty. Suz needed a break."

I pulled out my phone and scrolled. "She's not answering my texts."

"Not gonna, either. My Book Trout gals say she went for R&R."

"How do you know this, exactly?"

Lou rolled her eyes. "I said Trudy talked to her."

"You didn't say Trudy spoke to her."

"Yeah, I did."

"What else did she say?"

"Susan or Trudy? If we're solvin' this mystery, Mel, we gotta communicate!"

* * *

Lou snapped her fingers. "Did you hear what I said, Mel?"

I stared out the window, watching two people talk on the deck. "What?"

"Listen up: Suz ditched Art, the Glass Bottom guy. She needs to get her head on straight. Bring her liver back online. She's at the Dells."

"Okay."

"Steve-O and Max went back to the rental to write." She giggled. "Steve, I mean. Not Max. That dog can't type, but he could learn—are you listenin'?"

I nodded. "Susan is typing, and Max is at the Dells."

Lou looked outside. "Whoa, Cole's talkin' to Ericka. You're the body language expert. What's he sayin'? He finally givin' her the heave-ho cuz you told him to?"

I had no idea. Given our conversation earlier, I doubted it.

I sighed. "He needs to do what's best for him, Lou, no matter what anyone else says."

She patted my back. "You okay?"

"Yes, but I'm going back to town. I need to chat with Fern."

"Get a ride. I'm stayin' with the number crunchers to be sure Ali von Barstool isn't stealin'. There's a reception at the Glass Bottom on Sunday, the after-party for Curtis's funeral. I'm makin' desserts and need a pack mule. Plan on it."

* * *

I had two choices for the trip to town—either the ATV ice cream truck, where I'd be hydrated but the journey would take all day, or Captain Rand Cunningham.

I ran into him in the parking lot, within sight of Cole, of course, because perdition was the road on which my Northwoods vacation was traveling.

Ericka had disappeared. Perhaps she had departed for the Dells, too—for R&R, I hoped, and not ax-throwing lessons.

Rand wore slacks, a white polo that showed off his tan, and sunglasses. He looked like a casually dressed aviator pilot-god. If he were flying a trip through a hurricane in a paper airplane, you'd have complete confidence and buy a ticket.

"Rand, are you headed back to town?" I asked.

He hugged me. "Nice to see you, Mel. You look stressed. I heard you found a woman—"

"I need a ride to my rental. Are you headed to Copper Falls?"

"In a bit."

"Let's go."

He pointed to the lodge. "But I need to—"

I took his hand and spun him toward his white SUV. "Now, Rand."

* * *

I APOLOGIZED in advance for grilling Rand, and then I grilled him. "What's the gossip among the game sponsors?" I asked.

"Excuse me?"

We drove by a cliff, the treacherous drop-off where Steven had flung his manuscript out the window—had that been Monday, only three days ago?

It seemed like a year.

I grabbed the "Oh, Shucks" handle as we swerved. Even on a calm day, the water boiled angrily.

"What are the sponsors saying about Curtis Grey?" I asked.

Rand glanced at me. "The man who died on his pontoon?"

"Eyes on the road, please. Yes, that's the guy."

"Are you investigating his death?"

"Yes, please keep your eyes on the road."

"Don't worry," he patted the dash, "I've got this on auto-pilot."

"I prefer auto-Rand."

He swung—whoa!—into a gravel lay-by, a viewing spot overlooking the frothy drama below. Protruding rocks looked like shark fins, and waves crashed the shore.

A sign announced that we'd parked on Glass Cliff, a frightening concept if one thought about it.

Rand switched off the engine. "I want to help. What do you know so far about Grey's death?"

"Not enough. That's why I'm asking about chatter among the sponsors, one of whom was Curtis Grey until he canceled last-minute. You guys are the VIPs, the financiers, the power behind the throne. Someone must be talking about what happened."

Rand smiled. "You're claiming we're the power behind Bill Hartland's throne? He's not a golden chair type. He's more comfortable sitting in a bass boat."

True. Still, if there were palace intrigue, Rand would know. He had access to conversations above my pay grade.

"Did anyone have conflicts with Curtis?" I asked. "Was anyone angry with him?"

Rand extended an arm over my seat and leaned into me. Over his shoulder, I saw a familiar pickup cruise past.

Rats.

Sheriff Cole Lawrence slowed as though eyeballing a couple of teenagers who'd stopped to neck.

Rand brushed strands of hair from my cheek. "I regret our breakup, Mel. It was my fault. I traveled too much and took you for granted."

I shook my head. "It goes with the territory."

"I travel for a living, I know."

"I meant taking me for granted, but your job affected us, too."

* * *

FERN BUBBLE HAD JUST FINISHED her podcast, "Bubbles & Fiber," when I arrived at her condo.

She opened the door and saw my expression. "Bubbles for your troubles?"

I entered and saw a bottle on ice in the dining room. "Fern, how many old boyfriends, annoying cousins, and missing friends does it take to solve a mystery?"

"No idea."

I sighed. "Neither do I. This murder case is getting weirder by the minute. So much for my peaceful Northwoods vacation. It's been the opposite of that." I looked toward the kitchen. "Where's the hard stuff?"

"Whiskey?"

"Chocolate."

"This *is* serious. Have a seat in the living room. I'll get the Hughes'."

Hughes' "Hand Maid" chocolates were legendary. Formed by artisans in a basement workshop in Oshkosh and available only during certain times of the year, like the North Pole but in Wisconsin.

Fern always had a stash. After a minute, she brought caramels, toffees, and meltaways on a tray, along with a glass of milk.

She set the goodies on the coffee table. "I heard you found Dusty Grey."

"How is she?"

"Not good. The condo grapevine says she's in a coma."

"We need to find who hurt her."

Fern grimaced. "Are you sure that's a good idea?"

"I'm *not* going to quit. Susan could still be involved. What did the records search turn up?"

"Ali von Yaack is entangled in an ugly situation. The barstool company filed for bankruptcy last fall, and her condo has a large mortgage. She's in a tough spot financially."

"Could she benefit from Curtis's death?"

"She would, if she carried a life insurance policy on him. That's not unusual among exes in their wealth bracket."

"Anything else?"

"Greer and Dusty have financial problems. They closed their restaurant last year because of it." Fern sighed. "It's too early to say what Greer's inheritance could be, but it's substantial property-wise, according to my title search. Even if assets are locked in a family trust, Greer is set for life. The father's passing likely benefited his son. Possibly, Dusty, too."

I reached for a chocolate. "Was there talk of an affair? Could Greer have been cheating and wanted his wife out of the way?"

"I hate spreading gossip—do *not* repeat this—there's been infidelity on both sides."

I had no idea how Fern knew that, but she worked in PR, which included expert communication skills, psychology, and snooping around. If she said it happened, it happened.

"Susan Victory wasn't involved, I hope," I said.

"No, she was not."

"Are you aware she left town?"

"Who said that?"

"Lou talked to the Book Trout gals—"

Fern held up a hand. "Never mind."

"Rumor is Susan left for R&R because she's relieved at no longer being a suspect."

Fern studied my face. "What's wrong?"

"I came up here to spend time with Susan. I've called her, sent texts, picked her up when she fell off barstools. Told her to get help, call an attorney. She's ignored me."

"Aw, Mel, I'm sorry."

"Nothing I said made a difference. Now she took off and didn't tell me. I'm worried. What if something terrible happens?"

"I know. It's scary."

I felt tears sting. "I miss her, and our friendship."

"Have a chocolate, sweetie." She pushed the treats toward me. "Let it work its magic. Think about what you just said."

* * *

THE TREAT ENERGIZED me as though I'd had an espresso.

My brain began firing. "I made a mistake, didn't I?"

Fern tilted her head, and her glossy gray hair swooshed over an eye. "What do you think?"

"I acted like a parent to Susan, not a friend." I groaned. "No one wants to be nagged. Not kids, not teenagers. Especially not adults."

"You're right, but you were trying to help."

"It probably made her feel worse."

I thought about what I'd said to Susan during the past months. In truth, ever since last fall, I'd been overzealous, checking up on her as if she were a naughty teen.

I admitted I didn't trust her. "I'm afraid of the decisions she's making."

Fern reached for a cream-filled, then took a bite. "Don't be too hard on yourself. Mistakes were made on both sides. Susan is in a tough spot, and you're a caring friend."

"Why are friendships so hard sometimes?"

"Because, 'life is mostly froth and bubbles, but two things stand like stone—kindness in another's trouble and courage in our own.'"

"Wile E. Coyote?"

"Close. Adam Lindsay Gordon, an Australian poet."

I thought about how I'd spoken to Susan. Before coming to the Northwoods, I'd often lost my temper with her. It wasn't an effective way to encourage someone to get help. "So I should be kind to Susan, not nag or parent, eh?"

Fern nodded. "That's what I try to do. We both see she needs therapy and rehab, but we can't force her. No one wants to be lectured."

I looked at the chocolate. "It sure is a *rocky road*."

"A *whopper* of a problem, that's for sure."

I picked up a caramel. "What sort of epiphany brain food are these? If I eat more, can solve this mystery, and not make any more mistakes?"

She winked. "You could always be a writer. They don't make mistakes. They call them revisions."

I shook my head. "I've witnessed Steven's effort trying to get published. I'll stick with friendships and whodunnits. Those are hard enough."

* * *

FERN and I agreed to send a package to the hospital for Dusty.

"We'll send a healing prayer card for her, plus chocolates to the staff," Fern said.

I gave her cash for my half of the gift. Also, a phone number. "Please keep this source in the loop about Curtis Grey."

Fern looked at the number. "Who's this?"

"Jett McBride, a young police officer who wants to help."

She stepped to her desk and opened a red book, her lifeline of important info. She jotted notes. "Is this officer involved in the case?"

"Not officially. She's worried about the progress of the investigation and wants to assist without stepping on toes."

Worry lines formed between Fern's eyes. "Things could get dicey if the chief thinks she's undermining him. Let her know that."

"I will, in a kind, non-bossy way."

"How are things with Cole?"

"Fine."

"Really?"

"No, it's froth and bubbles at the moment."

She stopped writing. "You're in a dicey spot, too. He's law enforcement, and you're sleuthing under his nose. Plus, Rand showed up."

"It's fine."

"Anything I can do?"

I shrugged. "As Foghorn Leghorn says about love and romance, 'if you don't know where you're goin', any trail will get you there.'"

She shook her head. "That sounds more like your cousin Lou."

"Maybe, but I suspect they're the same person."

She hugged me. "Stay safe and trust your instincts. Call me when you need me. Give Max my love."

CHAPTER 42

Thursday, Later

I cruised the condo development, admiring its structures painted like trees.

I slowed by Susan's place. It was dark, the curtains closed, but the pots of geraniums on her porch were pruned, and the deck furniture's cushions were gone, stored safely somewhere. All actions that revealed Susan hadn't left in a hurry.

Ali von Yaack's condo, Throwing Shade, told a different tale. Branches were scattered on its deck, and a railing had broken. The place's siding had a moldy green tinge.

On the roof, eagles had left their calling card. It looked like someone had painted thick white streaks down the shingles.

I'd bet that Ali and the development's HOA had traded letters about the exterior. Perhaps eagles had been summoned as expert witnesses.

I looked toward the development's piers. *My Alibi* was up on its lift, its cover snapped tightly.

Did Ali travel to the Dells with Susan, or did she return to Chicago to resurrect the barstool biz? Because the two women left town, they couldn't be associated with Dusty's accident.

I exited the condos and drove toward Copper Falls. The Glass Bottom restaurant was located along the windy route.

I came around a curve and saw the pub—*what in the?* The place's sign was new: "The Glass & Bass."

Heavens to cowgirl cousins, Art Atkinson had rebranded!

Was he taking Lou's advice?

She meant well, but listening to her ideas was like consulting with Yogi Bear, Esq.

I slammed the brakes and marched inside, ignoring the "Closed Until Further Notice" sign.

The place was topsy-turvy. Broken barstools—a broken record now—were piled in the entry. Shelves had been emptied of their dusty knick-knacks, and the room smelled of paint and bleach. Someone clomped up the steps from the basement.

Art Atkinson emerged through a door behind the bar. He held a tray and looked disheveled. His shirt was ripped, and there were bags under his eyes.

He yawned. "We're closed."

"What are you doing?" I asked.

"Excuse me?"

"You're not listening to Lou Jingle to remodel, I hope."

"Who are you, again?"

"I'm Mel Tower, Lou's cousin."

"So you're not my ex-wife."

"N-no."

Why was I nervous?

"Or the county building inspector."

"No."

"Or my dead business partner." He cleared his throat and his voice deepened.

"I'm sorry about Curtis."

"Why are you telling me what to do with *my* restaurant?"

His eyes darkened.

Uh, oh.

One did not have to be a body language expert to recognize stress. I wouldn't pester him about Susan. No sense in poking the hodag.

I shook my head. "You just met Lou. She isn't someone to take advice from if you don't, ah, know her." My mouth felt dry, probably from the bleach smell.

"Lou has great ideas. I was searching for a new name. Everyone else's suggestions were crap." He crossed his muscled arms. "What kind of person are you, Mel Tower?"

Someone *not* smarter than the average bear apparently.

"My cousin's plans can be outlandish," I nodded toward the bar. "Before you know it, your staff will be dressed like Wally the Walleye and muskie martinis will be on the menu." I gestured toward the open space. "And a mechanical octopus will be installed for customers to ride."

"Why don't you let me worry about that?"

"Lou has wild ideas, and her time is not cheap."

That was a fib. But the guy was in the bar business. It didn't count. Tall tales and that milieu combined like curds and beer batter. Lou would never charge for advice. I said it to scare him. She'd dream up a Paul Bunyan steak special and bulldoze the parking lot for free.

Atkinson clattered a tray on the bar. "You're throwin' your cousin under the bus?"

Technically, it was under water because we were over a lake.

"Mr. Atkinson, my cousin means well, but—"

"Get out," he pointed to the door, "Get out, now!"

* * *

I DILLY-DALLIED on the porch of Lou's cottage like a kid who'd stolen candy.

I plotted my escape route before stepping across the threshold. I'd spent the last two hours driving around, pondering why I'd barged into the Glass & Bass and interfered with a man's plan for his establishment.

I was lucky my carcass didn't end up buried at sea.

If Art Atkinson had thrown me to the sharks and phoned Lou to say her cousin, Brutus (Mel Tower, same thing), had sabotaged her, I was in for a doozy.

I'd apologize. And then agree with what Lou said. Yes, I was a yellow-bellied rat fink! Then, I'd load Max in the car and escape for a quiet evening of respite from this disastrous vacation.

But you know what they say in the Northwoods—make plans and hodags laugh.

The door swung open. Lou wore jeans and a sweatshirt that said "Kick Some Bass." Her hands were free of rolling pins and iron skillets, thank God.

"Got a secret mission for us," she announced.

"I came to get Max. So tired." I yawned but kept an eye on her.

"You got skulkin' around to do tonight. Scavenger hunt for the games. Another pro-am, you and Steve-O. The rest of the team needs shut-eye."

"Oh?"

"We're goin' undercover. I'm drivin' the getaway wagon." She pointed to the driveway where a dark-colored van was parked. "Rebel Transport" was stenciled on its side.

"Whose van?" I asked.

"Need-to-know-basis only. Every team has stuff to find. We're gonna trespass, sorta. Cooked up the plan myself."

"Okay."

She squinted. "You're not sayin' it's nuts? Cole the Superman Sheriff could handcuff us?"

I shook my head. "I'm not like that—and whatever you hear tomorrow, Lou, *I didn't do it.*"

Her phone buzzed.

Please don't be Art Atkinson.

She glanced at it. Then: "Yeah, you're set in your ways, an oddball, but you wouldn't cross kin."

"Whatever is said, it did *not* happen that way."

"Here's how tonight goes down: Jason watches Max. You, Steven, and me roll out to get what we need at a certain place ... break in a little." She winked. "Then we hustle back to the cottage like wranglers with Scrooge McDuck's gold. I'll pick ya up at oh-twelve-hundred."

"Can't we just do it now?"

She looked around, eyes wide. "Are you kiddin'? This is a top-secret mission."

She partially closed the door. "Not even Jason knows the real deal.

Some stuff you don't tell your spouse. What he doesn't know could hurt him."

That made no sense, but Lou was a walking contradiction. Would her loyal, honest cousin point that out?

Absolutely not.

"Gotcha," I said.

"Wear black." She grinned. "Can you believe I'm finally tellin' you to wear your favorite color?"

I didn't answer.

Some things, like big mistakes, are better left unsaid.

* * *

WHAT'S the opposite of breaking into a restaurant with police tape across its side door?

Lou-the-Judicious explained the difference. She was a fake lawyer again.

We were parked behind Greer & Dusty's, hidden behind a dumpster. The sky was inky black, the air still. Not a creature stirred, not even a hodag.

Lou handed Steven a key. "Use this to go in the back. You guys aren't trespassin'. You're just a couple of squirrels lookin' for beer nuts. I peeked in the windows earlier. The only room cordoned off is the bar. The rest of the place is wide open."

"How'd you get a key?" I asked.

"Ericka thinks the 'True Gritty Charcoal Burgers' restaurant chain wants to buy the place. That gal will give up anything for a commission." Lou looked at Steven. "You're the writer. What's the word for a bunch of restaurant investors?"

"The mass noun would be a 'beef,'" he said.

She chuckled. "Good one."

Steven stared at the dark building. "Why this place, exactly?"

"We need somethin' with a logo. Relish tray, beer glass. Anything that says Greer & Dusty's."

I began, "But why this—"

"It's for points!" she said. "A win tonight will put the Cinnamon Shakers ahead of the BAs."

"We just dash inside, grab a tchotchke, and be done with it?" I asked.

She shook her head. "No, nothin' weird. Get a trinket."

"But a tchotchke *is*—"

"Steve-O, you get the goods. Mel, you check out where Dusty went down. Look for somethin' the bad guy left behind." Lou tapped her temple. "Act like Scooby Doo."

Which was better than acting like a traitor. She hadn't said anything about my disastrous convo with Art Atkinson, thank goodness.

"Anyone need a snack before ya break in?" Lou held up a bag of granola bites. "Just kiddin'. Don't trip on a broken chair. We can't sue Ali von Barstool if we're not supposed to be there, remember." She popped a bite into her mouth.

Steven took my hand. "Let's get this over with."

Like a couple of nutty squirrels, just as Lou said, we scampered across the lot, through the back door, and into Greer & Dusty's restaurant.

* * *

"HEY, Ichabod Crane, where do you think you're goin'?"

Lou shouted as loud as a cowbell. I was in the restaurant's basement and even heard her.

Ichabod?

That could only be one person.

I dashed up the steps, nearly crashing into Steven, who'd been snooping around the lobby. We banged out the back door.

Headlights blazing in the parking lot, and Hilarious Wilde held a camera, his arms in the air.

Lou stood by the van, legs spread, finger guns pointed. "Stop right where you are, big fella."

"It's Hilarious Wilde!" he yelled. "You were on my pontoon boat!"

"When? Where?" Lou asked.

"Sunday, four days ago ... remember the concert on the water?"

She stepped forward. "Why can't a Chicago Bears quarterback use his phone?"

"Because he can't find his receivers, you said!"

Lou nodded. "Yeah, it's you. Put 'em down."

Hilarious lowered his arms, then glanced from Lou to Steven, and then to me. His sky-high eyebrows revealed he was shocked at seeing a crowd at this hour.

"What are you doin' 'round these parts at one o'clock in the mornin', Hil?" Lou asked.

"I'm deputized by the police. What are *you* doing here?"

Just then, a white SUV raced around a corner and pulled into the lot.

Why was Captain Rand Cunningham here?

"My backup has arrived," Lou said. "Let's get to the bottom of this, shall we?"

* * *

NATURALLY, Cole drove in seconds later. His truck rolled over the curb like a tank. He parked, climbed out, and strode to us looking like Marshall Dillon quashing a dust-up—hat, boots, shirt that matched his eyes.

Seeing him shocked me, like plunging into a cold, Northwoods lake.

Lou began, "Your Honor—"

Cole ignored her. "Hilarious, what's going on?"

Rand cleared his throat. "Sheriff, if I may speak, Louella told me they were on a scavenger hunt and saw a man trespassing here at the scene of an unfortunate event earlier today."

"Trespasser turned out to be Hilarious," Lou said. "Pretty, funny, eh?"

Cole's gaze traveled from us—the Dirty Dozen (or so)—to the back door.

It had been pitch black when Steven and I scampered in, and there were no cameras. (Lou had assured us of that, but the chance of it being true was fifty-to-fairy-tale.)

The restaurant's back door had slammed shut when Steven and I emerged.

If our tour inside wasn't mentioned, there were no clues we'd taken a peek.

Hilarious covered for us. "It was a comedy of errors, Cole. I was out taking nighttime shots—I saw them, they saw me. It was a regular Keystone Cops moment."

"We surprised each other," Lou agreed. "Real goofy, a screw-up worse than an airline. No offense, Rand-O."

Cole sighed heavily, like a guy who'd had a rotten day.

"I'll vouch for the scavenger hunt," Rand said. "The teams are seeking items for a comprehensive list. They'll be collected and scored for the competition."

Lou nodded. "Yeah, we gotta scrounge up a muskie lure, a Brewers ball cap, and a Paul Bunyan knick-knack. Anyone got a coffee mug or somethin' with his picture on it?"

Rand stepped up to me, his expression looked odd. He took my hand. It felt familiar, strong. "I'd like to add something to support Melanie. I've never met anyone like her."

"She's a peach," Lou agreed. "Honest, kind, loyal. Like a golden retriever."

Rand continued, "This may not be the place to say it, but I'm still in love with her."

Lou smacked her thigh. "I did *not* have this on my bingo card! Some vacay, Mel."

I shook my head. "No—"

"What are you sayin', Rand? Are you askin' Mel to—"

I had to distract her. "Lou, have you spoken to Art Atkinson? Give him a buzz as soon as you can." I looked at Rand. "We need to talk."

CHAPTER 43

Thursday Night—Was I Dreaming?

Had the last few hours happened? Or was I in bed, dreaming about a disastrous convo with Atkinson, a "legal" break-in at a restaurant, and a near proposal from Rand?

My car rolled over a bump in the road and veered toward black water. I slammed the brakes—this definitely was *not* a dream.

I sped onward.

I'd ditched Rand and everyone else. I didn't appreciate being ambushed in the parking lot. It was time I took matters into my own hands.

Being a quiet observer served Mel Tower well, but at some point, she needed to come out of her shell.

I'd abandoned the scavenger hunt, hopped in my car, and raced to Cole's farm like a Pony Express rider on a midnight run.

The interior lights of the home were on. I got out, jogged to the front door, then knocked. *Ouch.* The solid door hurt my knuckles.

Cole answered wearing jeans and a denim shirt. He smelled of leather and pine.

"We need to talk," I announced.

He stepped out, then pulled the door shut. "What is it?"

"I had no control over what Rand said." I softened my voice. "I want to talk to you. Really *talk*. Like we did on the boat and at Bill's place. I can't stop ... thinking about you."

He shrugged.

"I know the investigation is stressful." I moved toward him, but he stepped back. "You and I have something, Cole. *We* should—"

"I can't right now, Mel."

"Yes, you can."

He glanced toward the door. "Not *now.*"

I sensed odd energy. "Tomorrow, then? Let's give it a few hours. Things always look better in the morning."

"How was the tour inside Greer & Dusty's?" He crossed his arms, changing the subject. "Was it just you, or did the whole gang go in?"

He knew ...

I answered vaguely, like a lawyer. "Individuals entered with a key, so technically, they had permission. The cordoned-off section was not trespassed. Legally, it's a gray area."

I smiled to ease the tension. Somehow, he and I had to get back to center, find common ground. There was an attraction between us worth fighting for. In the past, I would have let things go, but not anymore.

"I've arrested people for less," he said.

I wouldn't let his sternness deter me. "But you lean toward mercy, not cuffs. You're not the fire-and-brimstone type."

"I heard you and the big fellow from the BAs almost got into it."

I shook my head. "Ice cream soothed that savage beast."

He paused as though softening up. "How's Max?"

"Great, and he'd like you to visit Cinnamon. He'll take you to his favorite places—the dog park, the Dog Bowl. And the bowling alley. Off-leash, too."

"He's still in love with you, Mel."

I nodded. "Max loves me, yes. And someone loves you, Cole."

Just then, the door opened, and Ericka stuck her head out. "What are you doing?" Her jaw dropped. "*Oh, my gawd.*"

* * *

WHEN I ARRIVED at my rental on Lollygag, the sun had just cleared the horizon. It cast an orange glow on the cottage, making it seem like the tiny home was on fire.

I entered to find Lou in the kitchen wearing her "Cowgirls Do It Better" apron. The place smelled like a restaurant, basically—coffee, bacon, and onions. Casserole dishes sat on the stove, and juice carafes chilled on ice. Muffins were piled on a cake stand.

"Thought ya might be hungry," she said.

"Just coffee, please." Max tippy-tapped over to greet me. "Hey, fella."

"He was worried when you didn't pick him up from our place last night."

I patted the dog. "Sorry, Max."

"It's okay. We took a ride to find ya. Saw your car parked at Rand's rental."

"Yep."

"You want to talk about it?"

"Nope."

"I'll fix ya a plate."

"No, thanks."

"Brides!" She slapped the counter. "You gals want to lose weight before a wedding—"

"What wedding? *No one* is talking about that," I said. "Besides, you preferred Cole, I thought."

"I saw how pathetic he was with Ericka. Worse than the Bears in the Red Zone with a full set of downs playin' the Galloping Grandpas. Couldn't spot it any better, and they'd still fumble."

"What's the Book Trout gals' betting pool showing?"

She blushed. "How'd you know?"

"I have sources, too."

"The consensus pick for your weddin' has always been Rand. You guys were together for years. Long-distance, but you matched okay on paper."

"On paper?"

She held up a palm. "Trudy's the numbers runner, not me—she's our Bookie Book Trout. That's redundundant, I know, but don't be mad The gals are just havin' fun."

"May I have that coffee?"

She grabbed a mug. "Would ya like pretzels? I got some in those little packets. They'd make fun wedding favors. We'll print 'em with your initials—"

"*Stop*. Just cream, please."

"Last night in the parking lot, things got weird. Sorry about that. But you know what they say in families—bein' related means you never have to say you're sorry . . . much."

"I accept your apology, Lou. Remember that in case I have to say it to you."

"You apologize to me? That's the opposite of the way it usually goes between us."

I looked her in the eye. "Remember it, please."

* * *

I STEPPED out of the shower to see a text from Rand:

> Let's have a trip soon.

A vacation from this rotten vacation was an idea, but during our conversation last night I'd made it clear I was confused and not in the head space to spend time with him.

I wasn't wearing my reader glasses but replied with emojis.

Lou banged on the door. "Jason, Steven, and the team are here for breakfast. C'mon out."

"Should I put clothes on, or is the meal au naturel?"

She laughed, her voice muffled. "I always got that phrase confused with à la carte. No wonder why my catering biz never took off."

"I'm not hungry, but thanks."

"Pull on your britches and get out here. Got a team shirt for ya. Add a feedbag, and you'll match everybody."

"Go ahead and eat."

"About the competition today—"

"I'm taking the day off. The games will have to go on without me."

"Yeah, a spa day. I approve." She tapped lightly. "I gotta feed the boys, then we're takin' off. I'll leave food in the oven."

I wanted to ask a question, but then my phone pinged several times. I dug readers out of my makeup kit.

Bill Hartland wrote:

> Dress 911! Suko's coming apart—wedding hanging by thread—this is sew hard—meet her in town to find dress b4 she calls whole thing off!

I replied with a thumbs up.

Bill wrote:

> Eleven AM.

I scrolled, re-reading the prior text. My toes curled on the tile floor, and a chill traveled from feet to scalp.

The earlier text had not been from Rand—*it was from Cole.* "Let's have a talk soon," he'd written.

A *talk,* not a trip!

I'd sent a terrible response, an airplane emoji and a broken heart.

The moment was just *plane* awful.

* * *

MAX and I zipped to Fern's place. Who better to speak with during a communications crisis than a PR expert?

I lugged breakfast in a picnic basket, but Max brought vodka, Bloody Mary mix, OJ, and bubbles, in case Fern needed it.

We stood in her kitchen. Fern studied at my face. "What's wrong?"

"Dusty was found unconscious, and Susan is missing, but we think she's at a spa. Curtis Grey was killed seven days ago, and the murderer is still at large." I inhaled. "Max thought you'd like something to soothe your nerves."

"What else?" she asked.

I clacked like a teletype and recited the last twelve hours, outlining the confrontation with Art Atkinson at the new Glass & Bass, the ill-fated tour of Greer & Dusty's, and the miscommunication with Cole.

Fern told me to take a breath.

She ditched the booze and made spa water—cucumber, organic aloe vera juice, and lemon with a splash of Italian sparkling. Fresh-tasting and healthier than my idea.

She steered me to the sofa on the outdoor deck. "Shakespeare wrote that our good deeds are written in water, and our evil ones etched in brass."

I lifted my water. "Mine are in skywriting. Cheers."

"Remember what I said yesterday—"

"That opposites attract? Total myth. They miscommunicate."

"Take courage in another's trouble and kindness in your own."

I paused. "Are we drinking the same thing? That's *not* what you said."

"Cole will figure it out, Mel. Trust that he's courageous enough to handle Ericka, and your errant text. Give yourself a break. One miscreant text doth not ruin a relationship."

"Was that from *Much Ado About Nothing*? Shakespeare was way ahead of his time. Marlowe texted that about him, I read."

Fern sipped, watching me. "Where do things stand with Rand?"

"We're in a holding pattern." I stared at the lake. Fishing boats still lingered, but ski boats and their happy vacationers were dropping inner tubes in the water, preparing for a day of fun.

"What are you thinking?" Fern asked.

I sighed. "I worry that I can't help Susan. And that emotionally, romantically I'm confused. And because of that, both Rand and Cole will be the ones who got away."

* * *

FERN STEPPED INSIDE, leaving me on the porch. Max rested his head on my knee. I gently stroked his noggin.

Animals know.

Fern returned with chocolate. "Extra dark. Have one."

"Thanks, leave the box."

She patted my hand. "Kindness in another's trouble, courage in your own, remember."

"You're messing with me, Fern."

"What would you tell me if I were in this situation?"

I ate a piece of candy. "That you experienced a midsummer dream. While you slept, a sprite dripped potion in your eyes. You'll marry the guy wearing the donkey head. And if you don't like that, it doesn't matter because none of it happened."

She laughed.

I ate another chocolate. "That's from *A Northwoods' Night's Dream*, written by Bill Lakespeare, Will's Midwest relative."

"You'll manage, Mel."

"Maybe I'm supposed to stay single. Own businesses, let excellent people run them. Adopt rescue animals to overcome the trauma of the New York fashion industry. Be an amateur sleuth and solve mysteries. That's it, that's my life."

"As your public relations person, I say you're doing an excellent job with the businesses. As your friend, I say you scrimped and saved for your life *now*." She sipped spa water. "You've always been generous to my horse rescue, and Max adores you. You've solved one mystery, and you're working on another."

I lifted my glass. "It's decided, then. I'm Mel Tower of Sunnybrook Farm. Cheerful, single, and nosy."

Fern shook her head. "I've always thought there was a fellow for you."

"There are two. Both fabulous, and I'm messing it up."

"Timing is everything in relationships, Mel."

"But the Northwoods is on lake time. That means it doesn't exist, yet it moves too fast."

Fern stopped talking and poured us more spa water.

As a PR guru, she knew when to quit and communicate another day.

CHAPTER 44
Friday Morning

I left Max with Aunt Fern, then rushed to the bridal shop.

I was late, and my mess-ups were accumulating like unclaimed bags at an airport. A bell jingled as I entered "Lumberjill Bridal, elegance for all occasions," a boutique on Main Street.

Suko wore a plaid robe and a brilliant smile. "I can't wait to do a try-on, Mel. I'm so excited."

Bill's text to me claimed she was near panic, close to a runaway bride —had he purposefully been untruthful? Suko was the opposite of his text description. I expected a stressed bride-to-be but instead witnessed a cheerful songbird.

Suko hummed while Lumberjill's owner, Barb Blade, pulled gowns from racks.

Blade must have noticed my confused expression. "Are you okay, Ms. Tower? It looks like you have an ax to grind."

I played along. "A few problems came out of the woodwork, but they're nothing I can't hack."

"May I offer a Lumberjill espresso? Or a Harvey Wallbanger?"

There was a bar in the corner, with a coffee maker and drink fixings. Mugs and an assortment of glassware lined the countertop, along with oranges, cherries, and a jar of honey shaped like a canoe.

"Coffee, thanks," I said.

I stepped to a rack of glitzy pink robes. The place was Log Cabin meets Hollywood Glam.

Dresses hung from wooden hangers, and evergreen garlands and twinkle lights decorated shelves. Bedazzled accessories abounded, crystalized sandals, ball caps, and makeup bags glittered in display cases.

Suko gestured toward log benches circling an electric fireplace. "Wait here while I try on."

Coffee was delivered, dresses modeled. Barb Blade kept "logs" of every garment, and alterations would be completed fast, as in, "Chop, Chop."

After several gowns, Suko emerged wearing a stunner—a cream-colored mermaid with a sequin bodice. The sparkles reflected light toward her face like a personal spotlight. When she twirled, chiffon flowed around her like water.

"It's perfect," I said.

"This is the *one*." She glowed, and I couldn't have been happier for her.

Blade explained the dress was from a Northwoods designer, Holly Maple. "She's exclusive to Lumberjill and won't branch out, thank goodness."

Suko glanced at the price tag. Her glow disappeared like a blown fuse. Then, the horn at the front door blasted like a distress call from a Great Lakes shipping barge.

It sounded awful. Somehow, I knew the bell tolled for me.

Blade began, "What in the name of Paul Bunyan—why is Ericka here?"

Ericka Dimblé marched past the gowns to halt inches from my nose. "Mel Tower, you criminally trespassed at a crime scene, and you're squatting on a rental property. I'm having you arrested."

I gasped. Immediately, my temples throbbed and I felt faint—the lack of sleep and long morning was taking its toll.

Ericka sneered and clenched her fists. She looked like she wanted to slug someone.

She had me stumped, it appeared.

* * *

Kindness in another's trouble, a haymaker to a troublemaker's snoot in one's own.

Okay, not the quote.

Close enough.

Ericka erred in picking a fight—and in choosing a location where axes hung within arm's reach.

Barb Blade spoke first. "Ms. Dimblé, if this is about the dress you want, shouldn't you be engaged? Has Sheriff Cole asked—"

"He will, but this woman needs to be arrested."

Blade looked at me.

"I don't know what she's talking about," I said. "We should dia-*log*-ue before anything else."

Suko and Blade smiled.

Ericka reddened. She wore a crimson frock, and her skin blushed so quickly and violently it was like her body sucked color from the fabric.

"I'm not the enemy." I attempted to diffuse the situation and nodded toward the seating area. "If you're stressed, pull up a log. Let's talk about it."

Blade agreed. "I'll make alcohol-free Wallbangers."

"Ericka, I know excellent therapists," Suko added. "There's no need for this."

The blonde stepped back, eyes narrowed. "Mel Tower can go to jail or pack her bags and leave town. I've made a police report. I will not stop until she's gone!"

Gone, as in dead, or just axed from her vicinity?

She turned and marched through the store. She yanked open the front door, and the ship's horn blasted again.

I wondered if Ericka had played the drums in high school or competed in shot put—she possessed a lumberjack's touch with door-knobs. The noise she generated with a wrist could substitute for the village fire whistle.

Ericka shrieked!

Unfortunately for her, the only soul in town louder than she, walked in at the same time.

* * *

"I RUSHED over when I heard Mel was here," Lou announced. "Did one of your fellas propose?" She looked at the floor. "What happened to Ericka?"

The crash had tobogganed her across a leather bench like an Olympic bobsledder, then dumped her onto the plaid rug in a wipeout. She looked like roadkill, a flattened porcupine.

She was mad as a moose, though, and glared at me like I'd done the deed.

I stepped over to help her. "It's not what you think—"

She waved me off. "Save it. You're still going to jail."

"Who's goin' to jail?" Lou snorted.

Uh oh. Red flag, meet bull.

Lou swiped the rug with a boot, and her nostrils flared. "Where's Ali von Yaack?" she demanded. "In jail for pilferin' from the community? Or for sendin' her ex, Curtis, to the big Boat Show in the Sky? *What's her alibi?*"

"I have no idea!" Ericka cried.

Barb Blade dashed to the concierge desk and grabbed a mini-bullhorn. "Ladies, let's not bark at one another." She waved the horn toward the benches and fireplace, trying to herd us to the seats.

Ericka scrambled to her feet. Anger radiated from her body in shimmery waves. It was like watching heat rise from a griddle. "I should sue this place for putting a tripping hazard near the door. You haven't seen the last of me, Mel Tower. *Believe it.*"

* * *

ERICKA AND LOU TOOK OFF.

In opposite directions, thankfully.

Blade collapsed to a rocker, fanning herself. "That was alarming. I can't see the forest for the trees right now."

I stepped to the bar and brewed a ginger tea. When it was ready, I handed it to her. "This will calm your nerves. Stop the seesawing."

She smiled. "Thank you, dear."

I followed Suko to the changing suite and helped her out of the dress.

She slipped on a robe, staring at the gown. "It's perfect, but too expensive. I can't justify spending that much."

I hung it up. "You looked fantastic in it."

"Bill and I talked. He offered to buy it, of course." She reached for the garment, caressing the fabric with her fingers. "The man would lasso the moon if I asked, but this is *my* dress. I want to do it."

"I have an idea," I said.

"I can't ask you to buy it, Mel."

"That's not what I'm thinking."

She took out a tissue and dabbed her nose. "W-well, what?"

"Hear me out. I know a way for *you* to buy this beautiful dress for your wedding."

* * *

IF MEL TOWER'S wedding occurred and the groom didn't show, what would the event be called?

A towering disaster.

Not my best pun, but it's my pretend wedding, and I'll pun where I please.

I'd booked talent for a party in my future. Suko had agreed to sing for the gala, whatever it was, and I'd written a check as a deposit.

She'd used it to purchase her dream dress.

I climbed into my car—the steering wheel was *hot* due to the blazing sun— and imagined the party. Would it be a wedding? Probably not. Love was confusing, an emotion like plaid. Feelings and passion, reality and timing mixed like contrasting colors.

Shakespeare wrote that phrase in one of his comedies.

Or, I made it up. Take your pick.

But for a wedding, it is recommended that a groom is confirmed and the bride is convinced she's the marrying type.

Issues yet to be resolved.

The street rumbled, and my car shook. A pickup towing a massive pontoon pulled next to me, its brakes screeching like sirens. The rig was the size of an aircraft carrier. Battleship gray, too. It didn't just block the sun, it plunged my armadillo-shaped car into darkness, like I'd leaped from a cliff into black water.

I pressed the clutch and turned the key.

Bzzzz! Bzzzz!

I jumped at the robotic voice coming from the radio: "A summer storm watch is in effect," it declared. "Severe thunderstorms are expected in Buck County at fourteen hundred hours. Prepare for thunder, lightning, high winds. Secure outdoor furniture, garbage cans, yard items. There is a small craft advisory. Lake travel is not recommended."

I looked around. Beyond the shadow of the massive boat next to me, the skies looked crystal blue and clear. Hard to believe the forecast was the opposite.

CHAPTER 45

Friday Early Afternoon

When the Swedes took their turn at designing cars, they marched to a different drum. Drove a different path, if you will.

The engineers who made Saabs put the ignition down between the seats, not on the column. It was for safety reasons. Drivers don't break their knees by hitting the key in a crash.

Further, the cars are designed to withstand the impact of hitting a moose. Thus, I drove cautiously while skulking around the police station. Rusty, the equine officer, was big as a moose, and I had no intention of harming the precious creature.

I was searching for Jett McBride. I needed to hatch a plan with the young officer.

I drove slowly, which unfortunately made me look like a stalker, and who should be departing the building but a certain lawman?

I recalled the errant text I'd sent, the one with the airplane.

Cole motioned for me to pull over, pointing at a spot with yellow lines on the pavement labeled "Law Enforcement Only."

I parked, and he walked to the driver's side. He pulled a notepad out of his vest. "I'm sorry, ma'am, but this is parking space is restricted. I'll have to write a ticket."

"Cole—"

He interrupted, nodding at a sign. "Law enforcement vehicles and horses only."

"Sheriff—"

"May I see your license?"

I sighed. "Sure."

I rummaged in my purse and then flashed a picture of Max wearing sunglasses. "Here you are, sir."

He glanced at it.

No smile.

"You're currently not wearing glasses. Do you have a vision restriction to drive this vehicle?"

"I do not, but the dog does. Max has to wear his prescription lenses when he drives."

Cole scribbled, not looking at me. He wore cargoes, a denim shirt, and smelled like leather and pine. At this point, he should quit the force, open a cologne store, and make a killing at selling the men's fragrance of the Northwoods.

"Cole, can I please explain?"

"No, ma'am."

A ticket was fair game for the errant text. I wished we could start over with a date in his truck and a turtle sundae!

Mistakenly—I swear—I hit the windshield spray button. "Oops—sorry!"

The mist sprayed over the top of the windscreen. Water droplets sprinkled Cole's shirt. I got wet, too, because the convertible top was down.

"Sorry, Cole," I said.

He stepped back and handed over the note. "Please don't park in restricted zones, ma'am. Drive safely and enjoy the Northwoods."

* * *

I PUT off reading the note. It wasn't a positive message, I figured, after the miscommunication we'd had.

I spotted Jett McBride on the outskirts of Copper Falls. She was in a lay-by next to the road, sitting at a picnic table, an electric bike with a red light on it propped against a tree.

She waved me aside. "Step back. Racers are coming."

A rider on a mountain bike emerged from the woods. He blew past in a familiar black T-shirt, spraying leaves and gravel—WHOOSH! It was a BA, a Bad Address team member.

Jett shook her head. "Today's the bike-delivery race. That team is fast. They've lapped the others and are making up points."

Wind rattled the trees, and the pines swayed like green sails. That storm definitely approached."Do you have time to chat?"

She grimaced. "Yeah, I'm stuck here until the end, but don't get run over, please. They'll take my badge for killing pedestrians."

I moved away. "Have you heard anything about Susan Victory?"

"I overheard the chief say she's left town. D'you know where she is?"

"Is he looking for her?" I relayed that Susan had gone to the Dells for a spa weekend. "It's only a theory, though. Can you find out if she's there?"

Jett nodded. "I could do things on the sly."

"I'm trying to confirm her whereabouts. If you can find her, that would help. Ali von Yaack, too."

Jett's eyes widened. "She's missing?"

"She could have gone back to Chicago, but try to find both women. Any update about Dusty's condition?"

"She's stable, I heard. Has no idea who attacked her."

"Were there cameras in the area? Anything that would provide a lead?"

"The restaurant's cameras weren't operating, but a doorbell cam on a house nearby picked up an SUV. It was super dark, though. No plates or driver identified."

Another racer blew past—Steven of the Cinnamon Shakers. My friend looked intense, desperate. He vanished down the trail before I could shout encouragement.

The wind swirled.

A mini-tornado forced Jett to grab the notebook she'd been writing in. Pine needles and leaves flew in every direction. My car's top was down—an open invitation to the zephyr to come aboard and play.

The air danced on my seats. Tissues, receipts, and the plastic lid from a take-out cup burst upward like birds freed from a cage—and also the note from Cole!

Horrified, I watched the cream-colored ticket, previously tucked in the dash, soar upward and circle the treetops like a flat airplane. Then, as though late for a trip, the paper flew directly toward Glass Lake.

Unbelievable.

* * *

I COULD TEXT Cole with an airplane emoji again. Explain that the note flew off.

Not wise.

There was zilch I could do about the ticket that sprouted wings and soared off as though late on a mission.

"What's wrong?" Jett asked.

I pondered asking her to change her name. Aviation a sensitive subject, after all. I shook my head. "I'm worried about Susan."

"We need to stay in touch. We could solve this."

We made plans to talk later.

Jett was savvy to keeping our conversations confidential. "No texts or phone calls, easy to track. And, we can't meet at your rental—too many prying eyes."

She meant Ericka—the woman was a loose cannon. If E. discovered J. and M. were talking, E. could attempt to interfere with the young woman's job.

I told Jett about the incident at the bridal shop and the threat to arrest me.

"Oh, geez. I feel so bad for Cole," Jett said. "She just needs to find the right guy. Someone who gets her vibe and appreciates her. Sometimes, the solution is way easier than people think."

An interesting observation. Jett gave me an idea.

"If a warrant is issued for my person, I'd appreciate a heads up," I said. "I'll disappear to the Dells for a spa day, too."

Jett rolled her eyes. "I doubt Ericka's nonsense will go anywhere. But let's you and I meet out at the camp later. Tonight's the last event before the Glass Ball."

"The quiz show?"

She nodded. "Yeah, I gotta wear a box with a clue written on it. Bunch of us stand together while the teams guess the answer, which has to be in the form of a question."

"What's your clue?"

"The first round is easy: In hockey—"

"What is the penalty box?"

She smiled. "Yeah, and the second round is: A dog that—"

"What is a boxer?"

"You're good at this, Mel."

I didn't want to hash over my past life in New York City. I'd never been a partier. I'd stayed home, saved my pennies, and watched game shows. *Jeopardy!* always brought out my competitive side.

"You gotta help the Cinnamon Shakers tonight. They lost ground today."

That meant knocking around with Cousin Lou, and she'd "knock me around" if she discovered my indiscretion at the Glass & Bass.

Perhaps I'd stop back at the restaurant. Reason with the owner so he wouldn't throw me under the bus to my cousin.

Before leaving, Jett and I hatched a plan. I'd attend the game show incognito and dress as a box on the game board.

"Create your clues," Jett directed. "Write 'em with a black marker—big letters so they can read 'em."

She pulled out her phone and showed a picture of her costume. "Give a note to Bill Hartland, the emcee, so he knows your answers. Don't make the riddles too tough. They'll suspect you're a ringer."

It was a brilliant plan. In disguise, I could surveil the crowd and avoid Lou's wrath. Talk about a Daily Double.

I put the top up on the car before driving off. It was the opposite thing to do on a sunny day, but fool me once and all that jazz.

CHAPTER 46

Friday Afternoon

Question: These establishments were notoriously risky and often associated with gangsters.

Answer: What is a "whiskey" business?

I parked outside the Glass & Bass. No other cars were in the lot, but pontoons bobbed in the water, tied to the place's pier. Plywood covered the windows. The front door and steps were cordoned off by yellow tape. New developments since I'd visited yesterday.

To get in, I'd have to enter via the lower level.

The place would *not* be ready for a reception for Curtis Grey on Sunday.

Black clouds added to the restaurant's gloomy presence. I hesitated to go near the place, but I needed boxes to make my costume and sought to appease Art Atkinson.

Kill two hodags with one stone, as they say 'round these parts.

I approached the lower door. A pirate-themed sign warned, "Abandon hope, all ye who enter here."

The sign was sun-faded, tattered. Spooky looking. I wanted to scurry back to the Saab, but between enduring The Wrath of Cousin Lou or entering a condemned-looking shack, I'd take the shack.

I buzzed the rusty doorbell, but there was no answer. I stepped down a ramp leading to the boats. Perhaps there was a way inside through the boathouse. The ramp was slick with lake slime—I slipped and nearly went top over teakettle into the drink.

Did you hear about the fashion model who almost fell into the frothy, blue-black water of Glass Lake?

It was a *clothes call.*

A close call, indeed.

* * *

"WHAT ARE YOU DOIN' here?" Art Atkinson demanded.

It didn't take a body language expert to see that his mood hadn't improved. In the open-sided boathouse under the building, he stomped about *The Wilde Ride*, Hilarious' pontoon. Its engine cover was off. Atkinson must have been servicing it for Hil.

"Do you have extra boxes?" I asked. "Other places in town are sold out with the Deliveree Games going on. Everybody needs a good box at the moment."

White lie. But Atkinson was in the bar business. Didn't count.

"Why should I help you?"

"The faster I get a box, the faster you'll get rid of me." Wind whipped through the three-sided space. "I'm sorry for what I said earlier about the remodel ... I didn't mean to offend you about anything."

"Huh?"

Why did he have such an awful attitude—what had Susan Victory seen in him?

I raised my voice. "Looks like a storm is coming."

"I don't have boxes."

I pointed to cartons in a corner. They were thick cardboard, probably for beer bottles. "What are those?"

He grinned slyly. The *Ride* fell and rose violently, and seeing it made me queasy. "They're not really here. My beer distributor forgot to pick 'em up."

"How much for three of them?"

His eyes narrowed. "Ten a piece."

"I'll give you twenty if you load them in my car."

"Done."

* * *

WHILE SCRAMBLING up the slick ramp, I noticed two pontoons tied to the pier outside the restaurant. And old one, *The —ass Bot—*, and a shiny new one, *The Big Bottle*.

"Nice boat," I said.

"It's expensive," Atkinson grumbled. "Don't know what I was thinkin' buyin' it so soon with the remodelin' cost."

"Maybe you should have waited until it went on *sail*."

He ignored the pun and held up the boxes. "Where d'ya want these?"

I stepped to the Saab and opened the hatch. "In here, thanks."

"That'll be eighty—"

"Sixty"

"But with a tip, it's—"

"We agreed on sixty."

He sighed. "Tell your cousin we won't have that party here, and our deal's off. No excavating. The remodel is gonna take a while. I got no idea when I'll be ready to do the exterior."

His face contorted from a scowl to sadness, like he was overwhelmed by the decisions about the place.

I felt for him. He'd lost his partner, and to handle the emotion of it, from grief probably, he'd begun a frenzy of activity and now regretted it.

"Are you coming to the event tonight for the games?" I asked. "It might be a nice break for you."

He glanced at the sorry-looking building. "Too much to do here, and the storm tonight could mean the last of the place. Hope it doesn't tornado it into the lake." He grimaced. "That'd be a plot twist, eh?"

* * *

I ZIPPED back to the rental. An anonymous costume and surreptitious eyeballing of the suspects, er, players for the night's event was at hand.

For once, Lou's zany habit of packing like she managed of a troupe of actors came in handy.

Using a marker, I wrote an answer on the front of the box: "This iconic '70s film highlighted on-time delivery of a beverage and underscored obscure sociological conflicts between law enforcement, blue-collar workers, and marriage."

Smokey and the Bandit, obviously.

Too easy?

I thought the word "obscure"—a clue about smoke—gave it away, but I'd take the chance.

To make a costume, I sawed arm-holes in the box so it covered my torso. I wore a black turtleneck and jeans underneath. I found a red-head wig, a cowboy hat, and a lacy eye mask. If I lurked about the tent's edges, stayed to the side, I'd pull it off.

I was glad Max resided safely with Fern for the evening. Upon that thought, my phone buzzed. "Hi, Fern. How's Max?"

"He's good," she said. "We had a long walk before the wind picked up. Tonight looks bad, weather-wise."

I had an idea. "Maybe they'll cancel the final event. It's in a tent—"

"No, I talked with Lou. They're moving it inside the resort." She sounded tense.

"What's wrong?"

"I've got bad news."

"Is it Max? I'll be right there."

"No, he's fine. It's Susan."

My heart raced. The Dells was family-friendly—unless one was a risk-taker like Susan. There was a haunted pub tour, a museum of torture devices, and a Ghost Boat that ventures into spooky Cold Water Canyon. Had something gone wrong at one of these attractions?

"What happened?" I asked.

"She's missing."

"Was it the Ducks? Those amphibious vehicles are open-sided—"

"She never made it to the Dells." Fern spoke in clipped phrases, "I talked to Trudy ... who asked the other Book Trout gals ... Susan hasn't been heard from."

"Since when?"

"I confirmed it an hour ago."

"Does law enforcement know?"

"Not yet." She sighed. "She may have gone elsewhere for R&R. I'm hoping she entered a rehab facility. I'm concerned, but if I file a missing person report, it makes her look guilty."

Fern began crying.

Susan, where were you?

* * *

FERN SAID she was staying put all evening. "I'll keep making calls. My phone is charged, and I've got flashlights with fresh batteries in case the power goes out."

"I'm going undercover, no, 'underbox.'" I explained my costume. "If there's an emergency, if you can't reach me, contact Officer Jett McBride."

I hopped into the Saab. Well, no. I didn't hop—one cannot bend while wearing a box—so I dumped the carton in the hatch, climbed in, and then flew down Lollygag toward the resort.

While zipping through the town, I glanced in the rearview mirror. The red wig, hat, and mask made me look like Daphne Blake, one of Scooby's mystery-solving cohorts—but her nickname was Danger-prone Daphne.

Perhaps that was a poor comparison.

The wind had picked up and the sky looked menacing. It reminded me of that first date with Cole, the night a storm hit while we shared frozen custard, the evening we raced through a maelstrom and nearly collided with an ambulance, and the gruesome discovery of Curtis Grey on his boat.

The pontoon seemed alive at the time, bucking and destroying a pier.

I prayed the evening would not be a repeat of that fateful date, and that Susan had snuck off to rehab and would announce it when she was ready.

I respected her decision, even if it made her look guilty. It was the opposite of what I'd suggest, but it didn't mean she was wrong. Sometimes, opposite actions were complementary—the contrast provided meaning and harmonization.

Please, Susan, be safe.

I pressed the gas, mindful of the angry-looking waves on my left and giant boulders on my right. The scene felt confining, like I was boxed in by weather and circumstances.

If things went wrong, I had nowhere to escape.

CHAPTER 47

Friday Night, the Quiz Show

Dressing incognito had advantages if one were a.) solving a mystery and b.) observing one's suitors.

I'd dashed through raindrops to enter the lodge via the side door. The cavernous lobby had been transformed. If I stood still, I'd be decor. I'd never seen so many shiny boxes, dazzling pine trees, and lighted stars. It was like Las Vegas came to the Northwoods for a production.

At one end, there was a stage with a game board and space for human box-clues to stand.

Bill Hartland held a mic, cracking jokes. "Tonight's gonna be *crate*, folks. I hope ya polished your degrees from the U of *Box-ford*. Otherwise, your team will *fold* early."

People wearing box-clues mingled in the crowd. I silently guessed the answers: "This box plays music." *What is a boombox?* And, "A hockey-playing bird was put in the penalty box." *What is fowl play?* Easy ones. If I were forced on stage, I'd be final-round material and stay into the night, delaying my effort to find Susan.

No, thanks.

Look, there's Rand—he wasn't wearing a box. He wore a Hawaiian shirt with little airplanes on it ... and a tall redhead wearing a crimson dress. Okay, no, he wasn't wearing her, but the woman stood beside him at the bar, touching his arm and laughing.

Interesting development since he and I had talked. Rand had left our convo with a bad *altitude.*

I watched the pair. Upon second glance, they weren't together. She flitted from person to person at the bar, appearing to be a hostess for the event.

I couldn't think about Rand, though. I had to discover who killed Curtis Grey, who attacked Dusty—and locate Susan.

I halted next to a Paul Bunyan statue. He wore a white suit, Elvis sideburns, and held a shiny gold package. I scanned the room. Most people wore costumes. Could Susan be one of them—was she hiding in plain sight?

Also, was Cole here? If I spoke to him while solving these problems, good. I wanted to discover what he penned in that note without revealing it flew away like a gambler's last dollar.

I heard a conversation behind me.

Lou and Steven.

"Steve-O, you're lookin' ragged. Tough race today," Lou said.

"We lost ground," he replied. "The BA's big guy couldn't be stopped."

Lou explained how she fueled up the BAs. "I fed 'em breakfast, sorry. Gave the big fella homemade protein bars, too. He's a nice guy once ya get to know him. You seen Mel?"

"Nope."

"Rand's talkin' with Ericka's friend, that gal that looks like Jessica Rabbit. You wanna break 'em up, or should I?"

"Leave them alone. Rand can take care of himself."

"I wasn't gonna hurt her, just tempt her away with carrot muffins ... or a carrotini."

"Shouldn't you be watching the till in back?

"Yah, it's my last night of it, but I haven't seen Ali von Yaack, so I'm not worried about her filching money."

"I thought I saw her."

"No way!" Lou hustled to the bar, exiting through a door like a bettor racing to her bookie.

Steven cleared his throat. "Hey, Bandit, the coast is clear. You can turn around."

"How'd you know?" I asked.

"Great costume, but I knew one of your clues when I read it."

I scanned the busy room. "Did you really see Ali?"

He shook his head. "I said that to get rid of Lou."

"She's missing ... so is Susan."

"I thought she—"

"We can't find her. Keep an eye out, okay?"

"Did you ask her boyfriend? What about him?"

Steven's question zinged my brain like a slot machine hitting JACKPOT.

Did he mean Hank Leigel?

Hank was in Cinnamon doing lawyer things, like jotting notes on yellow pads and typing "Whereas." Maybe the Copper Falls police chef spoke to him, but I had no proof. I'd been so focused on Susan's erratic behavior that I hadn't thought about Hank other than to phone him with questions.

Hank and Susan were exes, but cared for one another, and I still thought of them as a couple—but I'd been focused on Susan's relationship with Atkinson, not Hank.

I'd kept the circumstances and the two men apart. Was Hank involved in Susan's disappearance? It was the opposite of the trail I'd been following.

Could Hank and Susan be together?

* * *

I WANTED to step outside and call him, but Steven stopped me. He glanced toward the bar. He must have spied Rand and the showgirl.

"Whatever happens, Mel,"—he thumped my cardboard costume—"you're the whole package. Don't let anyone get to you."

"Thanks."

The cheery notes of a game-show jingle began, signaling the event was starting. I was standing with my back, er, box, to the rest of the space. "Do you see Cole?"

"Yeah, he's behind you on one knee, holding a ring."

"*What?*"

"Just kidding. How's it going with him?"

"Flighty, honestly."

"For what it's worth, I heard he and Ericka had a bust-up fight at the resort. Word's out she was crushed."

I had an idea. "How well do you know the other competitors?"

"They're family now, even the BAs. Delivery folks support one another."

I smiled. "I'm glad you said that, Steven."

* * *

I GAVE STEVEN AN ASSIGNMENT, framing the deed as practice for a penning romance novel.

"I don't write those," he protested.

"You should. Think of the relationships author Steven Delavan could inspire. 'Ink is the great cure for human ills,' you know."

"Foghorn Leghorn?" he asked.

"Close. C.S. Lewis."

I kissed his cheek, then beetled toward the exit. Well, no. The box made me feel like a turtle, so claiming I moved quickly was false. The crowd had gained volume in voice and size. At the door, I tried to leave but struggled like a rectangular-shaped salmon swimming upstream. I stepped aside to wait.

A voice behind me asked, "How's the weather tonight, Cole?"

"Sunny. Hot."

Hilarious and Cole were talking.

I glanced out the doors. *Sunny?* It was a blue-black sky, and lightning flashed, silhouetting the trees, making them look like leafy ghouls. When the doors opened, the wind whooshed scents of earth and cedar to my nose.

The two men were speaking in code—did "hot" imply an arrest?

Please don't be Susan.

"The package is wrapped and secure?" Hilarious asked.

"Ten-four," Cole answered, his voice sounding stern, final, a Marshall Dillon baritone with a John Wayne chaser. His ominous vibe contrasted with the lively energy in the room.

"Bravo Zulu," Hilarious said.

I couldn't believe it. I was born at night, but not *last* night. Hil saying "well done" in military code-speak made me anxious. My box felt tight, claustrophobic.

Whisky Tango Foxtrot, they were not discussing clues for tonight's quiz show. Had Susan been arrested?

Was that what Cole wrote in the note? He'd given me a heads up about why she was missing.

But no, Susan was set up!

Question: This jewelry designer is being framed for a murder she didn't commit.

Answer: Who is Susan Victory?

CHAPTER 48
Friday Night, Desperately Seeking Susan

Like a mega-pontoon motoring against smaller ships, I pushed out the resort's doors and into the stormy night. Cold, damp air blasted my face, and I gasped.

I had to strategize with Fern—we needed to help Susan.

Hank Leigel could recommend a criminal defense attorney. He'd know one. Lawyers talk. They mingle at the same *bar*, right?

Good news was Susan couldn't be with Hank if she were in custody. Suspecting Hank was the opposite of my instincts about the man. It didn't make sense. He wouldn't harm Susan—unless he'd learned about her involvement with Art Atkinson.

I zoomed around a corner on the way to the parking lot, shaking my head at the idea. My barge-like costume crashed a smaller vessel. "Ope, sorry!"

The person wore a mask and a sandwich sign—smart choice. The get-up was more maneuverable than mine. The sign's quiz question caught my eye as I attempted it: "This movie is a favorite of boxes. In fact, it's great." I pondered. "No idea."

"What is The Crate Escape?" the person answered.

"Wait ... Jett?"

"Mel?"

I nodded. "Have you heard about Susan Victory? Is she in

custody?"

The young woman shook her head, and the mask slipped over her mouth. "Gosh, not that I know. But the chief would wait to release information. She has rights, too." Her voice sounded muffled.

"I'm headed to a friend's condo." I gave her Fern's information. "Susan is innocent. If you can't reach me, call this number. Please keep me updated."

"Will do."

Lightning split the sky, then *BOOM!*

We both jumped. Our cardboard costumes rattled as though made of metal. Well, Jett's did. I wondered what weapons she carried under the sandwich board—a handy concealment device.

"Be safe," I said.

"You, too. Gotta go."

I watched her jog toward the lodge, the board bumping against her back. After she'd disappeared, I skedaddled to my car, dumped my costume in the hatch, and zipped off toward Fern's.

* * *

THE PAVEMENT in my car's headlights twisted and turned like a snake —no, a hodag.

Rollercoaster hills resembled the mystical beast's humped back. The pointy white boulders lining the road looked like fangs. The rocks had a purpose—they kept cars from swerving into the drink.

Snakes vs. hodags.

Rocks vs. safety.

Opposing thoughts ping-ponged in my brain. I gripped the wheel. Driving while solving a mystery was tricky. I should be concentrating on lines and signs, but my mind drifted.

Opposites.

I glanced at the lake on my right. Black-blue water was a vast, dark shadow. Behind me, through the rear window, I saw streaks of lightning cross the night sky.

Water vs. sky.

Darkness vs. light.

Opposites.

The road curved toward town, civilization, Fern's place, my cottage on Lollygag.

My trip to the Northwoods was supposed to have been relaxing, with maybe a chance for romance. Instead, it turned out to be as calm as turbulence and romantic as being thrown in jail.

Rand vs. Cole.

Those two weren't opposites, they were similar. Captain Kirk and Marshall Dillon. Race Bannon and Spirit, stallion of the Cimarron. Strong, smart problem-solvers with a gentle side, and both men adored Max.

I was the opposing force. I was the zebra in the horse race, the vintage boat among yachts. I traveled with a personal jester, Cousin Lou, too. She was our foil, the spur in our sides, the burr under the saddle blanket. As frustrating as she was, Lou called out destructive behaviors among everyone.

I braked at a stop sign.

There were zero vehicles on the road—no headlights, no trucks pulling boats, no cars.

And no careening ambulances to sink at a boat launch, thank goodness.

Everyone in the county was likely at the resort, having fun, guessing answers to silly clues.

Question: This fashion model business-owner took a vacation and became boxed in by a mystery.

Answer: Who is Mel Tower?

Where should I go?

I glanced left, the direction that took me safely back to town, but a right would take me toward danger, Amityville Cove, the spooky bay where Curtis owned the boat launch and the Glass Bottom ... no, the new Glass & Bass.

I need to speak with Fern. *Turn left!*

In a moment of clarity—or its foolish opposite—I turned right, hurtling in the dark toward the unknown.

* * *

WHY DID the fashion-model-turned-sleuth dig for clues in Amityville Cove?

"Because she wanted to shovel her own grave," I muttered, peering out the windshield. A white, arrow-shaped sign said, "Elm Street. Nightmare. This way."

Kidding—what else did I have to do while working for years as a mannequin but make silent jokes?

I flipped on a blinker—*clack, clack*—and turned onto the gravel lane circling the isolated cove. Trees encroached immediately, and I feared they'd whip apples á la *The Wizard of Oz*.

I passed the driveway to Curtis Grey's manse. It fell off from the lane in a steep dive. The gravel path circled a ridge, and I drove on, passing narrow homes, just glimpsing roofs. Long driveways sunk to the gloomy haunts as though dropped from a cliff.

How the occupants climbed out during winter was a different mystery.

No lights were on in any of the homes. They appeared abandoned, ready for tear down, if their foundations had the droops, as Lou observed during our boat tour of the bay. The lane came to a dead end. I circled and crept back toward Curtis's home, the first one along the route.

The headlights of a dark SUV gunned up the drive nearest Curtis's and burst onto the lane in front of me, swerving and then overcorrecting.

Who was that?

I pressed the gas, and the gravel gave way. My car fishtailed and almost hit a tree—yikes!

I squinted at the SUV, trying to glimpse its plates or a silhouette of its driver, any clue. Ericka was the only person I knew with a vehicle like that, but were those her license plates?

Something seemed off.

Who'd been parked near Curtis's place in the dark?

* * *

THE SUV VANISHED into the night, driving so fast it rocked side to side. Black sky and lightning framed the cumbersome vehicle. It was like watching a pontoon disappear down the River Styx.

I didn't give chase to find out where it was headed.

Rain fell. The Saab's wipers swished the windscreen every few seconds. I pressed the clutch, shifted to neutral, and rolled past Grey's driveway. Castle Grey, my nickname for the dreary pile, was dark, too.

Where were Greer and Dusty? Had they been in the SUV?

I hadn't seen them partying at the quiz show. But that would be poor form. Curtis had passed just a week ago.

I'd met couples like G. and D. in New York.

That's why I left.

Okay, no. I appreciated good-looking, rich folks who seemed to have it all, and I wouldn't pass judgment. The truth about their lives was complicated. Mega money presented itself in peculiar ways. Financial affluence guaranteed opportunity, not happiness. Security, but not stability. Access, not success.

Opposites, one might say.

Raindrops tapped the car's hood. They were knocks, pulses, that fired my brain. I recalled what I'd seen and heard during the last week. I recalled the suspects in Curtis's death:

Ali von Yaack.

Greer.

Dusty—had she faked the accident in the restaurant to befuddle the police?

All three had motives, whereas Susan did not.

That's why she didn't do it.

There were other suspects: Art Atkinson, the restaurant business partner. He'd thrown Susan under the bus, according to Jett McBride.

Under the bus.

I put the Saab in gear, my mind engaging.

CHAPTER 49

Friday Night, Later

The funny thing about an old-school manual transmission like the Saab's was it reminded me of heavy machines—massive things like bulldozers and excavators. Earth-movers with buckets and tracking wheels.

That reminded me of Cousin Lou, who'd offered to knock down the homes of Amityville Cove due to their crumbly foundations.

Basements, in other words.

I wound through backroads toward the boat launch, the slippery, treacherous spot where Curtis's pontoon was found.

The Saab's trusty engine hummed, and the wipers kept up with the rain. No headlights in front or behind me—who'd been driving the SUV?

Perhaps *not* a civilian. It could have been the police. I assumed undercover officers were in the area to watch suspects' homes. But if Susan were in custody those operations would be canceled—they'd found the perpetrator, after all.

I called Fern to say I was on the way. "Hi, it's me—hello?"

"Call Failed," my phone read.

I tried again. "Fern, I'm coming over—"

Failed again.

I'd try when I got closer to town. I glanced in the rearview. The storm had calmed. The wind wasn't as strong, and the flashes and rumbles diminished in the distance.

A good thing because I wanted to stop and check out a theory. After that, I'd go straight to Fern's.

* * *

AT THE BOAT launch near the Glass & Bass, I texted Fern:

> I'm at the boat launch and the GB. If I'm not at your place in a half-hour, send Jett McBride, xx to Max.

I parked behind a tree to hide the Saab. It was a sight gag because the front and back ends of the armadillo-shaped cruiser stuck out. It was like concealing a chest freezer behind a lamppost.

Sorry, my expertise in amateur sleuthing amounted to late-night *Columbo* episodes. Mistakes would be made.

I stood a few yards from the car, wearing a fleece jacket to battle the chill. The rain had stopped, but the wind blew off the lake, and waves churned. The whitecaps made it look alive, possessed, like the gleaming teeth of a giant, writhing serpent.

I stared at the pier where Curtis's boat smashed posts a week ago, then looked at the launch where Cole went down, where the restaurant spotlights faced the slippery pavement. The spots were off now and the interior of the Glass Bottom, or the Glass & Bass, whatever its name, was dark.

Or was it?

Silently, I crept toward the place, feeling like a forty-five-year-old puma. I'd started the night dressed as a box, unprepared to become Inspector Morsewoods, but here we were.

I avoided the slimy launch and took the long way, traversing across the road, stopping behind trees, and eying the restaurant, which was built into a slope.

I'd erred when visiting on Thursday to chat with Art Atkinson. I searched for him in the bar, but he came up the steps from the basement, I'd assumed—*but what place built over a lake has a basement?*

I stepped closer to the building, wanting to examine the boat slip area underneath it and then dash back to the car.

The only sound was waves crashing the shore. Low, inky clouds blocked the stars.

"Stop right there!" a voice demanded.

* * *

"GIVE ME YOUR PHONE."

"Excuse me?" I said.

"Your phone!"

"What phone?" I lied.

The man shoved me. "I'm not kidding."

I jumped forward, thinking fast. It was dark, the slimy launch only steps away. I slipped and spun like a breakdancer. (Yes, acting was involved. I used to be a model, not a Rockette.)

Mid-cavort, I saw the guy: *Art Atkinson!*

"Gimme your phone," he demanded.

I wobbled, grabbing his shirt. If I went down, he was coming with me. We'd fight it out while sliding into the black water.

"I want your phone!" he yelled.

"*No!*"

I collapsed like dead weight. Down we toppled, and I jabbed him with an elbow.

He landed first on the greasy concrete: "Oof!"

I curled, then body checked him with a shoulder—crack!

"Ow!" he yelled.

Broken rib, I guessed—I shoved again, but couldn't get traction because we were too close. The launch was cold, wet concrete, and the man outweighed me.

"You shouldn't have come here," Atkinson growled. "I almost killed Dusty cuz she was gonna figure it out. I'll kill you if I have to!"

His breath reeked of beer. He stunk like he hadn't bathed—probably hadn't if he'd been busy killing Curtis Grey, ambushing Dusty, and gutting his restaurant—*and kidnapping Susan and blaming the death on her!*

"Where's my friend?" I yelled. "Where's Susan?"

"The same place you're gonna be—buried at sea!"

* * *

"MEL, HELP ME!"

Susan's voice.

It came from a boat. I was dark, but I squinted at the slips under the restaurant. A woman stood on a pontoon.

"The police are coming!" I called out. "Hold on, Susan!"

"Shut up," Atkinson ordered. "We'll be gone before they get h-here."

He coughed. He was on his back on the wet ramp. I pushed down, aiming for his ribs.

"Argh," he moaned.

The guy was beefy, tough. He grabbed my hair, pulling my head down. He cycled his legs, propelling us down the launch toward the black water.

I reached up and grabbed at his arm. He karate-chopped my wrist —*ouch!* "Stop! You'll drown us," I yelled. "Let me see Susan. *Please.*"

"Gimme ... your ... phone." He yanked down, then up. "I'll break your neck."

"It's in my pocket."

"Give it to me."

I flailed an arm. "Can't ... reach."

He yanked again. "Give it to me!"

Could the guy not see I was on my back, my head one way, my patoot another? I'd been a model, not a contortionist.

Rooaarrr!

An engine—what the heck?

I smelled oil and gas and heard the spunky sputters of an old Mercury engine.

Susan had fired up a pontoon!

* * *

Atkinson gripped my hair, but my head was turned in her direction.

Susan had flipped on the dock lights and now buried the throttle, reversing at top speed like a stunt driver in an action film.

The motor sputtered but miraculously didn't die at the tsunami of fuel that hit its four-stroke.

She was on my left, coming fast, "No Wake Zone" sign be damned. Atkinson and I were about five feet from the lake. Water roared at us, pushed by the reversing boat.

I heard boards groan and snap. Susan hadn't untied the lines, obvi, but that was the insurance company's problem, not mine. Then heavens to water hodags, the building lurched! Its pilings must have been toothpicks or Atkinson had sabotaged them.

I knew there was something weird about the place—that's why he'd remarked about the storm tipping it into the lake!

In the light cast by the boat, I saw the building downshift and half collapse on itself.

"Susan, over here!" I yelled.

Atkinson yanked my hair. I jabbed and kicked, hissed and scratched like a towel-wrapped cat at the vet. I broke free as the boat came closer. On hands and knees—the greasy launch felt *sooo* cold and my wrist ached—I scrambled to the water.

"Shut down the engine! I'm coming aboard!" I called out.

"You won't get away from me!" Atkinson growled.

"Suz, put out the ladder!"

The boat's wave crashed into the concrete, and I dove like a mermaid.

There was a steep drop-off. My world fell silent and dark.

I sensed the spinning propeller—the water vibrated like an earthquake. I prayed Susan would stop the whirling motor before the receding wave sucked me into its blades.

* * *

Atkinson was behind me. The busted rib would slow him down, I hoped.

Please, Lord, don't let him pull me under ... and DO NOT let me become model meat in the propeller!

The vibration stopped. I reached out and felt the metal hull of a pontoon. A bulbous fender splashed in the water.

I grabbed the oblong floatie, rocking in the waves alongside the boat. "The ladder, Susan, put it down!"

"I don't know ... w-where."

She was crying and slurring her words.

Maybe Atkinson drugged her. But good on Susan for having the wits to start the boat, flip on the lights, and back out from the slip.

I swam to the stern, and saw the pontoon's name—*The Wilde Ride.* If I remembered, the ladder was right of the engine.

"Watch out, he's c-coming," Susan warned.

She was standing, watching the water, looking like she was fighting through her confusion.

Good for you, Susan!

I began to shiver from the shock of the cold and my aching wrist. I pulled on the metal steps, freeing them from their bracket, and hooked the bars with an elbow. I put my feet on—then felt a yank on my soggy jacket.

Atkinson.

"You're not leavin!" he shouted.

"Susan, drive," I yelled. "*Go!*"

She cranked the engine, and I'd be darned if that motor didn't fire like a volcano. If Atkinson had tuned it, he'd transformed a putt-putt vintage pontoon into a mega-ship.

I shimmied off my jacket, one arm at a time, quick as a model swapping outfits for a show. Then I hooked an elbow around that ladder like my life depended on it—because it did.

Susan cranked the wheel and gunned it.

Bad for Atkinson.

He grasped my coat like a barnacle. Figured I was still in it, probably. The boat whiplashed and sent the propeller into his solar plexus like a blender on "Turbo."

The motor bogged, and Atkinson screamed!

Susan glanced back.

"Don't look!" I yelled.

The boat's lights were on and bright LEDs lit the floorboards. She saw how awful it was. Her eyes rolled, and I watched her knees wobble. She tipped over the fiberglass side into the drink.

I gulped air, and then heaved myself away from the boat, desperate to help my friend Susan.

CHAPTER 50

Friday night, Later

Question: What supplement did the brave young police officer ingest to pluck two women from the stormy lake?

Answer: Vitamin Sea.

Jett McBride showed up to fish us from our spot clinging to a broken pier. She carried lines and flotation devices in her squad, and possessed the training and smarts to rescue us before we were swept down a feeder river and into the Mississippi.

The woman will be a fabulous detective. Or chief, if she wants. Maybe even a sheriff.

She didn't arrive quick enough to stop *The Wilde Ride* from crashing into the restaurant and tipping most of it into the lake, but that wasn't her fault. The place was half-mast before the boat finished the job.

There was nothing Jett could do for Art Atkinson. She lassoed the body and tethered it, showing the poise and nerves of a boss mare protecting a herd.

Susan and I sat in her squad, wrapped in blankets.

"An ambulance is on its way," Jett said.

My teeth chattered, and my wrist was on fire. "P-please make sure it doesn't park c-close to the launch."

She smiled. "Already warned 'em, Mel. It'll be safe, I promise."

* * *

IN THE ER at Buck County Medical, Susan and I occupied the same room. The space was decorated like a log cabin with wildlife pictures on the cinnamon-colored walls and rocking chairs for guests.

In the ambulance on the drive over, she and I had talked. Susan was groggy, but coherent. She wanted to get help—immediately.

A nurse came in. "Ms. Victory, we have a room ready for you. I'll take you up in a few minutes."

Susan nodded, looking pale and exhausted. "I'll be here for a few days, then I want to go to treatment," she said.

The nurse patted Susan's arm. "I understand. We can help you. We have a therapy camp that's excellent. I'll send up an intake specialist, if you like."

"Yes, please."

"After that, we send you there in a covered wagon. We make it an adventure for our new Buckaroos." The nurse winked.

Susan smiled, a relief to see.

The nurse continued, "Welcome to the Sober Buckaroo Club." She pointed to a cowboy hat pin on her blouse. "I'm one, too. You'll do great."

Susan looked over at me. "Who doesn't want to be a Sober Buckaroo?"

"I'm so proud of you," I said. "You drove that boat like a champ."

"It won't be a problem to take care of my jewelry booth in the mall while I'm gone?"

I shook my head. "The only problem will be your customers asking when you'll return."

The nurse exited.

"I'm lookin' for cowgals sufferin' from hypochondria," a familiar voice said from the hallway. "They turned into popsicles in the lake."

Susan groaned. "I'm going to hear it from Louella."

Lou clattered in carrying a picnic basket and a cardboard coffee container. "Who needs a warm-up? You gals are chilled to the bone, I heard. It's June, but geez, that lake's still cold." She set the goodies on the sideboard. "Suz, you gave us a scare."

"I'm s-sorry." Tears brimmed.

Lou grabbed a coffee mug from the basket—"Cowgirls Do it Sober"—and poured in steaming liquid. She handed it to Susan. "It's the hypochondria. Extreme cold saps ya. 'Buck Up,' as they say in here."

"T-thanks."

She pulled out a giant box of tissues and set them on Susan's bed. "I know you talked with the po-po, but what the heck happened? Gimme the short version."

I stopped her. "Lou, they need to wrap up this investigation. Susan's attorney will—"

"Mel, it's o-okay." Susan dabbed her eyes. "I'll say a few things. Art and I got along okay. But looking back, he was setting me up for ... everything. He was ... after a life insurance policy, I believe."

Lou whistled. "Yep, seen it. I got a big, fat contract on Mel, just in case. People like takin' shots at her."

"*You do?*"

"Just teasin'. Go on."

"Art convinced Curtis to invest into the restaurant. He wanted to improve it but didn't have the money. Art wanted to do it *his* way. He did something unthinkable—killed his friend out of pure greed."

Lou shook her head. "Oh, what a tangled lasso some cowboys weave, when first they act like a Bears fan."

Susan smiled, weepy eyes glistening. "You have a unique way of putting things, Lou."

"Yeah. BTW, there's a shot of fireball in that coffee. Figured you'd want a last bender before ya head to Buckaroo Camp."

Susan coughed.

"Lou, *no!*" I said.

"C'mon, I'm kiddin'. Suz will be the bestest, soberest artist in your art mall." She hugged her. "From now on, your motto is, 'Whiskey in another's trouble, sobriety in my own.' You can do it, Susie-Q."

Lou moved to my bed. "Heard they got ya listed as a non-critical tenderfoot. But that wrist looks like crap. You couldn't ping a squirrel off a feeder with a slingshot at ten yards."

"Don't touch it."

"Nurse!"

"No, Lou—"

"But I told 'em I was your doc," she protested. "I'll order an X-ray."

"I'm waiting for one. Please just pretend you're my attorney and CPA."

"If you say so. That's not as much fun." She headed back to the sideboard and pulled more mugs from the basket—the thing seemed bottomless—and poured coffee.

She put a mug in my good hand. "Alie von Barstool was located, by the way. She was in Chicago this whole time."

"I'm glad to know she's safe," I said.

"You gonna stay a few days in here?" Lou asked.

"We'll see."

"But I booked ya a room on the Cougar floor." She winked at Susan. "You got two hotties after ya. That's where they put swingers like you."

Susan laughed.

"How's Max?" I asked. "I want to see my dog."

"Fern's bringin' him. She's on her way."

Lou looked at a wood-framed eye chart on the wall. "Would you look at that? All the images, top to bottom, are different kinds of cheese." She put a hand over an eye. "Third line: Curds. Basil-garlic. Pepper-jack. That's what I brought, just so happens. Carrot muffins for the staff, too. Who needs a snack?"

* * *

THE X-RAY REVEALED no broken bones, just my stubborn streak. In my private room, I protested to Fern: "Why should I stay overnight in the hospital for a sprained wrist?"

Doctor Mustache McGraw—I didn't catch his name, but that's how he looked—insisted.

Fern agreed. "Please be safe, Mel. They want to observe you for a concussion."

"Does that exist, or is it only in my head?"

"This is a lovely room," Fern soothed. "Not everyone gets the Pauline Bunyan suite."

I looked around. "Lou pulled strings. Or big ropes, to be accurate." It *was* nice. Oversized, pink-plaid furniture. Heated racks for fluffy towels, plus a view of the lake. I didn't feel great about bodies of water, but I'd get over it.

Max jumped on the bed. I stroked his fur while Fern and I talked.

"How'd you figure it out?" she asked.

"*I* didn't. Officer Jett McBride did. I was in the right place at the right time. Or, the opposite; the wrong time." I sighed. "Depends on how you look at it."

Fern nodded. "Officer McBride solved the mystery. Got it. As your PR person, I'll get that news out."

"Yes, to keep the peace among the officers involved, Jett is the hero." I scratched Max's chest. "She earned it, too. She came to me with a suspicion that Susan was being set up. Then she worked the case, went undercover, looked for clues."

"What happened at the quiz show?"

"Nothing was adding up: Susan was missing, supposedly. Then, I overheard a conversation and feared the opposite, she was in custody." I shook my head. "Since Curtis was killed, I've felt a yin and yang."

"Oh?"

"It's a vibe of light and dark, waves versus calm." I glanced at the table where Lou had set out baked treats. "Espresso frosting versus vanilla cupcake. It's a stage of life, I think."

"Up and down are on the same staircase, opposing forces are always interconnected." Fern smiled. "But my vibe is Mel Tower is experiencing personal growth."

"Is that only in my head, too?"

She laughed. "You're digging into who you are since moving back to Wisconsin from New York."

"Digging, and a staircase, were lightbulb moments, ironically. I visited the restaurant on Thursday and mistakenly assumed it had a basement."

"There's a boathouse under it, right?"

"Yes." I explained. "Just storage lockers for skis and inflatables. Atkinson kidnapped Susan and hid her there. She had room to stand up but not much else."

"Poor thing."

"She's stronger than she realizes."

Fern narrowed her eyes. "My take is Atkinson was at that party that night and killed Curtis for a life insurance policy. And, he likely sought to demolish the restaurant for another insurance payout. I'll bet he sabotaged the pilings during the 'reno.' That's why it toppled so easily."

"It wouldn't surprise me."

"Instead of the Glass & Bass, some folks are calling it the Dunk & Sunk."

"Let me guess, those 'folks' are Lou."

Just then, a giant vase of cardboard roses walked in, powered by my cousin. "These were just sent from the resort," Lou announced. "The quiz show ended hours ago. Steven's team won, and they wanted you to have 'em."

CHAPTER 51

Saturday Afternoon

At the cottage, a gift-wrapped basket filled with a toothbrush kit, hand sanitizer, and pretzels arrived, powered by a fellow in a uniform.

Rand stepped onto the deck and set the basket on the table. "For you, Mel." He kissed my cheek. "Feeling okay? There are air sickness bags tucked in there. Turbulent boat rides can have a lasting effect."

I smiled. "Thanks, but I'm fine. I mean, it's not like I see red or anything."

"Excuse me?"

"Nothing."

"How's the wing? Lou claims your career as a bulldozer operator is in jeopardy."

I held out my bandaged wrist. "My future in excavation is over before it began, but I'll be okay."

"Ouch." He peered at my swollen arm. "A job in flying is questionable, too. Aviators require a functioning wingspan to keep the aircraft up."

Max had been monitoring the perimeter fence—one never knows about squirrels—but galloped over when he saw Rand.

He leaped onto the deck and trotted straight to him. Rand scratched the dog's chest.

"You're still his favorite pilot," I said.

"And yours, too, I hope."

I sighed. "Mine, too. You'll always be my favorite flyer, Rand."

"So where do we stand?" He asked. "I shouldn't have put you on the spot in the parking lot the other night, but it's the way I felt."

I paused before answering. I had no concrete answer about Rand, Cole, or the relationship I sought.

The sun blazed, and a breeze swirled off the water. It felt refreshing, like an outdoor spa.

I was in a great place to figure it out, though.

"I don't know," I said, finally. "Since coming back to Wisconsin, I'm learning about myself." I tapped the bandage. "I'm digging into my personality, even with a bum wrist."

"I understand. Building a foundation takes time." He kissed me again. "Don't stress, though. I've known you for a long time, Mel Tower. You're pretty fabulous just as you are."

* * *

STEVEN ARRIVED after the last competition of the Deliveree Games. For the first time in the games' history, the Cinnamon Shakers won it in a dance-off tiebreaker. He and I walked Max down Lollygag for an afternoon constitutional. Horse-tail clouds swirled, and sunlight sparkled off the blue water.

Steven described the dramatic conclusion, "It was another musical box pro-am. Lou and I against Ericka Dimblé and Nate, the big guy from the BAs." Steven laughed. "Lou's a hockey player in a baker's body. We got points for speed, but those two were tough."

"Lou didn't body-check anyone, I hope."

"We came close, but I stopped her. And Ericka and Nate hit it off."

"Glad to hear it."

"I did my best to knit a story between those two—as you suggested."

I shook my head. "You're the writer. You plotted that romance novel. All I did was give a nudge."

"Nate seems to like her. How'd you know?"

We stopped to watch the glistening lake. Max trotted down to the little beach and dipped his paws in.

I watched the dog. "It was something Jett McBride said. Simple, practical advice to not overthink a relationship and go with a vibe. If that works for Ericka, and she and Nate get along, great."

My instinct said Cole had finally ended their relationship.

Not my business, though.

"Steven, at the quiz show, I overheard Cole and Hilarious talking in code. What do you think that was about? Give me your author's instinct."

He shrugged. "Could have been anything. An incident in the department they couldn't discuss in public, or a shower gift for Bill and Suko. Who knows?"

True.

I quizzed him again: "When I drove to Curtis's place, I saw an SUV. Could that have been undercover police?"

"Sure, but maybe it was renters who were leaving. Why don't you ask—"

"I'm staying out of it," I interrupted. "I didn't solve this case."

"Gotcha."

We started walking.

"Tonight's the Glass Ball, the big party celebrating the end of the games," Steven said. "There's another dance-off. Be my partner?"

I held up my wrist. "I'm feeling breakable at the moment. I'll pass."

The next day, however, I did attend a concert on the lake. It was an impromptu fundraiser to rebuild the Glass Bottom restaurant. Fern picked me up in the *Outlaw*, and we putt-putted to Hilarious Wilde's place and grabbed him, too. The Bill Hartland Trio put on another bash. Bill and Suko sang their hearts out, mining their set list for gold.

"You cats in the boats are lookin' sharp! Who's havin' fun?" Bill cried.

I was.

Yeah, I could dig it.

CHAPTER 52

Labor Day Weekend

Max and I returned to the Northwoods for the "Thrilla in a Flotilla," Bill and Suko's wedding.

A boat parade was involved, as was music, cake, and dancing. My wrist had healed to fighting form. Thus, Steven and I were paired in musical boxes. To paraphrase Vince Lombardi, life's battles go to the quick, the strong, and the cardboard savvy. From twenty paces, Steven could discern sturdy corrugation from paperboard that would collapse under the weight of twirling competitors.

Happily, we emerged gold-medal winners once more.

To the nuptials, Lou brought carrot muffins and Steven delivered gifts. Hilarious took photos, and baked a stunning masterpiece cake swathed in plaid frosting.

Cole was best man, so Max was my date.

He looked delicious in his duds.

Cole, I mean. (No offense, Max.)

During the Labor Day weekend, my best doggo and I stayed at my cottage on Lollygag. The sale went through, as I'd figured. I negotiated, but it was nice to have Hank Leigel on the phone as my wingman.

Speaking of, the wedding was outside on the resort's deck, and a plane flew over during the vows. Its wings flared to say congrats, I swear.

Rand and I hadn't talked much, but it was great to see him, even if it was from thirty-six thousand feet.

Cousin Lou and Jason, her better half, stayed at *their* new place for the holiday weekend. During the summer, Lou made an offer Ali von Yaack couldn't refuse—an all-cash deal and business advice.

At the wedding reception, Lou said, "I told Ali to stop makin' *grave* mistakes." She smiled. "Grave—and we got an excavatin' biz. Get it?"

I sure did.

Jason used his dozers on the houses at Amityville Cove, Lou explained. "But we call it Amicable Cove now. Much better energy, and way better drainage," she declared.

Susan and Hank didn't attend the wedding but came up for the weekend. She looked great, and Hank seemed delighted that they had reconciled.

Lou fed the masses because Greer & Dusty's and the Glass Bottom were closed for repairs. Rumor was a bigwig bought the buildings but no one knew the person's identity.

I gave the cottage a fresh coat of paint and a new name, "The Next Chapter."

I felt like I was turning a page. I still had to book Suko for a singing gig.

Maybe it would be for my forty-sixth, or Max's "Gotcha Day," which was in November.

Cole and I enjoyed a horseback ride one sunny afternoon. The "ticket" he'd written when I parked in the police-vehicle spot was an invite, he'd revealed, and I happily accepted the consequences. A summons ordering me on hooves instead of wheels was one I'd willingly pay.

We also had a boat day on *The Root Beer Float* and shared a perfect afternoon on glass-like water. Cole blew up floaties while I prepped snacks.

Before jumping in, he said, "Don't tell the tourists, but September is the best time up here."

The night before I left to return to Cinnamon, we went out for a treat—root beer floats instead of frozen custard. We sat in the cab of his truck and enjoyed the lake view as the ice cream stand's giant illuminated cone reflected off the shimmering waves.

Cole kissed me, then handed over a frosted mug. It felt cold but smelled luscious—a combination of vanilla bean and nutmeg.

"Care to dig in?" he asked.

I stared at him.

Eyes like the Northwoods sky.

"Sure," I said.

Louella Jingle's Carrot Muffins

Lou's carrot muffins are famous in Cinnamon. Rather than break bread, she breaks muffins.

"They are delicious as is," she says. "You can add cream cheese frosting if ya like, but there's no need. Sift powdered sugar over the top to make 'em pretty, and you're good to go. And ya can mix 'em by hand with a whisk, a good workout for your arms!"

LJ Carrot Muffins

1 1/2 cup flour
1/2 tsp baking powder
1/2 tsp baking soda
1 tsp cinnamon
1 tsp nutmeg
2/3 cup vegetable oil
1 tsp good-quality vanilla
1 cup granulated sugar (Lou has tried half-granulated, half-brown, too. Up to you.)
2 eggs, beaten
1 cup grated carrots
3/4 chopped walnuts (optional)

Preheat oven to 350 degrees. Spray 12 cup muffin tin with nonstick spray

Sift together dry ingredients. Combine oil, sugar, vanilla, eggs. Mix by hand with a whisk until blended. Then add dry ingredients. Mix well. Stir in carrots and nuts (if using the nuts.) Bake in muffin tin 20 minutes, approx. Should make 12 muffins. Let cool. Sift powdered sugar over the top, but that is optional.

Dear Reader

Welcome to my world! I sincerely hope you enjoyed the Northwoods, and Cinnamon, Wisconsin, and Mel and her family and friends. I write stories for readers who want to laugh and escape, who seek a break from the busyness of life to stop in a land of beautiful countryside, lakes, pine forests, cows, and cheese. Wisconsin is my home, and I love sharing it with readers. Feel free to join me on social media, where I discuss writing and books, and share sunrises from my very special backyard. Take care and happy reading, TK.

Acknowledgments

Life is mostly froth and bubbles, but two things show you're a Midwesterner: You bring a casserole for another's trouble, and bake carrot muffins in your own. To Midwesterners who make life in Wisconsin a joy, thank you. This place is unique, beautiful, and different, and it is like having a million friends willing to laugh and help one another. To my writer friends in The Wisconsin Writers Association, Sisters in Crime, and the Blackbirds, thank you for the support. To my writing sisters, Valerie Biel and Kerri Lukasavitz—*thank you.* I cannot do it without you! To my cover designer, Patricia Moffet, a big THANK YOU from across the Pond. It takes a village to create a novel—I'm glad you're all in mine in Cinnamon, Wisconsin.

Milton Keynes UK
Ingram Content Group UK Ltd.
UKHW020754130524
442628UK00001B/134